Sexy/Dangerous

He walked in, the dogs with him, and the canines went straight to the bed where she lay.

"That you, Doc?" she asked groggily. She was lying on her stomach on top of the indigo quilt his mother had given him for his birthday last year. She was wearing a lightweight gray sweatsuit. The top was loose fitting and had short sleeves. "Can you unhook my bra? Arms won't bend back there. Had to shower in it."

Adam went still. "Let me go get Kaitlin."

"Just unhook the damn thing. Please? If the dogs could do it, I'd ask them."

Adam stood there for a moment and met the eyes of the dog Ossie. Adam swore the dog shrugged. He glanced over her tall body with its fine behind, and in the end decided to get it over with. He sat down on the bed. Reaching over, he found the clasp through the soft fabric of her top, and the heat of her skin seemed to run up his arms. He undid the placard, and the sigh of pleasure she gave in response put a big-time crack in his celibacy vow.

By Beverly Jenkins

SEXY/DANGEROUS
BLACK LACE
THE EDGE OF DAWN
THE EDGE OF MIDNIGHT

BEVERLY JENKINS

SEXY/DANGEROUS

HarperTorch
An Imprint of HarperCollins*Publishers*

This is a work of fiction. Names, characters, places, and incidents are products of the author's imagination or are used fictitiously and are not to be construed as real. Any resemblance to actual events, locales, organizations, or persons, living or dead, is entirely coincidental.

❦

HARPERTORCH
An Imprint of HarperCollins*Publishers*
10 East 53rd Street
New York, New York 10022-5299

Copyright © 2006 by Beverly Jenkins
ISBN-13: 978-0-06-081899-9
ISBN-10: 0-06-081899-9

First HarperTorch paperback printing: November 2006

HarperCollins®, HarperTorch™, and ❦™ are trademarks of Harper-Collins Publishers Inc.

Printed in the United States of America

Visit HarperTorch on the World Wide Web at www.harpercollins.com

10 9 8 7 6 5 4 3 2

To Alicia T. for asking what if?

Prologue

Tuesday, May 9, 2006
Madrid, Spain

Dr. Adam Gary tugged his tie free then tossed the length of blue silk onto the big bed of his hotel room. He was dead tired, he realized, stretching the muscles of his neck in an attempt to rid himself of some of the day's tension. He shrugged out of his suit coat, then while opening the upper buttons of his white shirt, stepped outside onto the small wrought-iron balcony attached to his hotel room. The night air felt good, and after being cooped up for the past twelve hours attending lectures and sitting on panels, the lights of Madrid twinkling against the darkness were calming.

He'd been the hit of the three-day conference on alternative energy sources. After his presentation many of the attendees came up to offer encouragement and congratulations on his revolutionary breakthrough in fuel cell research. Currently, most of the fuel cells being developed required the inclusion of expensive metals like gold and platinum, but Adam had come up with a device based on the cheaper and more plentiful carbon. The prototype still needed tweaking before it could be marketed, but he was confident the bugs would be worked out, and once they were, the device he'd named Black Satin would have limitless potential, whether it be heating homes or powering the engines of interstellar probes. The big oil companies weren't going to be happy with his discovery, but that was their problem.

He turned his attention back to the lights of Madrid and wished he'd had the opportunity to see some of the sights, but he'd been so busy there hadn't been time to do the tourist thing. Maybe he'd have a chance in the future.

Adam stretched his arms wide and felt the tiredness in his bones. All he wanted was a hot shower and a big room service dinner. Some of the other scientists he'd met had graciously invited him to join them for dinner and to explore the city's nightlife, but he was just too whipped, so he'd declined.

Stepping back into the luxurious suite, he picked up the phone and ordered what he wanted to eat from the hotel's restaurant menu. When he was told it would be at least an hour's wait, he didn't fuss. He headed to the shower instead.

He emerged a short while later feeling much better. Wearing a pair of sweats, an MIT T-shirt, and some flip-flops, he did some preliminary packing in anticipation of tomorrow morning's flight home, then sat down with some of the articles he'd picked up at the conference. He was reading one on cold fusion when a knock sounded at the door and a Spanish-inflected voice called out, "Room service."

Pleased, Adam opened the door and all hell broke

loose. Two men immediately forced him back into the room but Adam fought to get free. He had no idea who they were or why they were there but he wasn't going to let them kick his ass while he found out. Lamps hit the carpeted floor, tables were turned over, and chairs toppled as the battle escalated. Adam took a few hard punches to his stomach, but instead of throwing up like he wanted to, he gave the man nearest him a vicious elbow to the nose that made him back off and cry out. The other man punched him in the jaw and sent him sprawling, but Adam came up with a lamp in his hand and doing his best Hank Aaron imitation connected with the assailant's face. The man screamed in pain and immediately dropped to the floor.

Breathing harshly, Adam turned on the remaining intruder—the one he'd elbowed. Blood poured from the broken nose. Adam smiled ferally and held the lamp out in front of him, waving it back and forth with the slow, deadly rhythm usually reserved for switch blades. "Come on," he taunted. "You're so bad. Come on."

The man's eyes shot hate, and he pulled out a gun. "We didn't expect you to fight, Dr. Gary."

Adam eyed the weapon. "I'm full of surprises. Who are you? What do you want?"

"Some people are interested in your invention."

"They ever hear of a phone?"

The man coughed and spit blood onto the carpet. "My wife will not be pleased when I come home with a broken nose." He paused for a moment to wipe the blood on his sleeve, and that's when Adam launched himself like a linebacker on a quarterback. The impact sent them crashing to the carpet. The gun went sailing, and Adam's fists made sure the man didn't get up to go after it.

In the silence that followed, Adam staggered to his feet. His knuckles were bloody and felt busted. His face had taken a beating and his stomach felt like hamburger, but he was still standing. The room was in shambles. The man who'd been taken out by the lamp lay on the floor whimpering in pain, his still unconscious accomplice nearby. Adam stepped around him to pick up the gun. His breathing labored, he scanned the trashed suite for the phone. Finding it, he dialed the front desk.

When the concierge came on the line, Adam said, "This is Dr. Gary in 532. Send the police to my room."

Without offering any further information, he set the phone back in its cradle then dropped down onto the overturned sofa to wait.

One

Wednesday, May 10, 2006
Manhattan, New York

Jan Kruger hated Manhattan. The traffic, noise, and the melting pot population were all symbols of a political system he found abhorrent. Given a choice, he'd rather be sitting at home on his veranda enjoying the company of his wife and watching the South Africa sunset, but instead he was stuck in New York traffic with a hired limo driver who smelled of curry.

As a member of a South African trade group, Jan had been forced to come to the U.S. more times than he'd wished, but his many visits gave him a keen sense of how America worked, and that knowledge had come in handy when a junior position in the South African embassy opened up and he was hired. Now, five years later, he held the title of Assistant to the Ambassador, a woman descended from the Zulu king Cetshwayo, whose forces had defeated Jan's ancestors and the British army at Isandhlwana in 1879.

He hated the ambassador as well. She represented the new South Africa, a country determined to eschew its glorious past in favor of a future built upon the deluded visions of ANC terrorists like Mandela and Walter Sisulu. Jan championed the old South Africa—its eliteness, its pride, its apartheid—and he was not alone. For the past few months he and a small cadre of like-minded Afrikaners had been meeting to formulate a plan that would restore that glory in a new country they would call their own.

There'd been a setback, though. This morning he'd gotten a call from his people in Madrid. The kidnapping of Dr. Adam Gary had been botched. The two operatives sent to his hotel were in a hospital and Gary was on his way back to the States. No one had expected the scientist to put up a fight, so now Jan knew that he and the others had to come up with another way.

Traffic was still stopped. Jan glanced at the heavy gold Rolex on his wrist. If it didn't clear soon he was going to be late for his meeting, and military men— especially the United States variety—were sticklers for punctuality, at least on the surface. In reality, in return for the money he'd promised them, the generals would wait until hell froze over if necessary. He knew how America worked.

The driver finally got the car moving again. The tie-up, caused by the collision of an airport shuttle van and a cab, had drawn the police and a crowd of curious New Yorkers. As his black limo crept by the wreckage, a grim Jan sat back against the plush seat. He had to figure out a way to get his hands on Dr. Adam Gary and that prototype, because the prototype was one of the necessary keys to their plan.

Friday, May 12, 2006
Detroit, Michigan

Mykal Chandler slid the file across the desk to Max Blake. She opened it and looked at the color photo. The head shot was of a good-looking, brown-skinned brother. Beard, moustache. Hair graying slightly at the temples in a distinguished sort of way. Grown and sexy, as Baby-face would say.

"Name's Dr. Adam Gary," Mykal explained.

"Doctor of what?" Max studied the face for a few moments longer. *Nice mouth.*

"Astrophysics, for one."

Max was impressed. "Really?"

"Supposedly, the brother's invented something that's going to revoulutionize everything from heating homes to space travel."

Max stuck the pic back into the file. "What is it?"

"Some kind of device that produces its own energy."

"I'll bet the gas and oil companies aren't happy about that. So what's going on that we're involved?" Mykal headed up a secret crime-fighting group called NIA, and Max often moonlighted as one of its operatives.

"Somebody tried to kidnap him a few days ago at a conference in Madrid."

She glanced up.

"He thinks they were after his prototype."

"Where is he now?"

"At a government-owned house on the western side of the state."

"You want me to go up and evaluate the security?"

"No, I want you to *be* the security. He doesn't even have a chicken on the place."

She was confused. "If this is such big-time stuff how come there's no security?"

"He doesn't want any. Says having a lot of people around will interfere with the flow of his work."

Max drawled, "You know I don't do crazy real well, Mykal. That's why I have two ex-husbands."

He grinned. "He's not crazy. 'Eccentric' is the word everyone is using."

"Educated crazy, then."

"Bingo."

She sighed. "Okay, so how do we work this?"

"I'm sending you in as his new housekeeper. The old one quit about a month ago."

"Why?"

"Husband retired and they moved to Florida."

"Okay. I haven't exercised my pots and pans in a while. Might be fun. Does he know I'm coming?"

"Yes, but all he knows is that the person is named Max Blake."

"In other words, he doesn't know I'm female."

"Correct. I didn't want to waste time arguing with him about it. If he throws a fit, I know you'll handle it."

"True, that."

Myk had no doubts about Max's abilities. She was a former Marine and had cut her intelligence teeth in the rebel-infested jungles of Colombia. She was tough, efficient, and smart. Today she was wearing a pair of cowboy boots; black jeans; a black halter top with a red cami underneath; and a black Stetson. Her attire spoke to her free spirit. When the Department of Defense had called him to send an agent up to take care of Dr. Gary, Max immediately came to mind.

"You're the best person for the job, Max," he told her

now, "so don't worry about Gary trying to get you replaced. Ain't gonna happen."

"Thanks." Max yawned and then stretched her arms
and shoulders. The plane ride to Detroit had been a
long one. Sometime in the near future she'd need a real
night's sleep.

Myk asked, "Any questions?"

"Nope.

"Okay. Check in when you get there. If you need a
map to his place, there's one in the file."

She stood up, showing off her five-foot-eleven-inch
frame.

"Good luck, Max."

She threw him a loose salute and strolled out.

The only person allowed to call her *Maxine* was her
mama, Michele. To everyone else she was simply Max.
Because of her height and take-no-prisoners attitude, it
was a name she wore well.

She was driving up Michigan's west coast to rendez-
vous with Dr. Gary. The day was beautiful and singer
Anthony Hamilton was on the in-dash CD player lyri-
cally begging Charlene to come home. Max had been
driving for almost five hours, but the May breeze flowing in through the open windows of the rented Honda
SUV felt good.

She glanced up at the rearview mirror to check on
the big male rottweiler lying on the backseat. "How're
you doing, Ossie?"

The black and tan Ossie slowly lifted his massive
head, and the misery reflected in his eyes broke Max's
heart. "I'm sorry, baby. The GPS says we'll be there in
a few. Just hang on."

Car travel always made him sick. Vets had prescribed everything from patches to pills but nothing seemed to help.

On the other hand, Ossie's sister, Ruby, belted into the passenger seat next to Max, scanned the road with eager eyes. Ruby liked riding, whether by car, plane, or boat, and the longer the journey the better. Ruby's first love, though, was the convertible Max bought last year. Anybody who didn't believe dogs smiled had never seen Ruby riding in the T-Bird's front seat. The first time Ruby rode in it, she refused to get out after the drive was over. In fact, the dog proved so stubborn, Max wound up letting her sleep in the convertible overnight.

Both dogs were extremely intelligent, but Ruby was the smarter. She had a way of reacting to situations Max swore bordered on human. She could roll her eyes, dismiss you with a look, and, like her brother, understood English and Portuguese, thanks to their breeder and trainer, a Brazilian friend of Max's named Portia. Max loved both her dogs, and like the famous credit card, she never left home without them.

She punched up the GPS screen on the dash. The display showed their destination to be less than a mile away. "Almost there, Os."

He whimpered mournfully.

"Poor baby," she said sympathetically, and turned off the main road onto an unpaved one marked PRIVATE. The bumps and lumps tossed the Honda's occupants this way and that. Knowing all the bouncing wasn't helping Ossie's condition, Max did her best to avoid the deeper ruts, but it was next to impossible. For his sake, she prayed they wouldn't have to go much farther.

The fates were kind. Around the next bend the road dead-ended at a large rusted wrought-iron gate that looked to be about eight feet high. The address on the cylindrical mailbox matched the address she'd been given for the Gary residence. "Looks like we're here," she said, peering through the windshield at the gate. The fence stretched as far as she could see in both directions. Inside, she saw a forest of cloud-kissing trees. She had no idea how far away the house might be, but she set aside her curiosity for now. Cutting the engine, she opened her door and got out so she could open the hatch and tend to Ossie.

The liquid brown eyes staring up at her were as sad as a carsick child's. "Come on, Os. Let's get you out so you can feel better."

Ossie slowly lifted his 110-pound frame, then gingerly moved from the SUV to the ground. Max knelt beside him and hugged him close. Gently stroking his head, she said, "Let me get Ruby and I'll be right back."

Once Ruby bounded out of the seat, Max leaned into the car and dug out their bowls. Filling each with bottled water from the cooler, she let the dogs drink while she pulled out her cell phone. She wanted to let Dr. Gary know that she'd arrived, but she got his voice mail instead. She left a short message and waited to see if he'd call back.

Ten minutes later she was still waiting. The dogs were done drinking, so she dumped out the remaining water, restashed the bowls, and checked out the gate.

There was a call box on the front, so she opened it and pushed the button labeled Talk.

After a few moments of silence she heard a female voice ask, "Yes?"

"I'm here to see Dr. Gary."

"He isn't seeing visitors today. Please call back and make an appointment."

Click.

Surprised by the abrupt ending, Max hit the button again, but this time there was no response. "Well," she said, not pleased. Ruby was watching her. Ossie was lying on the ground, his head on his black paws.

Undeterred by the woman's rude attitude, Max scanned the gate for the best way in. She noticed the thick rusted chains wrapped around the base of the gate and the ancient-looking padlock anchoring them. "You think this is what passes for security around here, guys?"

Not waiting for an answer, Max walked to the back of the SUV and dug out a pair of long-handled bolt cutters. A few minutes later she was driving slowly through the open gate while Ossie and Ruby loped alongside.

The narrow road twisted, turned, and climbed. The pines lining the way were so tall that for part of the way the sunny day became shadowy as dusk. Once the trees cleared and the sun came out again, Max was treated to a view of the sparkling blue waters of Lake Michigan that was awesome. Having traveled all over the world, she'd seen her share of beautiful vistas, and this one ranked in her top ten. She studied the house as it came into view. It was a large brick structure with Tudor lines that seemed more suited to an old world city like Boston. Her briefing materials from NIA mentioned that some of the houses along this stretch of the Lake Michigan coast were originally built during Prohibition as summer homes for Chicago's mobsters. She wondered if this stately old mansion had been one of those. She had a thing for historic architecture, and looked forward to checking out the inside.

With that in mind, Max led her canine escorts up the wide steps and rang the bell. No response. Keeping her temper in check, she hit the bell again, leaning on it for a good fifteen seconds or so.

Moments later the door was snatched open by a short, brown-skinned young woman dressed like someone in the Junior League. She had on pearls, a gray silky blouse, a navy skirt, and black patent stiletto pumps. The pearls weren't real, and neither was the weave, but the hostility in her eyes sure was. She snapped, "We're not . . ."

The words died away as she actually looked at Max and her attire.

Max didn't take offense. She assumed the household didn't get a lot of callers wearing sunglasses, black Stetsons, and green snakeskin boots, so she let Ms. Junior League get a good look, then said, "I'm here to see Dr. Gary."

. The woman seemed to regain her composure, and with it, her bad attitude. "Dr. Gary doesn't see anyone. He's in the middle of a project." She cast a disgusted look down at Ruby and Ossie. "And he doesn't do dogs at all."

Max had no idea who this weave-wearing young woman might be. The child didn't look a day over twenty-five, and there was nothing pertaining to her in the Gary file. On one level, Max was glad to see that Gary at least had someone guarding his door, but she hadn't traveled all this way to be chased off by a Chihuahua in pearls. "Dr. Gary is expecting us."

"No, he isn't. I'm his secretary and there is nothing on his calendar. You'll have to make an appointment. Have a good day."

She made a move to close the door in Max's face, but Max pushed it, and her, out of the way. "Excuse us," she said calmly.

Outraged and wide-eyed, the woman shouted, "You can't just bust in here!"

By now Max and the dogs were already past her. Max told the dogs, "Find the doc, would you guys?"

The dogs split up and took off.

The woman yelled angrily, "I'm calling the police!"

Max didn't break stride. "That's your choice, but I'd hold off on that if I were you."

Max passed room after room. All were empty. No furniture. No drapes. Not even a lawn chair. Why no furniture was a mystery to her, but it would have to wait. She had to find Dr. Gary first.

Down in his basement office, Dr. Adam Gary was more tired than he was willing to admit. He'd spent the last few days and nights in his lab trying to come up with a way to get the prototype to generate more heat and to do it for longer periods of time. Right now, Black Satin could only produce heat for a little over an hour. He knew he was on the edge of a breakthrough—he could taste it—but no matter how many times he fiddled with the formulas or studied the models generated by his computers, the solution still eluded him. Looking at the equations on the monitor now, all he could say was, "What am I doing wrong?"

That's when he saw the dog. It was a big rottweiler, and the sight of it standing in the open doorway where nothing had stood seconds ago rattled him so badly he almost fell off his stool. Wondering how the animal had gotten in and where it had come from took a backseat to getting the hell away from it. His heart was pounding, he was sweating, and his basic instinct was to run, but he knew better. "Go!" he yelled at it. "Get out of here!"

The big dog raised its head and barked. Adam frantically scanned the paper-strewn office for something to throw or to threaten the canine with, then just as quickly changed his mind. Agitating the animal might provoke an attack.

Then, suddenly, another rottweiler appeared in the doorway, and beside it stood a tall woman with skin the color of old gold in the sunshine. She was wearing jeans. The thin straps of her low-cut, green tank top showed off bare arms that were sleek and toned. Dark glasses shaded her eyes, and the permed hair showing beneath the black Stetson was short, brown, and softly spiked. Adam was six-foot-three, and she was tall enough to look him in the eyes.

"Good job, Ossie," she was saying to the dog, giving it a fond pat. Her soft voice was sweetened by a faint southern twang. Only after thanking the dog did she turn her attention to him. "I'm Max Blake. This is Ossie and Ruby."

Before the shocked Adam could recover from that bombshell, Kaitlin marched in, saying, "I told her you were working, and I told her you don't do dogs."

Adam was still trying to make sense out of this. *Max Blake? My security expert?* Not wanting Kaitlin to know that he didn't have a clue as to what was going on, he said to her, "I've been expecting her." It was a lie, of course. He'd not been expecting a woman, and he certainly hadn't been expecting dogs! He looked her up and down. Chandler's people were supposed to be sending him a security expert, not a woman in a cowboy hat! "Get those dogs out of here," he growled.

"They're clean."

"I don't care."

Though Max hid her irritation behind her shades, she didn't like his attitude or his tone. The angry looks he kept shooting at Ossie and Ruby made her wonder if there was more going on here than just a fear of dog germs. She held off on quizzing him, though. Instead she turned to Kaitlin and asked, "Can you walk them back out to my car, please? The doctor and I need to talk." Max met his eyes and noted that his held not an ounce of welcome.

Max's request had obviously offended Kaitlin, who drawled, "Adam, tell her that I am *not* a dog walker."

"Just go, Kaitlin, so she and I can talk."

She huffed in response and crossed her arms.

Max knelt next to the dogs and said, "Kaitlin's going to take you guys back outside, so be nice to her, and I'll see you in a bit."

The dogs looked up at Kaitlin with such expectant faces she seemed caught off guard for a moment. Then, with her young pretty face set tight with anger, she turned on her heels and stomped off. The dogs padded along silently in her wake.

Once she was gone, Adam said to Max, "Nobody told me you were a woman."

Hoping to lighten the tension, she tossed back,

"You were expecting maybe mouse and squirrel?"

His stony face said he didn't care that she had jokes. "Why wasn't I told?" he asked pointedly.

Tough crowd, she said to herself. "Because it didn't matter." Max took a casual look around the small wood-paneled space. Judging from the racks cut into the walls, it must have served as a wine cellar once upon a time. The space was below ground, and the bright bare bulbs strung across the ceiling for lighting made it feel like a cave. There were a couple of computer monitors, a few tables and chairs, and against one wall sat an old tan couch. Every flat surface was covered with stacks of papers and leaning piles of books.

"And the dogs?" he asked bluntly.

She turned back to him and the matter at hand. "What about them?"

"Do you always take your *pets* on a job?"

"They're not pets. They're part of my team."

"Oh, really?" he drawled, sounding unimpressed.

"Yes, and their security clearance is probably higher than yours, Doc." Max didn't see any beakers or any other nerd gear she imagined scientist types would have around, so she asked, "Where do you do your real work?"

That seemed to throw him for a moment, and it made her wonder if he'd thought her not smart enough to know this wasn't his lab.

He finally answered, "Through there." He used his head to indicate the small door at the back of the room. "But it doesn't matter because you won't be staying."

She casually folded her arms and gave him a cool smile. "Oh really?"

"Really."

Max knew from the file that he'd be a good-looking man, but it hadn't prepared her for his arrogance. "They're not going to replace me."

"Yeah right." He pulled out his cell phone.

Max shook her head at his obstinance and took a seat. Removing her Stetson, she finger-combed her short hair. While he waited for the call to go through, she went back to sizing him up. He was built. No Poindexter here. The way his razor-cut moustache flowed around the sexy mouth and down into the jaw-hugging beard gave him a dangerous outlaw sort of look. Had she met him at a club, she would have been subtly and sinuously all over him—until she realized he was a jerk. He looked tired, though. There were dark circles under his brown eyes and weariness in his face. Whatever he was working on must be kicking his butt, she decided, and she wondered when he'd last had a full night's sleep. Probably the last time she'd had one, she noted as she yawned and stretched. She'd gone from Osaka to L.A. to Texas and here to Michigan in what seemed like a day. Tired didn't begin to describe how she felt, but the fatigue took second place to knowing Mr. Wizard was going to have to eat his lab coat when he learned that she wasn't going anywhere.

Holding the phone to his ear, Adam waited for Myk Chandler to pick up. Adam was convinced he'd have no trouble getting rid of the woman watching him so silently from behind her shades. All he had to do was say the word and her butt would be outta here.

Wrong.

"What do you mean, you won't replace her?" he

snapped into the phone. He watched her remove her sunglasses to reveal amused green eyes set in a face fine enough to stop a man in his tracks. Adam blinked. He turned away and forced himself to pay attention to what Myk was saying on the other end.

"The Department of Defense approved her, so she stays."

"And I have no say?"

"She's a former Marine. She worked Homicide here in Detroit. She cut her security teeth in the Colombian jungles."

"I don't care about her credentials," he said evenly, "I want her and the damn dogs gone."

"Adam," Myk said reasonably, "she's there for security, that's all. Let the lady do her job so that you can do yours. Okay?"

For a second or so Adam was too angry to answer, but finally said, "Yeah."

"Good," Myk replied, sounding weary. "Now, anything else?"

"No."

"Talk to you later, then."

"Later." Adam closed the phone and studied the woman seated across the room. *This is a disaster waiting to happen,* he told himself. *A disaster.* Determined not to be distracted by how good she looked, and not caring if she heard the annoyance in his voice, he said, "Kaitlin can show you where you'll sleep. I have work to do."

Adam then walked to the door of his lab and without another word closed himself in.

Max sat in the silence wondering how much jail time she'd get for cutting off the nose of a top-secret government scientist. His attitude toward her didn't really matter; she'd worked for bigger jerks. She just wished this one weren't so seriously fine. Sighing at the injustice of it all, she stood up and strode off to find her rottweilers and the Chihuahua.

Two

The dogs were outside resting on the grass by the Honda, but Kaitlin was nowhere to be seen. Max leaned down and rubbed their necks affectionately. "She abandoned you all, huh? Well, come on. Let's go for a walk."

She started up the drive and marveled at the stately pines towering over the front portion of the property. They were magnificent, but from a security standpoint, their size and numbers could provide excellent cover for lurkers, so she made a mental note to get Benny up here to install some surveillance cameras. Another problem was that ancient gate she'd used the bolt cutters on. The whole thing, gate, fence, and all, needed replacing yesterday. It didn't provide an ounce of deterrent. As it stood now, a squirrel could jack the place.

After a while the meandering walk took Max and the dogs back the way they'd come. On the side of the house, they discovered a crumbling brick archway that led to the rear of the property and onto a very large cement patio that offered a breathtaking view of the lake. "Wow," she whispered with awe. Behind her was the large wall-sized window of the living room, and she could see Kaitlin watching her from inside. Max ignored her and walked to the edge of the fenced-in patio and looked out. She'd had no idea the house offered such a panoramic view nor that it was built on a sandy bluff that had to be a good fifty feet above the beach below. Gulls circled overhead on the thermals of the gorgeous day. Their cries and the waves breaking against the shore were the only sounds. The peacefulness Max felt was welcome. Having been on the move from country to country for what seemed an eternity, she was glad to have an assignment that might have a slower pace. Yes, she was here to do a job, but she looked forward to sitting out here at the end of the day and breathing in all this serenity.

The dogs, on the other hand, had their attention dead set on the water. Rottweilers love to swim, and Ruby and Ossie were no exception. Max looked to the left and saw a set of wooden steps carved into the face of the bluff. A metal handrail ran down their length to the beach. "You two want to swim?"

Both dark heads turned her way and the excitement in their eyes made her grin.

She gave them the go command with her hand, and they took off down the slope, leaving her to navigate the steps.

While the dogs played in the lake, Max stood down on the beach and looked up at the house. With her shades on she could see many large windows. She counted three balconies attached to rooms on the second floor. She'd known the place was big, but from down here she saw that it was even larger than she'd initially believed. Were the rooms on the second floor as empty as the few she'd seen on the main floor? She knew scientists could be eccentric, but surely the house had furniture somewhere.

From a security standpoint, the elevated positioning was a good thing. The steepness of the dune was also good. She wished there was a way to neutralize the steps, however, and planned to think about it. Surveillance cameras would be needed on this side of the house, too, as would motion detectors. If perps were coming by sea, she needed to know before they knocked on the patio door.

After, the dogs shook themselves dry. It was time to climb back up the bluff to the house. Max jogged up the stairs while the dogs loped up the face of the dune. They beat her, of course, and when she did arrive, every muscle in her body burned from the exercise, but the former Marine was still in excellent shape.

Max pushed open the large patio door and stepped into the cavernous unfurnished living room. In the center of the empty space stood Kaitlin. Max slid off her sunglasses. The young woman didn't appear any friendlier than she'd been earlier, but Max didn't let that bother her. "Dr. Gary said you'd show me where we can sleep."

"Why are you here?" Kaitlin demanded.

Max wondered if there was some kind of microbe in the local water supply that made these folks so rude. "I'm the new housekeeper."

"What?" Disbelief filled Kaitlin's face and then she began to laugh. "You're kidding, right?"

"Nope," Max responded easily. "I'm here to cook, clean, and help the doc out any way I can." Max's attention strayed to the large stone fireplace built into one wall. It wasn't in very good shape. The dark grate looked to be filled with dirt, cobwebs, and lord knew what else.

"I don't believe you."

Max shrugged. "Doesn't matter what you believe. I'm here. The dogs are here. You and I can either get along or not. Makes no difference to me." Max waited.

Kaitlin responded with, "There are three bedrooms upstairs. Take your pick." That said, she turned, and with her stilettos clicking on the dusty wooden floor, left the room.

Max shook her head at the woman's attitude and walked over to let the dogs inside. The dirt on the floors made it impossible to know the wood's true color or condition, so she didn't think it mattered if Ruby and Ossie tracked in more. However, once she had the place cleaned from top to bottom that would change, and other arrangements would have to be made for the dogs' entrances and exits. For now, though, she was content to have them with her as she explored the house.

Just as she'd feared, the place didn't hold a stick of furniture. Not in the large dusty library where the books on the shelves were so old that when she pulled one free it crumbled into dust and pieces in her hand; not in what appeared to be an old ballroom where the peeling wallpaper looked to be fifty years old; not in the once grand dining room with its wood-paneled walls and tin ceiling.

The kitchen, however, held a 1950s gas stove, an ancient refrigerator, and a single enamel sink. There were spaces on the surrounding walls that showed someone had removed most of the cabinets and had even primed the empty areas in between as if planning to paint, but the job must have been abandoned. The two small cabinets that remained hung on the walls like orphans.

"This is a mess," she said aloud. She looked down at the dogs.

When Ruby barked as if agreeing, Max cracked, "You can say that again. Let's go see what the upstairs looks like."

Kaitlin had been right. There were three bedrooms, but not one of them had so much as a lightbulb inside, let alone a bed. Sensing she was genuinely going to need a whole lot of patience to survive this assignment, Max pulled out her phone and put in a call to Mykal Chandler.

After he picked up, she explained her dilemma. "I've seen anthills with more furniture than this place. The appliances are something out of *Leave It to Beaver*, and there's no place to sleep because there are no beds."

"The place is government-owned. Maybe he's been waiting for them to provide furnishings. Give him the benefit of the doubt."

She walked to the windows. With the heel of her hand she rubbed at the grime covering the glass until she could peer through. The view of the lake would be spectacular from the room once you were able to see out. "I'm giving him that and more, believe me, but I need to get some contractors up here to look at the wiring. I'm sure his lab is state of the art, but this house can't possibly be."

"You'll definitely need to make sure the wiring is up to code if you're installing cameras. As for the appliances, beds, and furniture, you'll have to talk to him. Even though the government holds the title, he's the tenant. If he agrees, bill me and I'll bill DOD. If they can pay thousands of dollars for toilet seats, I don't think they'll mind springing for some improvements, but talk to him first."

Max sighed. "Okay. I'll see what he says."

They then moved on to discuss Gary's issues with the dogs. Max stated bluntly, "He's just going to have to get over himself on that. According to the file, he's not allergic, so there are no medical issues. The dogs aren't going to be in his lab unless its absolutely necessary anyway, so . . ." She let her voice trail off.

"I agree, but keep me posted, okay?"

"Will do."

She ended the call and snapped the phone back onto her belt. She wasn't looking forward to another confrontation with the good doctor, but there was no way around it.

After leaving the dogs in the room, Max made her way back down to the cellar.

When Adam heard the knock on the door, he ignored it. He knew the sound and cadence of Kaitlin's knock, and because it wasn't hers, he assumed it was Max Blake's. A second knock sounded, firmer this time, and he ignored that one as well. Then he heard her shout, "Dr. Gary!"

He studied the door, then barked back, "Go away! I'm busy!"

"We need to talk!"

"Later!"

"Now, dammit!"

In contrast to the darkness of the outer office, the walls of his lab were white as snow. Computer monitors were humming, the lights in the ceiling above were sharp, bright, and state of the art. His work was his life, but this woman seemed set on messing up both.

An unhappy Adam slid from the stool, did a quick save to his work on the computer, and with tight jaws went over and opened the door. "What do you want?"

"To have a conversation."

Adam wasn't accustomed to a woman tall enough to look him in the eyes, nor one fearless enough to challenge him like this. "Kaitlin can answer any—"

"Forget Kaitlin. This is between us."

Adam's jaw tightened. Stepping out into the gloom of the cellar, he closed the door on the lab. "What?"

"First of all, why isn't there any furniture in this house?"

Adam studied her. "Not my job."

"How long have you lived here? Five years?"

"Give or take a few months, yeah."

"Have you ever had the electricity checked, or the furnace cleaned, or done anything else to maintain the house's systems?"

"Nope. Haven't had time."

Max stared. "Well, before I install security cameras, this place needs to be inspected and brought up to code."

"Fine," and with that he turned to the door.

"We're not done, Doc."

He stopped.

"I'll be replacing the appliances in your kitchen, too."

"Why? They all work."

"But they worked better in 1957. How do you cook in there?"

"I don't, but Mrs. Wagner never complained."

Max knew from the file that Mrs. Wagner was the old housekeeper. "Well, if I'm going to be doing the cooking, I'll need something a bit more modern."

Adam's lips thinned. "Do whatever you think needs doing, just keep the noise down and leave me the hell alone." He went back into the lab and slammed the door.

Max stared at the closed door and toyed with the idea of lobbing a Molotov inside, but it was just fantasy. No way would she let the fact that she couldn't stand him impact his research, but sooner or later the two of them were going to have to talk about the security issues, otherwise she was going to run this operation the way she wanted and to hell with his input or his complaints.

Not pleased, Adam sat in the silence of his lab. The only thing he was supposed to be concentrating on was perfecting the prototype, not kidnappers, and definitely not the distracting Max Blake with her arresting green eyes and svelte curves. Just looking at her, he never would have guessed that she carried such impressive credentials. Marines. Homicide. The dogs notwithstanding, if she'd been sent by the Department of Defense, she had to be good at what she did. Which was what? Admittedly, he didn't know a thing about security protocols. He knew computer firewalls and how to keep a lab from blowing sky high, but this was unknown territory. Myk said to let her do her job so he could do his, and in reality that was the only logical choice. Adam wasn't stupid. The kidnapping attempt was dangerous business, and they'd try again, so just because he didn't want Max Blake around didn't mean he didn't need her.

With that in mind, he knew he needed to stop grumbling and cooperate with her because the sooner he did that, the sooner he could give full attention to his work.

That decision made, Adam walked back over to the

computers to resume his quest to fix the prototype, and as he settled in, there was no other place he wanted to be. For him, scientific discovery was an exciting, exhilarating love affair that had begun in the second grade when his teacher, Ms. Rogers, brought a cocoon into the classroom and placed it inside a glass aquarium. Over the course of the semester, he and his classmates were treated to the metamorphosis of a monarch butterfly. No one was more mesmerized than Adam's eight-year-old self. From the moment the orange and black monarch came out of the chrysalis and spread its distinctive shaped wings to dry in the classroom's warmth and light, he became hooked on science. Been that way ever since. It was an obsessive, all-consuming love that came before fiancées—he had two broken engagements as proof—before sports—although he did take a peek at the NFL and his beloved NBA every now and then—before friends—he hadn't talked to anyone in over a year; before everything.

His mother, Lauren, to whom he did talk frequently, warned him that one day he was going to come out of his lab and find that life had passed him by. Adam imagined she was right. Over the years, he'd spent so much time in the lab that the days would pass unnoticed. Tuesdays would melt into Fridays and Fridays into Mondays, but the sleepless nights and the lack of a social life were minor prices to pay in the real scheme of things. The Black Satin Project was on the cusp of changing the world in ways more far reaching than the discoveries of radio, the combustible engine, and penicillin combined, and for Adam, being able to positively affect and impact the lives of people not only in industrialized countries but in small underdeveloped pockets of the globe was what being a scientist was all about.

He'd be the first to admit that he lived the life of a recluse, though. If he ever expected to have the family he wanted, he was going to have to live aboveground long enough to find a woman willing to marry a man who otherwise doubled as a troll. She'd have to be unique, but not as unique as Max Blake, he mused sarcastically. He wondered if Ms. Texas was married. Any man in her life would have to be a strong one. It was also a given that a sister as fine as that didn't sleep alone, or at least not for long.

Max and the dogs were outside enjoying the sunset. The lack of chairs meant she was sitting on the concrete, but she didn't mind. The sun was descending into the lake in a fiery blaze of oranges and reds, and the scene was relaxing and peaceful. She was surprised to see Dr. Gary step out to join them. Even though he was not one of her favorite people, she was a Texan and raised by her mama to be polite, so she said, "Evening."

He nodded a short silent response. She watched him checking out the dogs lying at her feet, and noted that he didn't come any closer. Max supposed he was afraid of catching something, or scared he'd take some dreaded doggie virus back into his lab. She mentally rolled her eyes and rubbed her hand along Ossie's muscular back.

He asked her then, "What do I need to do to make this security thing work for both of us?"

Max studied him. Was he finally surrendering? "You need to know that the dogs and I are here to keep you safe, and that all you have to do is let us do our job." She turned her head so she could see his face. "You look tired."

"Goes with the territory."

For a moment Max saw him as a human being, but then he said, "I expect the dogs to stay outside at night, and that you alone will be responsible for removing any feces they leave on the grounds."

So much for the human moment, Max noted sarcastically, before saying aloud, "I brought my scooper, but there's no place for them to stay outside, so they'll sleep in the room with me."

"Get somebody to build them a pen. They can't be running loose in the house while I'm sleep."

Max took offense. "These dogs are government trained. They don't 'run loose.'"

He appeared to have more to say but instead looked out toward the lake and kept whatever it was to himself.

Max thought that wise; she'd had just about enough of him and his demands. "Friends of mine will be up to put surveillance cameras on the premises in a few days, then lay in a more secure gate down by the road."

He didn't respond but she saw his bearded jaw tense.

She tossed out, "For somebody who was almost kidnapped, you don't seem too concerned about your own safety."

"Oh, I am. I'm just not happy with the way it's affecting my work."

"According to my handlers, everybody and their mother wants what you've invented—the Russians, the Saudis, the Eastern Europeans. Big countries, little countries. If your prototype does even half the things it's supposed to, you're about to put OPEC and the rest of the energy cartels out of business. Do you know what that means?"

He held her eyes but didn't respond.

"There are probably people somewhere who want you dead—yesterday, because your research is about to send them to the poor house. Think about it, who's going to want to pay for oil or gas to heat their homes when they can use a simple device that can generate its own heat?"

"It isn't perfected yet."

"Doesn't matter, Doc. The potential is there, and that's what counts. You're supposedly one of the biggest brains on the planet, and you're a *brother*, this can't be news to you."

"No, it isn't," he admitted. "I just want to work."

"Then how about we get on the same page so that you can do that?"

He met her eyes and said, "Fine."

Max felt relief. Was she finally going to get some cooperation? "How long has Kaitlin worked for you?"

"About two months."

"That long?" She found that interesting. "I'd've thought it was longer."

"No."

Max sensed there was more to the story, but apparently he wasn't going to offer any details. So much for the cooperation. "Did you hire her personally or was she sent over by a service?"

When he didn't respond right away, Max explained, "I'm not trying to get in your business, but I need to know who all the players are, and their roles. We can't protect him if we don't know the good guys from the bad, right, Ruby?" Max rubbed her behind the ear and Ruby barked.

Max smiled, but when she looked over and saw the granite set of Gary's jaw, it faded. She said to him softly, "You know, they really are wonderful animals. They're smart, loyal, loving."

"They're dogs," he responded coldly.

"And both of them would give up their lives for you, even if you don't deserve it."

Having reached the end of her patience, Max stood. "You and I will talk tomorrow. The dogs need to run twice a day so we're going to go and take care of that. When we get back, we'll sleep in the car."

With that said, she gave the rottweilers a hand command and they took off down the steep dune. Max had to walk by the silent scientist in order to reach the steps leading down to the beach. She passed him without a word. Even though she could feel the heat of him as she did, the steely jawed Max ignored him because she was done with Dr. Jerkyll for the day.

Adam tried to feign indifference to her declaration about the dogs being willing to die for him, but the tug on his conscience was real. The last thing he needed was a woman in green cowboy boots calling him out. Although he'd never admit it to her, the snatch attempt had scared him, otherwise he would never have agreed to security being on the premises. The memory of the Madrid incident's outcome gave him a grim satisfaction, though. Both thugs had to be taken to the hospital by ambulance. *At least they know I'm not a punk*.

He turned his attention down to the beach where she was playing fetch with the dogs using pieces of driftwood. The trio was outlined against the descending sun like a shot from a movie. Her laughter and their responding barks rose clearly to his ears. They were having a good time. Her tall fit frame drew his eyes in ways no woman had done in quite some time.

"Is she really going to be the housekeeper?"

Adam turned. The irritation on Kaitlin's face was easy to see. "Yes."

"Why?"

"Because I hired her."

"From where, a circus? We don't need her here or those dogs."

Adam ignored that and asked instead, "Isn't it about time you went up to your room and e-mailed your father or something? I'm sure he'll be interested in your opinion of Ms. Blake."

Kaitlin's chin rose. "You make me sound like some kind of spy."

"Aren't you?"

"Of course not," she responded, as if offended. "You invited me here, remember?"

"No, you invited yourself."

"Daddy said you needed a secretary."

"Correct. Daddy said. I didn't." Daddy was Dr. Sylvester "Sly" Kent, an old mentor of Adam's determined to ride to fame on the tail of his lab coat.

"But I've been helpful."

"Yes, you have." And she had, Adam admitted to himself. In addition to tackling his piles of unopened mail, she'd done up the schedules for the grad students who would be working with him this fall. She also brought him bagged breakfasts every morning, and in the evening she ordered in pizzas or subs. She was going to make some brother a great wife one day, but the brother's name wouldn't be Adam Gary. He might be a scientist, but he wasn't a fool. Kaitlin had been sent to the house with two missions: One was to keep her father on top of his research, and the other to see if she could interest him in a relationship that resulted in making Sylvester Kent his proud father-in-law. *Not a chance.*

"Adam?"

Her voice brought him back. "Yes?"

"So, what are you going to do about her?"

Adam turned back to the beach. They were heading away from the house. The dogs were at Max's side, pacing like sentinels. He had to admit they seemed well-trained, but his attention was trained on the fluid, mesmerizing walk of their owner. "Nothing. She starts tomorrow."

Kaitlin looked displeased, but Adam didn't think he owed her anything other than, "See you in the morning, Kaitlin."

He went inside and left her to fume alone.

Three

Jan Kruger was alone in a London hotel room reading over the reports sent to him by his associates. The ancillary elements of the plan were coming together, and that pleased him. The contacts he and his group needed inside the various U.S. military and intelligence agencies were on board and awaiting further instruction. In today's corrupt world it hadn't been difficult to find people willing to betray their country's trust in exchange for cash. The dreams of Kruger and his associates to establish a new order had been embraced not only by people in the U.S., but in many of the European nations as well. He'd just returned from a secret meeting with some of Great Britain's military and could now add their support to the pledges he'd extracted from others in France, the Balkans, and the Soviet Union. As far as Jan knew, the South African government didn't have a clue as to what he and his people were embarking upon, and he planned to keep it that way.

The highlight of today's reports had been the information on Gary. Thanks to a newly recruited woman who worked as a secretary in the Office of Homeland

Security, they now knew where Dr. Gary was living and working. Although the mole hadn't been able to find out if there were any security people on the property, Jan didn't think finding out would be too difficult. Knowing Gary's location had been a burning question they now had the answer to. Included with the Gary info had been the addresses and pictures of his famous parents in case pressure needed to be applied to make him cooperate. The device Gary had invented was a potential gold mine, and if he could get his hands on it, he could rename himself Midas.

In the interim, though, he'd be leaving London tomorrow for another round of secret talks, this time with a Danish arms dealer with ties to everything from automatic weapons to black market F-16s. All for a price. If the man could deliver on his claims, he knew he would be able to cross off one more item on his now shrinking to do list, and that pleased him as well.

Max awakened around six-thirty in the morning, stiff but rested. The folded down seats in the back of the Honda had served as a makeshift bed for her and the dogs. Not exactly five-star accommodations, but for one night it hadn't been bad. Lying in her sleeping bag idly stroking the warm backs of the still snoozing rottweilers, she thought about the day's plan. Before going to sleep last night, she'd spent a few hours on the phone with Myk and on her laptop contacting contractors from a list of trusted companies. Many of the workers would begin arriving this morning, so she hoped Adam Gary was ready. He probably wasn't, but that's why she had been assigned: to get him ready whether he was down with the program or not.

When Max and the dogs entered the house a short while later, Kaitlin was dressed and in her pearls. Since Max hadn't seen her driving in or out, she assumed the Chihuahua had spent the night on the premises. "Morning, Kaitlin."

"Good morning," she replied, barely parting her lips. "You don't have to make Adam breakfast, I'm on my way to pick something up."

Since Max hadn't seen any food in the house anyway, she shrugged. "Fine with me. I need a shower. Which bathrooms work?"

"Mine does, but I'm not sure about the others." She then added pointedly, "And no, you may not use mine." She then fished around in her designer handbag. Pulling out her car keys, she looked up at Max and said, "And I mean it."

Max wondered if the girl knew just how close she was to being smacked. "Any cleaning products around?" If the dust and cobwebs flourishing everywhere else in the house were any indication, the bathrooms would probably need a good scrub-down before they could be used. If they worked at all. Max had been using a small one off the '50s kitchen for her needs until now.

Walking away, Kaitlin tossed out, "Look in the kitchen under the sink." Today's skirt was red, tight, and short. The heels, spiky as the patent leathers she'd worn yesterday, were red as well. *All booty, no brain,* Max said to herself, then she and the dogs headed for the kitchen.

She took a look around at the kitchen and swore this was the same one Aunt Bee used to cook in for Opie and Andy. Tossing that silly thought aside, she walked to the sink. Inside the small cupboard she saw a can of bathroom cleanser and a half-used bottle of dishwashing liquid. That was it. No sponges, no disinfectant, no nothing. Sighing, she grabbed the cleanser.

Last night she had been so disgusted by all the cobwebs and dust infesting the bedrooms, she hadn't even bothered to inspect the bathrooms. So this morning she took her first look at the one connected to the bedroom she planned to have as her own. To her relief, the small bathroom wasn't bad. The cabbage rose wallpaper was hideous and peeling in spots, but there was a small pedestal sink, an ancient-looking but functioning toilet, a tub, and a shower head. There was no shower curtain but the rusted rod to hold one was in place. The faucets appeared to have been copper once upon a time but were now green with age.

Max turned on the water in the tub and a reddish brown stream spewed out.

Ruby barked at it.

"Yuck, is right," Max told her, patting the dog's neck. Ossie took one look then walked out. Max watched him find a spot on the far side of the bedroom, where he laid down as if to say, *Call me when you're done.* She smiled.

It took a while for the water to run clear, but the way it swirled down the drain indicated that the pipes weren't plugged, which was good. Max shook cleanser into the now wet tub. Finding a small roll of paper towel inside the cabinet door above the toilet, she used some sheets to scrub the white enamel until it glowed.

She had concerns, though. Every time she turned the water on, the pipes in the wall set up a racket like they were trying to shake loose. Hearing it, she was glad she'd had the foresight to include a plumbing service in the folks coming out to evaluate the house today. It sounded like their expertise might be needed.

Now that the tub was clean, Max raced the dogs out of the room and down the stairs to the car so she could grab the overnight bag holding her toiletries. She'd cart in the rest of her luggage later. Laughing, she raced them back inside, almost knocking over the returning Kaitlin and her bags of fast food breakfast.

"Sorry!" Max called to her, but by then the dogs had bolted up the steps and Max was last again. *Damn!*

Not caring if Kaitlin tattled to the principal in the basement about her and the dogs running through the house, an invigorated Max stripped out of her clothes, turned on the water gently so it wouldn't splash out of the tub, then stepped into the shower's weak but warm stream. The pipes began their knocking. That worry, coupled with not knowing how long the hot water would last, made her wash quickly. When she finished, she reached to turn the hot water spigot and it came off in her hand. Alarmed, she tried to shimmy it back on, but her efforts only increased the water force until it was roaring out of the shower head like the Hoover Dam. It happened so fast, she was under assault before she realized it. The pipes were screaming and so was she as she fumbled to turn it off. The pounding force had the ancient shower head spinning like Linda Blair's and throwing water everywhere. It finally ripped free and the spray blinded, cursing, Max felt for the Cold. It turned, but not off. Water as frigid as the Bering Sea began pelting her full force. She screamed at the shock and stumbled out of the tub. The dogs began barking with concern outside the door, and a soaked Max stared at the water now pouring out of the shower pipe. It was coming too fast for the drain to handle. Water began backing up into the tub at a rate that signaled disaster if it weren't turned off soon.

She grabbed a towel and quickly fastened it around her wet self. She ran for the stairs with the dogs on her heels.

As Max came tearing down the steps, she spotted Kaitlin. "Where's the house's shutoff valve?"

"What?" Kaitlin's eyes were large as saucers as she looked the wet Max up and down.

"The valve that turns off the water!"

"What are you talking—"

Max was already on her way to the basement.

In the lab, Adam was staring at equations on his computer monitor when a sound unlike any he had ever heard before began emanating from the pipes. It wasn't unusual for them to make a groan or two when water was turned on because it was an old house, but this sound? Sensing something wrong, he saved his work and hurried to the door, opening it just as Max was about to knock.

She shouted, "Where's the water shutoff valve?"

Stunned, Adam looked at her in the towel she was clutching to her wet body and blinked. He was so busy staring at her long legs, the damp glistening slope of her bare arms and shoulders, and the soft tops of her dewed breasts rising above the towel that he didn't hear the question.

"Where's the damn valve?" she shouted again.

Adam shook his mind to clear it. "What?"

"The shutoff valve! Where is it?"

"I don't—"

She cursed. "Find a flashlight. Come on!"

Speechless, he watched her and the dogs run off.

Hearing the pipes roaring like a wounded beast seemed to wake him up, though. He hurried into the lab, grabbed a flashlight, and took off in pursuit.

Max found the water heater in a space not too far from the lab and hoped the valve would be on a wall someplace near, but it was dark as hell. She couldn't see a damn thing and she was having a heck of a time trying to hold onto the towel. Feeling her hands along the wall while praying the water upstairs hadn't overrun the tub, she toyed with the idea of just turning the water off at the water heater. That would stop more water from coming into the tank, but the water already in the tank was feeding the shower's pipes and would continue to flow until it was empty. Suddenly, there was light. "Hallelujah! Hand it here."

He gave up the flashlight, and she focused the beam on the dark walls. Snaking it up and down, she finally found what she was after. The small wheel was positioned about waist high. Accustomed to relying on the dogs, she said, "Ossie, quick. Come hold this."

The big male trotted into the light. She placed the barrel of the flashlight in his mouth, and the dog held it trained on the spot while she tried to turn the valve. It was stuck. Straining, she said, "Dammit, turn!"

She tried again, but it refused to move. She tried again, groaning with the effort, and lost her towel in the process. Embarrassed but cool, she snatched it up, wrapped it around her once more and hoped Gary hadn't fainted.

Adam was certain that quick glimpse of perfection would have left him blind had he been a character in a Greek myth. He had to shake himself to keep the scene from playing over and over.

"Let me try," he said.

When his eyes met hers, Max gave him a look that dared him to say anything about her towel. He didn't, but she swore she saw him smile as he turned away.

"What is this thing again?" he asked, straining with the effort to turn the old valve.

"Your water shutoff valve. Controls the water coming into the house."

He stopped. "Really?"

"Yes, and if you don't hurry the hell up, the whole upstairs is going to flood. The faucets in the shower broke off and the water is on!"

That seemed to get his attention. Finally, strength prevailed over rust and age and the valve began to turn. Max listened to the pipes. They were still clanging. "More," she told him. "More."

He turned the wheel until it wouldn't turn anymore, then came silence.

Max wilted with relief.

He asked her, "Now, how did this happen again?" All he could think about was her nude frame.

Max took the flashlight gently from Ossie's mouth, then related the story.

When she was done, he said grimly, "I suppose I should get the pipes looked at."

"You think?" she asked, then added, "How can you not know where your shutoff valve is?"

"Never needed to know. I've lived in apartments and condos most of my life."

Max shook her head at his ignorance. Growing up, her mama Michele made sure she and her sister JT knew as much about keeping the house maintained as they did about applying makeup. "I'm going to dry off.

There's a thousand people coming today, and the first thing they're going to fix is that plumbing."

"A thousand?" he asked, sounding alarmed.

"More like two thousand," she tossed back, just to mess with his mind. She slapped the flashlight into his palm, then she and the dogs left.

Alone now, Adam trained the light back on the valve. Who knew? And who knew he'd be shown one of the sweetest female bodies he'd seen in quite some time. Not that he'd been eyeballing her, but his mind's camera must have been because his memory was filled with vivid flashes of those long golden legs, small perfect breasts, and the way her trim waist flowed into that gorgeous behind. He shook himself. He'd been celibate by choice for the past two years because of the demands placed upon him by his research. Women were a distraction he couldn't afford while bringing the Black Satin Project to life. Even now, with the prototype in the final stages, concentration was vital and discipline essential, but as the vision of her bending over to pick up the towel replayed itself yet again, the image set off a stirring in his groin that was achingly familiar.

Upstairs, Max put on her clothes, then used a towel to mop up the water in the bathroom. Luckily, she'd found the valve before the tub overflowed and disaster struck, but the walls and the floors were still soaked. The memory of losing her towel came back to embarrass her, and she wondered what Gary had thought of the accidental striptease. She'd tried to play it off by acting as if it weren't a big deal, and he seemed to do the same, to a point. Had he been smiling or not? It hadn't been one of her best moments and she'd been embarrassed, but she hoped he didn't think she'd dropped it on purpose. She knew that there were women who did dumb things like that to catch a man's eye, but she wasn't one of them. Gary was cute, and had that pirate look about him, but he wasn't really her type. Making love with him would probably be like being immersed in ice water. She preferred her loving at a much higher temperature.

When Max and the dogs came downstairs, they found Kaitlin at the front door arguing with six or seven men dressed in work clothes and holding tackle boxes in their hands. Apparently, Ms. Chihuahua was playing guard dog again and trying to make them leave, but the men arguing and shaking work orders in her face weren't buying it.

Max stuck two fingers in her mouth and let fly a piercing whistle that quieted everyone in mid-shout. In the silence, she and the dogs walked forward. "Gentlemen, I'm sorry for the confusion. I'm the housekeeper. I didn't tell Kaitlin that you were coming. My bad."

The men were staring at her as if she had just stepped out of a UFO. Max didn't know if it was her height, her color, her skinny blue halter top, jeans, or matching blue boots, but since she was accustomed to folks staring at her, especially men, she let them look while she said, "Is there a plumber here?"

A Black guy raised his hand.

Max smiled. "Okay, I'll see you first. The rest of you give Kaitlin your names, make yourselves comfortable, and I'll be back to put you to work."

Kaitlin was staring, too, but as if Max had lost her mind.

Max gave her a wink then walked off with the brother plumber and his two-man crew.

For the rest of the morning, the plumbers worked on the pipes and bathrooms. Painters stripped wallpaper and brought in dry wall. Brick masons were turned loose on the crumbling archway adjacent to the house, and electricians roamed the place in search of frayed wiring. Even though all the contractors had passed NIA's security checks, she kept an eye on them nonetheless. By noon the house was a hive of noisy activity and Max was the queen bee.

To Max's surprise, Kaitlin was a good second in command. Armed with a clipboard and a no-nonsense attitude, she made sure the workmen stayed on task and turned a withering eye on anybody trying to hit on her. Her dislike of Max was still intact. She spoke to Max as little as possible. But she took care of business, and that's all Max cared about.

In the basement, Adam threw up his hands. How in the world was he supposed to concentrate with all the racket going on upstairs? Hammering, drills, men yelling back and forth. *This is not going to work.* He'd agreed to have a few things done to the house, not erect the Sears Tower.

Planning on giving somebody a piece of his mind, he left the lab and went to find the woman in charge.

The upstairs looked like a construction site. He'd never seen such chaos. Noise, men carrying paint cans, women carrying lumber, saws going, plaster dust everywhere. He looked around for Blake. He didn't see her or her dogs but he did see Kaitlin.

He yelled angrily over the wail of circular saws, "Where is she?"

"Kitchen!" Kaitlin shouted back. "I tried to stop her!"

Grim, Adam set out in that direction. He was so intent upon his mission he walked directly into the path of a wheelbarrow. "Hey! Watch out!" the man pushing the thing warned loudly. Adam jumped out of the way just in time. Cutting the man a look, he moved on.

The state of the kitchen left him speechless. The place was so torn apart it looked like a pipe bomb had gone off. The sink was gone, the stove disconnected and pushed aside. A man with a sledgehammer was knocking holes in the wall. She was on the far side of the room wearing a yellow hard hat and watching the workers removing the countertops. When had he authorized that? More amazing were the dogs. They had on canine versions of hard hats that looked like miniature bike helmets complete with chin straps.

"You need a hard hat in here, man," one of the men carrying out the countertop said to him.

Adam had no intention of putting on a hard hat. Instead he turned to Max and gritted out, "May I speak with you please, Ms. Blake?" Then he added for emphasis, "Now."

She met his eyes and shrugged. "Sure." But before leaving she said to the dogs, "Ruby and Ossie, stay back out of the way."

When the dogs backed up, Adam shook his head, latched onto her arm and very gently but pointedly bum-rushed her out onto the patio. Turning her loose, he asked, "Who said you could turn this place into mayhem?"

"You," she said firmly. "You said to do whatever I thought necessary, remember?"

Adam did remember. He also remembered her losing her towel, and that only added to his mood. "I didn't know it would be all this."

"The house is crumbling around your ears, Doc. Weren't you with me this morning when I starred in *Waterworld,* or was that a clone?"

He sighed angrily and looked away. "I can't work with all this going on."

"Then do something else for a while. Watch the news. Take a walk."

Max saw Kaitlin on the other side of the glass watching them. She had her clipboard clutched tightly against her chest and her face was grim. Max asked, "Will you please tell me what is the deal on her? Are you two engaged or what?"

"Not engaged. Although her father would like that."

"Who's her father?"

"Dr. Sylvester 'Sly' Kent. Helped me get my first lab. Now he wants to be my first father-in-law. She's the bait."

Max thought she understood the girl's attitude now. "She's cute if you like them young."

"I don't."

The eyes staring into hers were frank; male.

Oh my, Max said to herself. Leaving that alone, she brought the conversation back to more immediate issues. "The electricians need to cut the power so they can do some rewiring. What day is good for you?"

Adam could smell the faint notes of her perfume, and it was as distracting as she. "None."

Max was puzzled. "Don't you have a backup generator for the lab?"

"I do."

"Then why are you being such a pain in the butt? Pick a day or I'll pick one for you. Today is Tuesday."

He met her eyes, and when she didn't flinch, he again wondered how such a beauty could be so tough. "Tomorrow," he mumbled. "Get it over with."

"Thank you." Max wanted to throw up her hands. She'd never had an assignment drive her insane on the first day.

"When will the dog pen be built?" he asked bluntly.

Max sighed. "What is it with you and my dogs?"

"When?" he asked quietly.

"As soon as possible."

"Good." He stared over at her for a long moment, then said, "I have to get back to work. Try and keep it down."

When he was gone, Max shook her head and went back inside.

Downstairs, Adam surrendered. No way could he concentrate with the bedlam going on upstairs. He'd asked her to keep it down, but apparently she had a different definition for the phrase because the noise sounded louder. Disgruntled, he slid from the stool and took off his lab coat. He'd never had anyone call him a pain in the butt before, and he wondered if her military training was responsible for her fearlessness or if she'd been born that way. From her point of view, he supposed he was acting like a pain in the ass, but she didn't seem to understand he had no room in his life for upheaval. *And she'd only been around a day.* He couldn't imagine what things would be like in a month. The dogs were bad enough, but now he had to contend with wheelbarrows, drills, and dust. To make matters worse, every time he looked at her, his memory kept flashing back to her in that towel; the droplets of water on the edge of her neck, the imprint of her nipples pressed against the damp towel, the sleek firm muscles of her legs and thighs. He ran his hands over his eyes. He had to stop. If he didn't get those images of her out of his mind, his commitment to celibacy was going to crumble around his ears just like his old house.

To do something with his restless energy, he changed clothes and went to work out on the weights he had set up in one of the basement's other small rooms. He pumped iron for a good thirty minutes, but it didn't help; all he kept seeing was Max.

Four

Max took Adam Gary's grumbling about the noise into consideration, but because no one in the work crew spoke *drill* or *saw,* it was hard to tell the machinery to hold it down.

By five o'clock that evening the workers were packing up for the day. They'd all be back first thing in the morning. Although the house was still torn apart, the various projects were proceeding well. According to the electricians, the wiring was so old and substandard the place was a potential fire trap, but they'd made good headway pinpointing the areas needing to be worked on first. Max was pleased because Benny, with his fiber-optics equipment, would be coming tomorrow to lay in the cameras. The plumbers had also given her a report. They'd turned the water back on and their diagnosis of the pipes had something to do with air chambers and ratios. Since Max didn't have a clue as to what they were talking about, she simply nodded and told them to take care of it, and they had. The faucets were fixed in her shower, and when she turned on the water, the pipes protested for a moment but then went silent. A new shower head had been installed as well. When she stepped in to wash off the plaster dust and the rest of the day's grime, the experience was blessedly drama free.

After the shower she dressed and, refreshed, went went on a search for Kaitlin. Max wanted to know if there was a decent restaurant nearby that didn't involve clown's crowns or paper bags. She was hungry and in need of a good meal. However, she hadn't fully explored the house and so had no idea where Kaitlin's office might be. "Ruby, find Kaitlin, please."

Ruby stood still for a moment, then moved her head a few degrees to the right and left as if listening. When she seemed satisfied, she began walking up the hall. Max could have just as easily yelled out Kaitlin's name, but every opportunity she had to work the dogs kept them keen.

Ruby made a turn and led Max and Ossie into a hallway Max had never seen before, and then up an old rickety staircase. Max asked, "You sure this is where she is, girl?"

Ruby kept going. At the top of the stairs was a landing. Set back a few feet stood a large wooden door bordered with carvings of mathematical equations and chemical symbols. Ruby walked to the door and sat down. Max, confused, stood on the top step. "Okay, if you say so."

Just as she raised her hand to knock, she heard Adam Gary ask, "What are you doing?"

Max turned and stared into his suspicious eyes.

"Looking for Kaitlin."

"She's not in there."

"According to Ruby, she is."

"Well, the dog's wrong. That's my room. Kaitlin knows it's off limits."

His room? Max had wondered where he slept but assumed he had a place connected to the lab. "She's usually right."

"This time it's not."

"She's not an it," Max gritted out. *What was it going to take to get him to lighten up?*

He came up the stairs, brushed by Max and opened the door. Lo and behold, there stood Kaitlin, looking for all the world like a kid caught rummaging through her parents' room.

Seeing Gary's thunderous face, Kaitlin spoke up quickly, "I—came to see if you had any laundry."

He folded his arms. "Laundry," he echoed skeptically.

Max didn't believe her for a moment.

"Yes, you asked me to take your sheets to the Laundromat. Remember?"

Max could see him scanning the room as if looking for her real purpose.

"I remember," he said, "but I also remember telling you not to be in here without permission."

She smiled that cute twenty-five-year-old smile that probably made lesser men believe her every word. "I know I'm not supposed to be up here, but sometimes, Adam, you get so busy that you forget stuff like washing your sheets."

"Oh really?" He looked her up and down, then said harshly, "Get out, Kaitlin."

Her shocked eyes morphed to hurt. "You don't have to be so mean, Adam Gary."

"Out."

With her lip quivering, she shot Max a nasty look, then made a hasty exit.

Max waited until she was gone to say, "Guess Ruby was right, after all."

He didn't say anything.

Max wasn't surprised, so she asked instead, "Do you keep anything connected to your work up here?"

"One of my desktops is over there."

Max could see the screen saver on the computer's monitor. Multiple strands of Einstein's famous equation $e = mc^2$ floated lazily over the screen. "Check and see if she logged on or tampered with your disks. If she was up here after sheets, I'm five-foot-two."

Max thought he smiled in response to her quip, but like last time, it vanished so quickly she wasn't sure.

While he sat down and booted up, she checked out the room. This was obviously the attic. The space was circular, with walls paneled in cherrywood. Large windows overlooked the lake. Built-in shelves, filled top to bottom with books, dominated one wall, and a huge black metal bed covered with a beautiful indigo quilt dominated another. Where his downstairs outer office resembled a cave, this space with its plush gold and ivory Turkish rug, framed artwork, and neatly stacked audio components resembled a cocoon. Also unlike the office downstairs, the bedroom was barracks clean, not a book or paper out of place. The room exuded haven, and she thought it would be the perfect place to cuddle in and let the world go by, but she doubted he knew anything about that. On the other hand, she liked seeing him in real clothes. He was wearing an old MIT T-shirt, jeans, and Reeboks. Without the lab coat, the lean muscles in his arms showed themselves for the first time. He had a trim waist and the jeans fit real nice. *Not bad for a brother made out of ice water.*

To put herself back on track, she asked him, "Any idea what she really might have been doing?"

He shrugged. "No telling. Nothing seems moved or out of place, though."

"I'll have a lock put on tomorrow."

"Good." For a moment there was silence as he did a quick scan of his programs, then said, "Nothing indicating she logged on so far." Adam clicked on his mailbox and saw a message from his mother. Smiling, he opened it. A digitalized picture began to load and seconds later her face appeared. Her brown eyes, so like his, were filled with intelligence, and as always a spark of mischief. He glanced to the bottom of the pic and froze. Beneath the picture were the words: *Will the lioness fight as fiercely as the cub? Have a good evening. Your friends in Madrid.*

Max saw him stiffen. "What's wrong?"

"They're threatening my mother." Adam quickly pulled out his phone. If they went anywhere near her, he'd kill them with his bare hands!

Max read the message and whispered, "Good lord." Seeing the phone next to his ear, she said, "Are you calling her?"

"Yeah." He stood and began to pace.

"I'll call Myk and let him know."

Adam turned his attention back to his own call. His mother's voice mail kicked in. Disappointed, he kept his voice as normal as he could. "Hey, Mom. Just checking in. Call me when you get a chance. 'Bye." As he ended the transmission, his worry increased in proportion to his anger. If the people responsible for sending the e-mail wanted to tangle with him fine, but leave his mother out of it. Grim, Adam punched up his stepfather's cell number. Ray's phone rang a few times, then Adam was sent to his voice mail, too. Tight-lipped, he forced his voice into the same calm tone he'd used before and left Ray a similar message.

At that moment Adam felt like a terrible son because he had no idea where his parents were. He remembered his mother calling to say she'd be going on a trip to West Africa, but he'd been so obsessed with the prototype that he hadn't paid much attention to the dates or to her itinerary. Had she gone already? Had she returned? How long did she say the trip would be? He ran his hand over his hair. He didn't know. The same held true for his stepfather. The last time he'd talked to Ray had been two weeks ago. Or had it been longer? Once again he couldn't recall the conversation clearly, and now there was no way to be sure they weren't in danger unless they called. If anything happened to them he'd never forgive himself.

Max was on the phone with Myk. She had him hold on for a moment while she spoke to Adam. "Did you get your stepdad's voice mail, too?"

He nodded. "Neither of them answered. She said something about going to West Africa but . . ." He shrugged.

Max relayed that info to Myk. She and Myk talked for a few more minutes then she closed her phone. "Myk's tracking down your parents right now. He'll call back soon as he can. If it's any consolation, Myk and I are both betting they sent this to scare you."

"And they're doing a damn good job."

Max sympathized with him. "I'm not going to tell you

not to worry, because if it were my mama, I'd already be on a plane for home. We'll just have to wait and see what Mykal finds out."

Adam nodded but all manner of disturbing scenarios filled his mind. For the first time in a long time his work on the prototype took a backseat.

"Who else knows about this invention of yours?" Max asked.

"Most of the scientific community. I took the wraps off at the Madrid conference and referenced some of the work that went into it."

"Exactly how much referencing did you do?"

"Enough for them all to know that I'm just a heartbeat away from perfecting it."

"I see." Max rolled that around in her mind for a moment, then asked, "So can the people who sent the e-mail do anything with the prototype if it's not finished?"

"Depends. Lot of people out there with bigger brains than mine."

"Could anyone you know be helping them?"

It was a question he'd been asking himself since leaving Madrid. "Not that I know of." Adam wished he knew where his mother was.

"You have firewalls on your computers?"

"Yeah."

Max was glad to hear that, although the Madrid people had somehow accessed his mother's screen name in order to lure him into opening the message. "Myk's going to contact a friend and have her try and find out where that e-mail really came from. What about Ms. Kaitlin, could she be a mole?"

"Only for her daddy, but he doesn't have access to a

lab, as far as I know, and you'd need one to finish the prototype."

"He's a scientist?"

"Yeah. Got himself kicked out of the community, though. A couple of his assistants popped up pregnant and took him to court."

Max's empty stomach growled loud enough to be heard in Tokyo. "Sorry," she said apologetically. "If I don't get something to eat, I'm going to keel over. I was looking for Kaitlin originally to ask if there were any real restaurants around that delivered."

"Danny's. Over on Third."

"What kind of food?"

"Basic stuff. Best sweet potatoes, greens, and ribs this side of Detroit, though."

Max was impressed. "There's a soul food place up here?"

"Yep."

"This Danny's a Black man?"

"Nope, Polish, but when you taste his food, you'll swear his mama was a Black woman from the South."

Max smiled. "Okay." She could see that he was still worried about his mom, and she couldn't blame him. "If your mama is anywhere on the planet, Myk Chandler will find her."

"Thanks."

"Whoa!" she exclaimed.

He stared. "What?"

"I didn't think you knew that word."

His dark eyes flashed irritation.

Max quickly defended herself. "I was kidding, goodness. You really need to lighten up, Doc. All that darkness is gonna turn you into Darth Vader one day."

He smiled.

She was so astonished she laughed, then said to the dogs who were lying by the door, "And he can smile, too, guys!"

Ruby barked twice in happy response and Max saw Adam freeze. The stony set of his face made her study him in the silence now filling the room. She said to him quietly, "You really need to tell me what's going on with you and the dogs."

He looked away and didn't respond for a few long moments. Finally he said, "Two rottweilers attacked me on the way home from school."

Max's heart twisted. "How old were you?"

He met her eyes. "Twelve. I was hospitalized for ten days. Had to have seventy-five stitches put in my jaw and lips. Another fifty in my back and shoulders. The beard is mainly to cover the scars."

Max could only imagine the pain he must have endured. "I'm so sorry. That's why you don't do dogs."

"Exactly."

She understood now. She walked over, knelt next to the dogs and said just as quietly, "Ruby and Ossie, go wait for me down by the steps. I'll be there in a few minutes."

Ruby stood and left. Ossie stood, too, but he stayed. When Max looked down, she saw that the dog's eyes were focused on Gary. It wasn't like him to not comply with a command, so she said, "Go 'head, Os,"

The big male gave the scientist one last long look, then trotted out.

Max said to Adam, "Being around them must be hard. There was nothing about the attack in the file I was given."

"Not something I talk about. Grown men aren't supposed to be afraid of dogs."

She understood that, too. "I feel really bad. I'm so sorry. I can be like a bull in a china shop sometimes."

"I've noticed that."

"Bet you have."

They both grinned this time, and the effects of his soft one seemed to slide right through her. *Oh my,* she said to herself.

Adam had been affected by her as well and found himself wondering what it might have been like had they met each other under normal circumstances. "What would you like from Danny's?"

"The yams and ribs sounded good. Do you have a menu?"

"Yeah. Hold on." He walked back over to the desk and opened a drawer. Pulling out the menu, he handed it over.

Max read the selections then said, "Yep. Yams. Ribs. Collards. And throw in a piece of coconut cake because I've been such a good girl."

He chuckled, "Oh really?"

"Yes," Max said with mock attitude. "You don't think so?"

Adam stilled. He knew how he wanted to respond to the provocative question, but he'd known this woman less than a week and he was supposed to be practicing celibacy.

An amused Max asked, "No comment?"

His eyes sparkled. "No comment."

Max was pleased that the ice between them seemed to be thawing, even if it was only a small crack. It made her wonder about the man beneath the scientist.

He made the call to Polish Danny's Soul Food. After ordering for Max, himself, and out of courtesy, something for Kaitlin, he closed his phone. "About thirty minutes."

"Okay. I'm going to hang out with the dogs until the food comes." Then she added, "And Adam, I am sorry about what happened to you. Ruby and Ossie would never hurt you. It's not how they were raised."

He didn't speak to that, but did say, "If I hear from my mother I'll let you know."

"And I'll let you know if Myk calls me."

"Sounds good."

Unspoken words passed between them then, and Max sensed he was as aware of her as she was of him. "I'll see you later," she said in parting, and left him alone in the room.

Adam walked over to the windows and looked out over the lake. He was so concerned about his mother, she was all he could think about. *Did those men have her?* Once again hundreds of ugly scenarios played in his mind with such vividness he finally had to force his mind onto something else. The dark clouds forming out on the horizon signaled rain. Usually, watching a storm roll in was one of the joys of living there on the lake. Adam was as fascinated by weather and storms as he was with every other branch of science, but this evening his excitement was muted. The swan-shaped glass barometer mounted on the wall beside the window had been a Christmas gift from his mother a few years back, and the sight of it sent his thoughts to her again. *Where is she? How is she? Is she safe? What about Ray?* The glass swan measured barometric pressure by the movement of the red dye resting in its belly. The dye was rising into the neck, which meant the pressure was dropping rapidly, indicating the approach of a big storm. Sure enough, Adam could see thick dark clouds filled with flashes of lightning sweeping across the water like dust from an advancing herd of charging buffalo.

He wondered if Max enjoyed storms. He had no idea why he'd told her about his issues with the dogs. As he'd said, the attack wasn't something he usually talked about, especially not with strangers but with her he had. In his younger days he would have been all over the foxy, green-eyed Max Blake. His attraction to her was growing by the moment, but the reality of the now was that he needed to stay as far away from her as possible. She came across as a woman who captained her own ship and as a result had probably left behind a trail of broken male hearts a mile long. He had no plans to become a member of the club. His work was a jealous mistress, but a woman like her could inspire a man to greatness.

He shook off the fantasies of the tempting Ms. Max and turned his thoughts to Kaitlin. What had she really been doing up here in his room? Could she and her daddy be connected to the threatening e-mail? He hoped not. He was sure Kaitlin had contacted her old man about Max, however, and equally sure that Sylvester Kent would be showing up in the next couple of days, ostensibly to check her out.

A soft rumble of thunder brought Adam back and he looked out at the lake. The storm clouds were now smoke gray and hugging the lake surface in a way that made them appear to be forming from the water. He could see shards of lightning flashing periodically inside them and he estimated the brunt of the storm to be about twenty minutes away. The red water in the swan barometer had risen high into the neck now, which meant the pressure was still dropping. The storm was going to be a wild one. It was not the time for anyone to be on the beach. A storm spawned by such low pressure would be packing winds capable of taking out large trees. He checked his watch to try and gauge the delivery from Danny's. If the driver was lucky, he'd be here and gone before it hit.

Adam turned away from the window. He wanted to power down the computers. Lightning liked to snack on silicon the way tornadoes liked trailer parks, but out of the corner of his eye he saw Max and the dogs jogging down on the beach. He looked at the approaching storm and the wind-whipped water and then back at her with amazement. He assumed she knew a storm was coming, so what the hell was she doing on the beach? She was the tallest thing out there for miles. Was she trying to be a lightning statistic?

The faint rumble of thunder shook the silence again. The sky was turning black. Tight-lipped, Adam hurried out of the room and down the stairs.

Outside, Max and the dogs jogged back toward the house. Fat raindrops were beginning to pelt them, so Max increased the pace. Being out here in the storm was part of the training Portia wanted Max to maintain. The dogs never knew what kind of weather they'd be working in, and Portia and Max wanted them to be comfortable in all types of conditions, but this jog might have been a mistake. Max could see the lightning. The clouds looked like fat black cabbages. Since she was the tallest thing on the beach, she hoped Mother Nature didn't mistake her for a lightning rod. A flash of lightning struck the water about two hundred feet out, and the thunder was so loud, Max felt the ground shake beneath her shoes. Blinded by the rain now coming down horizontally, she signaled the dogs to take off, so they'd at least be out of the wet, but they kept pace beside her. Grinning at their loyalty, she kicked into a sprint.

The beach was muddy now, though, and she was having trouble breathing because of the fierce winds, but they made it to the stairs. The wind had increased threefold in a blink of an eye, and Max found it hard to see, let alone make any headway up the steps. She grabbed hold of the railing to keep from being blown to Chicago and realized the very serious mistake she'd made underestimating the weather. She'd not only endangered herself, but her precious dogs. The dogs, built lower to the ground, seemed to have hunkered down and were attempting to break a path through the screaming wind and hurricane force rain. Max put her head down, gripped the rain-slick rail and forced her body to conquer the weather that was trying to push her back. Her hand slipped and she lost her grip. She managed to grab hold again just as the angry wind slapped her spine back against the iron rail. Her back screamed with pain. Then a strong hand grabbed her around the waist. She looked up into the grim, wet, bearded face of Adam Gary.

"Come on!" he yelled over the swirling wind and rain.

Max was grateful for his presence but she could see Ruby struggling to go forward. "Go ahead!" She pointed at Ruby. "I need to help her!" she shouted.

Holding tightly to his hand, Max made her way over to the canine. The rain and wind were slapping her face with so much force it kept snatching her breath. Her back protested when she lifted Ruby, and Max wasn't sure she could carry her the whole way up. Ruby was ninety pounds of bone and muscle, and she was heavy.

Max saw Gary pick up Ossie with no problem. He wrapped his other arm around her waist, and as she carried Ruby, they battled their way up the stairs.

Once they were safely inside, Max and Adam slid to the floor with the dogs. They were all soaked and breathing heavily. Glad to be out of the raging storm, Max tried to catch her breath. She swore never to do anything that asinine again. Ever. She hugged the drenched and panting Ruby. "You okay, girl?"

Max checked her over for any obvious scrapes or injuries but saw none. "I'm sorry. My fault entirely."

She could see Adam's tight face. He was so wet he looked like he'd taken a shower with his clothes on. "If you have something to say, please say it."

Ossie was standing beside him panting with exertion. "A woman with your training should have more sense."

"I know. Thanks for the rescue."

Her attitude seemed to have caught him off guard.

She asked, "Did you expect me to argue with you?"

"Yes," he said frankly.

"Excuse, me," Kaitlin said, coming into the room. "While you all were out chilling in the storm, dinner came. I'll eat in my room." She set the bags down on the floor at her feet.

Adam warned, "Just make sure it's *your* room and not mine."

She showed him a sour face then left with her portion of the delivery.

Max was still lying on the floor. "If you don't like her, why is she here?"

"It's complicated."

Max could feel her back stiffening like a board. She went to stand up but the pain refused to allow it. Gritting her teeth, she forced her body to obey the command and struggled to her feet.

Adam saw her stiff movements. "You need a hot shower and some ibuprofen for that back."

Outside, the storm was still wailing.

"I'll be fine."

"Are you always so hard-headed?"

"Always. Ask my mama." She took a few stiff-legged steps that made her wince. The dogs looked up with concern. "I'm okay," she told them. "Just moving a little slow, that's all."

She saw Adam shake his head at her stubbornness, and said to him in response, "I'll take the shower and the pain meds, but first I want to get out of these wet clothes, then I plan to eat."

If he had another comment to offer, he kept it to himself. On the other hand, the thought of walking up the steps and the struggle she knew she'd have getting out of her wet clothes were daunting even to a former Marine. Once again Rita Risk Taker, the name given her by her mama when Max was growing up in Texas, had bitten off more than she could chew. Max viewed her back injury as divine payback for foolishly placing the dogs in harm's way, so she accepted her punishment without whining and reminded herself that she'd done far harder things, like surviving the Marines' Crucible, hunting and eating lizards in the jungles of Colombia when the rations ran out, and making a fifteen-mile walk across the Afghanistan countryside to Kabul on a badly fractured foot. With those accomplishments under her belt she could certainly drag herself up a measly flight of stairs.

Drawing in a deep breath to strengthen her resolve, she placed one wet sneaker in front of the other and climbed to the top.

Five

By the time Max stepped out of the shower, her back hurt so badly every breath brought agony. She managed to drag on some clean panties and a pair of sweats she dug out of the duffel she'd brought in from the car that morning, but she had neither the ability nor the inclination to do anything about her pancake flat hair, so she decided to avoid mirrors instead. She cupped her hand beneath the running stream of water coming from the tap in the sink and swallowed some of the over-the-counter meds she carried in her medicine kit. She hoped the relief would kick in soon because her back was on fire. It crossed her mind that her injury might be more serious than she'd first assumed, but she wasn't going to deal with that possibility, either, at least not for now. For the moment, all she wanted was a bed so she could fall out.

But she didn't have a bed, she reminded herself. She knew Kaitlin wouldn't give up hers without a death match, so that left the SUV, but no way was she going to crawl into the back of the Honda, not in her condition. Instead she left the bedroom and took a slow walk down the hall and up the set of rickety stairs. He was going to throw a fit, but she didn't care. She needed to lie down, and his bed was the only game in town.

Downstairs, Adam stripped off his wet T-shirt and tossed it to the floor. He was hoping she'd be back by now. The dogs were lying on the floor by the patio door, watching him. He was still amazed by the fact that he'd picked up the one she called Ossie. Instinct, he supposed. It had been so chaotic out there, his aversion to dogs hadn't even crossed his mind.

He studied the canines. Even though he'd rescued the big male, Adam still didn't like them, and he certainly didn't trust them, no matter how well trained she claimed them to be. The terror associated with his own vicious attack still lived inside as raw and real as the day it happened.

Ten minutes passed and still no Max Blake. He didn't know what to do about the dogs in her absence, but he was wet and in need of a hot shower himself, so he decided not to make it his problem and started toward the stairs. The dogs got up and slowly followed. He felt a frissom of panic but took a deep breath, stopped and told them, "Stay."

They stopped, looked up at him and sat.

Pleased, Adam walked away. The dogs got up and trotted behind him.

Adam said firmly, "You are not going with me. Stay here. She'll be back."

This time they didn't sit. Instead they gave him the impression that they were waiting for him to climb the stairs and that he was just wasting his breath trying to convince them to do otherwise.

Sighing his surrender, he gestured toward the staircase. "Go on, then."

As if that was all they'd been waiting to hear, they bounded up the steps. Adam shook his head and followed.

To his displeasure, the dogs were now walking up the hallway that led to his room. The workers had left all manner of items stacked up against the wall, and plaster dust was everywhere. When the dogs began to climb his short stairway, he asked testily, "Where the hell do you think you two are going? Go find your mama."

Adam hadn't seen or heard anything that indicated Blake's whereabouts, but the scent of vanilla lingered fragrantly in the air. The dogs were now sitting by the open door of his bedroom. Since he still hadn't seen Blake, the idea that she might be in his room tightened his jaw. He walked in, the dogs with him, and the canines went straight to the bed where she lay.

"That you, Doc?" she asked groggily. She was lying on her stomach on top of the indigo quilt his mother had given him for his birthday last year. She was wearing a lightweight gray sweatsuit. The top was loose fitting and had short sleeves. "Can you unhook my bra? Arms won't bend back there. Had to shower in it."

Adam went still.

The dogs were as close to her as they could get without jumping onto the bed. "Hi guys," she said softly without moving. "I'll be better in the morning." Then she called again. "Doc?"

Adam approached the bed. "Let me go get Kaitlin."

"Just unhook the damn thing. Please? If the dogs could do it, I'd ask them."

Adam stood there for a moment and met the eyes of

the dog Ossie. Adam swore the dog shrugged. Taking a deep breath, he walked to the edge of the bed. For a moment he hesitated like a man contemplating a lit stick of dynamite. He ran his eyes over her tall body with its fine behind, and in the end decided to get it over with. He sat down on the bed. Reaching over, he found the clasp through the soft fabric of her top, and the heat of her skin seemed to run up his arms. The vanilla scent he'd noticed in the hall wafted temptingly across his nose. He undid the placard, and the sigh of pleasure she gave in response put a big-time crack in his celibacy vow.

"Thanks," she said softly, and a blink later she was asleep.

"Hey!" Adam said, alarmed. "You can't sleep here."

But she was out. He looked down at the dogs. They made themselves comfortable on the plush rug, rested their heads on their paws, then closed their eyes.

Adam threw up his hands. Mad and outdone, he stomped into the room's connecting bathroom to take a shower.

When Max heard the water turn on, she smiled sleepily, then drifted off to sleep for real.

Inside the shower stall, Adam washed and simmered. Where the hell was he supposed to sleep now? Truthfully, he hadn't used the bed in weeks. He'd been crashing on the old sofa in the basement because it was closer to his lab, but that wasn't the point. The point was: The bed was his, and the only women allowed in it were the ones he was sleeping with. She and her damn dogs were taking over his life, and he couldn't believe she'd asked him to undo her bra. She acted as if she asked men to do that every day. Maybe she did, but he didn't want his name on the list. Her sigh of pleasure when the bra came undone had made him hard as an eighth grader on a school bus, and he wasn't happy about that, either.

Done with his shower, he shut off the water and grabbed the towel. After drying, he saronged it around his waist and padded barefoot back out into the room. He opened the dresser and pulled out a set of fresh boxers and another T-shirt. Casting an eye over to Ms. Texas sleeping cozily on his bed, he watched her for a moment. Lord, she was fine. That golden brown skin, that tall svelte frame. The green eyes only added to the overall allure. Adam glanced at the dogs. Ossie was watching him back, and Adam jumped. Cursing softly, he resumed his search for socks and a pair of jeans. Ignoring the silent scrutiny of the dog, he carried everything back into the bathroom and dressed. When he was done, he gave Sleeping Beauty one last look, then quietly left the room.

Downstairs, he grabbed his cold dinner and started to the kitchen to warm it up, then remembered the house no longer had a kitchen. He gave another dissatisfied sigh, turned to head down to the cellar and froze. Ossie was sitting in the hallway.

"If you're trying to scare me to death, you're doing a damn good job, dog."

For a moment the two males eyed each other silently. Finally, Adam asked, "What do you want?"

Of course, the dog didn't answer, Adam shook his head for even starting the conversation, but he felt compelled to say, "Look, I'm scared of you, okay. If you're messing with me because you sense fear, it's not funny, my man. Not at all."

Ossie yawned, then stretched out and settled his head on his paws.

"Aren't you supposed to be up there guarding the woman who jacked my bed? I don't blame you for wanting to take a break, though. Being around her has got to be tiring."

Adam really wanted to go to the lab, but the dog was blocking his exit. "Look, man. Been nice talking to you, but I have work to do. I don't want to bum-rush you and freak you out but you're going to have to move so I can get by."

Ossie stood, turned and walked off.

Adam didn't know what to think. Had the dog understood his words? Adam now had a clear path. He carried his cold dinner toward the basement stairs, and when he realized Ossie was trotting behind him, he sighed again. Something told him it was useless to try and get rid of the animal, so rather than waste his time and breath, Adam ignored him, but the dog didn't seem to mind.

Adam stuck his cold dinner into the microwave in his outer office and stashed Blake's uneaten food in his small dorm-sized fridge. While he ate, he called his mother again, and again got the voice mail. He tried to distract himself by reading some of the scientific journals he'd not had time to check out previously. Every now and then he glanced over at Ossie, who'd made himself comfortable in the doorway. The big dog seemed content even if Adam wasn't.

By midnight Adam's eyes were glazing over from all the reading and the lateness of the hour. It had been quite a day; from the construction crews this morning to the threatening e-mail to the evening storm and the jacking of his bed. He thought about his mother and the woman asleep upstairs. There was no doubt in his mind that if they ever got the chance to meet, they'd instantly like each other. Both were independent spirits with minds of their own. He just hoped the bull-headed one upstairs in his bed hadn't cracked her spine or injured herself in some other equally serious way. Memories of the vanilla scent she wore came back to mess with him and to remind him that it had been a long time since he'd undone a woman's brassiere or smelled perfume on her skin. Realizing his mind was taking him down a slippery slope, he pushed the thoughts of her aside and walked over to the big, old-fashioned wooden chest on the floor next to the couch. Lifting the lid, he took out a pillow and a thin blanket. He tossed both onto the tan couch and took off his jeans. Ossie watched silently.

Adam said, "I'm going to bed. If you're staying, I snore. Just so you'll know."

He didn't want the dog in the room while he was sleeping, but didn't seem to have much choice in that, either, so he stretched out on the couch, pulled the blanket over him, and doused the lamp on the table near his head. Once he was comfortable, sleep refused to come. His concern that his parents might be in danger kept him wide awake. He tossed and turned for what seemed like hours, then finally his eyes closed and he went to sleep.

Jan Kruger was in the Copenhagen airport waiting for his noon flight back to the States, where the time was approximately six A.M. He wondered if Dr. Gary had enjoyed the e-mail. Thinking about it made him smile. Truthfully, he hoped the message had scared the scientist to death, because he planned to use any means necessary to accomplish his goal, even if it involved dangling Lauren Gary's life as bait.

Eventually, Jan know that he and the good doctor would meet face-to-face, but that time had not come; there were other details to attend to first, such as finding out what the security protocol surrounding Gary's residence entailed. Was it large, small? Was Gary still living at the address? None of the moles had been able to glean the answers, so the only option left to him and his associates was to send someone to Michigan to take a look around.

After a long and sometimes heated debate, and over his objections, Vlad Oskar had been chosen. Jan didn't trust him, mainly because the mousy Oskar was not Afrikaner and had no real ties to their cause other than the money he'd been paid. Granted, Oskar's contacts had been the ones to appropriate Lauren Gary's screen name so that the threatening e-mail could be sent, and with his background in fuel cell research he'd be the person heading up the analysis of the prototype once Jan's group finally took possession. However, under pressure, Oskar sweated profusely. He called it a genetic disorder, but Jan thought it stemmed from fear.

However, the others had insisted on using Oskar as their eyes for this mission. No one else in their inner circle had the technical expertise necessary to evaluate the security, and now that their plans were under way, they didn't want to waste the time or the money bringing in another electronics expert, so the job was Oskar's. Jan hoped the choice didn't blow up in their faces. Too much was at stake.

In other developments, his meeting with the arms dealer had been successful. Orders had been placed and money deposited. Between the e-mail to Gary and the fruitful negotiations with the dealer, Jan was feeling rather good. Oskar was a fly in his pudding, but he set that worry aside for now. A few minutes later he was boarding his plane.

Max awakened disoriented and sore. For a moment neither sensation made sense until her brain shook off the last vestiges of sleep and the memories of last night rose up to make everything clear. She gave her spine a short, careful move and was pleased that it felt no worse than it had before she fell asleep. It hurt still, but not with such agony. She wondered if Dr. Gary was still mad about her taking over his bed. She felt guilty about it and promised to make her apologies as soon as she ran into him.

Turning her head on the pillow, Max saw Ruby lying on the floor looking up at her, and she gave the dog a small smile. "Morning, girl. Where's your brother?"

Ossie wasn't in the room, but Max was sure he was in the house because if he weren't Ruby would have let her know the moment he disappeared. Max just hoped that he wasn't somewhere scaring the hell out of their host. After learning of Adam's terrible mauling, she planned to be more considerate of the doc's feelings. But having seen him pick up the 115-pound Ossie during the storm like he weighed no more than a package of Oreos let her know the brother doctor was a lot stronger than the average nerd, and that maybe he wasn't as afraid of the dogs as he believed.

Max sat up gingerly and slowly swung her feet over

the edge of the bed. Her back protested in a way that let her know more pain meds would be needed just as soon as she found some food. Thinking a hot shower might help with the stiffness, she stood. Ruby stood, too, and looked up expectantly.

Max sighed. "You probably need to go out, don't you?"

Ruby waited.

"Okay. Go on downstairs. I'll follow fast as I can."

Max looked at the clock on his nightstand. Six A.M. In three hours the workmen would be knocking on the front door and she needed to get it together.

Adam was in the middle of his morning run. He supposed he should have left Max a note explaining his whereabouts, but he'd needed to get out of the house. The sun was just coming up, the air was clear, and the only sounds were the circling gulls, the water lapping against the shore, and his measured footfalls. The daily two-mile jog along the beach kept him in top physical shape and usually helped clear his mind as well, so he could focus. The solitude often made him feel like he was the only person in the world, and he did some of his best thinking on these runs, but this morning his mother was on his mind, and he had company. Running alongside him was Ossie the rottweiler. The dog seemed to be trying to turn him into a friend, but Adam wasn't about to add a rottweiler to his buddy list. His hope was that Max would know how to stop this attempt at dog bonding. Yes, he had carried the dog in from the storm last night, but that didn't mean he wanted to get married.

* * *

Max let Ruby out through the patio door and then followed her outside. She still had no idea where Ossie had gotten to, and she assumed Adam was in his lab. Ruby began to bark, and Max looked down the beach. The surprising sight of Dr. Adam Gary jogging alongside Ossie made her walk to the edge of the patio to get a closer look. Sure enough, there they were. Ossie was running easily and the doc was, too. Adam had the stride of a trained athlete; smooth, easy, and he looked real good in his shorts and sleeveless sweatshirt. On a more serious note, she wondered if he'd heard anything from Myk concerning his mother. Max prayed the woman wasn't in danger. If she were, this baby-sitting operation would take on a more deadly tone. Down on the beach, he was hitting the stairs and Ossie was loping up the face of the dune.

Max's back reminded her that she hadn't taken the pain meds she'd promised it when she got up, but she wanted to check out the Ossie and Adam connection first. When he reached the patio, he bent over to catch his breath, then checked his watch. After a few moments he straightened, wiped his face on the towel hanging on the wrought-iron railing, then looked her way.

Max found it hard to ignore the hard lean muscles of his brown legs, but said easily, "Morning."

Still winded a bit, he nodded. "Morning. How's your back?"

"It's been better, but I'm okay. Did Myk call?"

"No."

She sensed the tight response was rooted in his concern, and she wasn't mad at him for it. She noticed that Ossie was standing right next to him. "Ossie seems to have taken a liking to you."

"Yeah."

Max studied Adam's face. He didn't look real happy. "It's probably because you rescued him from the storm. I told you they were loyal."

"He slept in the office with me last night, too. Can you make it stop?"

Max felt bad. "Sorry." She called Ossie, "Come here, boy."

He trotted to her side. Max got down to his level, aching back and all, and said quietly, "The doc doesn't like you hanging around. You make him uncomfortable. No more playing shadow with him, okay?"

Max looked up at Adam's tight face, then back to the rottweiler. Ossie sat and gave a soft whimper. Max stroked his back. "I'm sorry."

"He acts like he's disappointed."

A terse Max didn't respond. *How can a brother who's supposed to be so brainy be so clueless?* Instead, she struggled to stand straight again. Trying to hide her wincing, she told him, "I have to get something to eat. Did my dinner get put away last night, I hope I hope?"

Adam could see how much pain she was in and it concerned him. "It's in the fridge in my lab. There's a microwave down there. I can heat it up if you want."

Max was pleased by the offer. "Thanks." She needed to take her meds but she needed food first.

"Be right back."

After his departure, Max slowly made her way inside, too, and wondered if he was genuinely trying to be nice or just attempting to atone for hurting Ossie's feelings. Deciding that an answer wasn't necessary, she eased herself down the living room wall until she reached the floor, then sat and waited for her own personal Einstein to bring her breakfast.

When Adam returned, he was carrying a plate holding her warmed-up food in one hand and a carafe of coffee in the other. Seeing her seated on the floor made him embarrassed that he had no furniture for her to sit on. She was the type of lady a brother wanted to be on his best for, and show his best to, and all he could offer was a spot on the old wood floor.

He was handing her the plate when his phone vibrated against his waist. "Excuse me." He took the call. It was Mykal Chandler and he had good news.

Adam placed his hand over the phone for a moment and said to Max, "They found her. She's in Senegal."

Max saluted him with a forkful of yams. "Yay!"

He grinned and returned to Myk's voice. The two men talked for a while longer, then a visibly relieved Adam closed the phone.

Max asked, "Feel better?"

"Much. Myk said she's on her way back to the States today. He's going to have someone watching her as soon as she touches down."

"Good. What about your stepdad?"

"Toronto. Myk's made contact with the police there and they've promised to keep an eye on him until he comes back to the States. Myk's people will take over then."

"Sounds like all the bases are covered."

"Yes it does. He's going to send some FBI agents around to see them when they get back, to tell them the government's got me on lockdown until the prototype is finished and that I'll call them when I'm done. Since they're used to me being out of touch when I'm work-ing, they won't worry."

"Now if we can find out who sent the e-mail, maybe we can all relax."

Adam nodded. Relax and go back to debating with himself why being mesmerized by a green-eyed sister named Max was a bad thing. He watched her eating her ribs. Her fingers were stained with the sauce, and the sight of her elegantly sucking them clean made him hard as a length of pipe. "I'll get us some coffee cups."

His abrupt exit made Max look up quizzically and wonder if she'd missed something, but because she had no way of knowing, she went back to her break-fast.

When her plate was clean and her stomach stuffed and happy, Max gulped down the meds with some wa-ter, and was one contented cookie. Adam was seated on the floor nearby drinking his coffee and enjoying his morning with her. Over his coffee cup he said, "Break-fast with ribs and yams has to be different."

"Different is a breakfast of roasted Peruvian liz-ards," she countered.

Adam stared.

"They tasted like stringy pieces of burnt chicken. We cooked them on sticks over a pit."

Adam made a face and drank down some coffee. "Have to admit—never had the pleasure."

"There was no pleasure involved, believe me," she tossed back with amusement in her voice. "Just neces-sity."

Adam smiled. He decided she had to be one of the most intriguing people he'd ever met. Roasted lizards.

He wouldn't eat lizards if someone offered him a million dollars. "Do you like your life?"

Max nodded. "I do. Not many people have seen sunsets all over the world."

"Or eaten lizards in Peru."

Their smiles met and they studied each other in the silence that rose between them. Max said, "Underneath all that science, you're not such a bad guy, Doc."

"You're not too bad yourself." Adam wondered what it might be like to watch sunsets with her.

Kaitlin walked in then. Neither of them seemed glad to see her but she was so caught up being herself she didn't notice. "Why are you two sitting on the floor?"

Max said, "We're having a picnic."

Kaitlin rolled her eyes. "Adam, I'm going for breakfast. Want me to bring you something?"

"Yeah. The usual."

"Okay," she said, then added, "I really wasn't doing anything in your room yesterday."

Adam said wearily, "Just get breakfast, okay?"

Today's attire was blue. Blue shoes, skirt, blouse, and pearls. "Okay. Back shortly." She shot Max a frosty look then departed.

When she was gone, Max cracked, "Maybe she'll get lost and not come back."

"We should be so lucky."

They both grinned.

Max said, "I need to get up and get this day started." She glanced at her watch. "The workers will be here in one hour. Is there anything in your lab or in your room that needs to be added to their to do list?"

"Not that I can think of."

"What about Ms. Thang's room? And where is it, by the way?"

"Which room did you take?"

She told him.

"Then she's down the hall and around the corner. Can't miss it. There's a monogrammed K on the door."

"You're kidding."

"Nope, and I'm pretty sure she doesn't need any work done. It's pretty pimped out as it is."

"Pimped out?"

He grinned. "When you see it, you won't believe it. Trust me."

Max shook her head. "So what are you going to do today now that you don't have to worry about your mom?"

"Shower so I can be out of the way when all the hammering begins, then head to the lab."

Max's meds were finally kicking in, but getting to her feet was still a pain-filled struggle.

Adam could see the discomfort on her face. "You ought to be in bed."

"I don't have one." Finally on her feet, she took a few seconds to catch her breath.

"Then use mine. You didn't have a problem taking it last night."

Max's guilt returned. "Sorry about that, but I really needed to lie down."

"Evidently," he said softly.

She looked up into his eyes. "Thanks for helping with my bra."

"Now how is a man supposed to answer something like that?"

Max had no idea but she enjoyed seeing him flummoxed. "I'm sure you'll come up with something." Tossing him a smile, she made her way to the stairs and disappeared.

The amazed Adam drained the last of his coffee. He'd planned on insisting that she spend the day in bed, but she'd somehow managed to make him forget all about it with her outrageous self. Burying fantasies of helping her out of more than just her brassiere, he supposed the only thing he had left was to clean up after their picnic. He set the cups on her plate and grabbed the empty carafe. As he took a look around to make sure he had everything, his eyes strayed to the dogs outside on the patio. He could see Ruby looking out at the water, but Ossie was lying by the door, watching him with sad liquid eyes.

Adam's guilt gave him a tug. Had he really hurt the dog's feelings? Realizing how ridiculous that sounded, he stashed the dishes in the bathroom sink, then headed to the shower. When Kaitlin returned he'd eat breakfast and get to work, but in the back of his mind he knew he was going to spend time wondering what type of bombshell his "friends" from Madrid would lob next.

Six

At nine A.M. sharp the workers began arriving, and once again the house was plunged into a beehive of activity. The hard-hat-wearing queen bee, feeling better now that the pain meds were working their magic on her sore back, spent the morning directing traffic, supervising the installation of the new kitchen appliances, and answering questions like what to do about the colony of wasps currently living in the downspouts on the front of the house and how long would the power be off. The electricians had turned off the juice at nine-thirty. It was now 10:45.

At 10:55 the power came back on and Max, flanked by the helmet-wearing dogs, continued her rounds.

Kaitlin had taken off right after breakfast, saying all the noise was giving her a headache, then added, "I'm going to the mall. I'm through playing your unpaid slave."

As the girl stalked off, Max took a deep breath and prayed for the patience she was going to need to keep from smacking Kaitlin every time they met.

By the end of the day the kitchen's new sink, dishwasher, and appliances had been installed, and the kitchen walls were primed and painted and waiting for the new cabinetry scheduled to be hung tomorrow. It pleased Max that she would no longer have to forage for food. She'd even found a local grocery that delivered, and the new fridge was stocked and ready to rock. She hadn't seen Adam since their peaceful morning, and she made sure Ossie stayed close and didn't wander down to the cellar to say howdy. Content with the new kitchen, she happily started dinner.

Downstairs in the lab, Adam lifted his head. He smelled pork chops. Who was cooking pork chops? At first he thought he might be imagining the down-home aroma, but it was way too succulent to be imaginary. Somebody was frying pork chops, and he got up to go find out who.

He didn't know why he was surprised to find Max standing over the skillet in the kitchen with a long-handled frying fork in her hand. As far as he knew, Kaitlin didn't know a ladle from a can opener.

When she turned around, she said, "Hey. Do you want to eat?"

He met those green eyes and said, "If it's as good as it smells, yes ma'am."

She gave him one of those smiles he was beginning to crave and said, "There are plates and silverware in that box over there." She moved some of the pots from the stove and set them on the newly installed countertop. "Help yourself."

Max back was mad that it hadn't had any pain meds since noon. She'd been so busy with the workmen she hadn't had time. Now, she wished she'd made the time. Between the dull ache and the stiffness, she wanted to lie down, but eating overrode everything. This would be her first home-cooked meal in a long time and she planned on enjoying it, messed up back or not.

Adam couldn't believe the food. There were pork chops, wild rice, broccoli, corn bread, and spiced fruit. "You make all this?"

"Ruby made the corn bread," she told him, "but I did everything else."

Kaitlin walked in. "There's some man named Benny at the door. Says you're expecting him?"

Max replied. "I am, let him in. I'll be right there."

"No need, babe," the male voice said. "You know how I hate being kept waiting."

Max turned, and there stood Benny's six-foot-two-inch handsome self. She smiled broadly and went to get a hug. "How are you?"

"Still trying to recover from you leaving me, girl," he said, looking down into her eyes.

She chuckled. "Yeah right. What's the latest pole dancer's name?"

"Lola."

"Lord."

He kissed the top of her hair.

She could see both Gary and Kaitlin staring on in interest, so she made the introductions. "This is Dr. Adam Gary and Kaitlin Kent. Benny Watson."

Adam came over and shook Benny's hand. "Nice meeting you."

Kaitlin walked over to the dark-skinned Benny and said, "Pleased to meet you, Mr. Watson."

Benny gave her the smile that rendered most women mindless. "The pleasure's all mine, baby girl."

When Kaitlin giggled, Max rolled her eyes and said to him, "Benny, if you want to eat, grab a plate. The doc and I will be outside." Then she added drolly, "I'm sure Kaitlin will show you where everything is."

"I'm counting on it," he replied, still smiling down at Kaitlin.

Max fixed her a plate, Adam did the same, and the two of them walked onto the patio.

A breeze was blowing gently in off the lake. Out on the horizon a freighter could be seen slowly making its way upstream. Adam asked, "How long have you known Watson?"

"Seven or eight years. He's one of my ex-husbands."

A stunned Adam stopped and stared, but she walked over to the new patio table and took a seat beneath the colorful umbrella as if she'd said nothing at all.

Adam followed and took a seat. Unable to hide his astonishment, he asked, "*One* of your ex-husbands? How many do you have?"

"Two." She met his eyes without a hint of shame, then shrugged. "Sometimes things don't work out. How about you? Any exes?"

"Two. Fiancées."

"Ah. We have something in common," she said, pausing for a moment to take the pain meds her sore back had been begging for.

He cut into his pork chops. "I guess you could say that." He forked a piece of the meat into his mouth and groaned, "Oh, this is good."

"Why thank you."

"No, thank you for this great food." *Fine and can*

cook, too? Adam felt as if he'd died and gone to heaven. "Not many people work with their ex."

She shrugged. "Benny's a good man, but monogamy wasn't—isn't—his thing."

He looked up. "Thus your question about the pole dancer?"

She smiled. "Yeah. It's a running joke now, but when I was married to him it wasn't funny. At all."

Adam saw her in a new light. Because of her vibrant, headstrong ways, he'd assumed she'd be the one doing all the heartbreaking. "How'd you get into security?"

"After I resigned my job in Detroit no other police department would hire me, so I started my own firm because I had bills to pay."

"What happened in Detroit?"

"My partner shot a kid, then planted a gun to make it look like a righteous shoot. On the stand, I told the truth. The powers that be didn't like it and they asked me to resign."

"So, you did."

"Yeah, and then I got the best lawyer I could find, sued their lying butts, and won."

"Good for you."

"In some ways, yes, but they won, too, by keeping me from working."

The conversation slid into silence. Adam found himself wanting to know all he could about this unconventional woman. He would never have expected her to have two bad marriages. She'd told him about Benny's infidelity, and it made him wonder about the circumstances surrounding her other ex. Had he been unfaithful, too, or had she been the cause of the breakup?

Benny stepped out onto the patio and said to Max,

"I have to find a motel and get a room. Kaitlin's offered to drive me around."

"Okay. See you later."

Benny waved Adam's way. "Nice meeting you, Doc."

Adam said, "Same here."

Once they were alone again, Adam asked, "Is Kaitlin in trouble?"

"Up to her weave."

He chuckled, then left the table to go back inside and grab a couple more pork chops.

When he returned, he said casually, "Do you regret the divorce?"

She chuckled. "Oh no. Benny and I can work together, play poker together, whatever, but that's as deep as it gets. Benny's about drama, and I'm too old for that these days."

"You play poker?"

She nodded.

"You any good?"

Her eyes flashed humor. "I'm okay. You play?"

"I used to in college and med school."

"You any good?"

"I used to be."

She checked him out over her fork of rice. "Well, whenever Benny's around, a game's sure to follow and he's very good. Just so you'll know."

"Thanks for the warning, but I don't have time for poker."

"You don't have time for much of anything, do you?"

He met her eyes and found himself wondering what it would be like to wake up and see those eyes each morning, but in reply to her question, he shrugged.

"All work and no play makes doc a dull boy," she pointed out.

"Some women like dull."

"They're lying."

Adam laughed at that. He couldn't help it. "Oh, really?"

"Any woman who claims she likes dull is lying not only to her man but to herself. Bank it," and she used her fork for emphasis.

Adam didn't want to admit how much he was enjoying her. "Thanks for clearing that up."

"No problem. Just one of my many services."

"Think you'll ever get married again?"

She seemed to consider the question for a moment and then shook her head. "Nah."

"Why not?"

"Not into being controlled or sitting at home while my husband is out looking for fresh honey."

"You sound bitter."

"I'm allowed."

"Not all men are that way."

"Probably not, but I'm done with the heartache."

Adam wondered if she was this honest with everyone. "So you've sworn off men."

"Oh, no. I didn't say that," she said, chuckling. "Men do have their uses. They're good for poker, going to games with, even hanging out with, but not for saying 'I do' with."

Adam wondered about the men in her past. Men being men, there were undoubtedly some who had tried to cage her. With her height and beauty, she was as exotic and as compelling as something mythical, and a man's first instinct would be to hoard her like dragon treasure, but if she were as complex a personality as he sensed her to be, she probably didn't do cages well.

Max didn't mind the personal questions. Allowing him to know more about her personal side was a good way to build trust. She also hoped him getting to know her better would keep the ice breaking. "So tell me what it was like growing up with famous parents."

"Great, crazy, sad."

He quieted, and Max saw him look out toward the lake as if reliving a memory only he could see. She said softly, "Not trying to bring back old pain."

"No, it's okay. When you're fifteen and your parents divorce it rocks your world."

She gently moved her now empty plate aside. "Back in the day, I remember seeing pictures of you in *Jet* magazine, but I never realized you and that boy were the same until I read your file." His mother was the award-winning African American essayist Lauren McDonald Gary, his stepfather the legendary R&B singer Raymond "Sweet Ray" Gary. Sweet Ray adopted Lauren's five-year-old son Adam as his own a few days after their marriage in 1972. Max remembered her mother recently describing the marriage of Lauren McDonald to Sweet Ray Gary as being equivalent to Marvin Gaye marrying Alice Walker.

"I was lucky in the sense that my mother never denied Pops visitation," he said after taking a swallow of the lime Kool-Aid she'd made to go along with the dinner. "Even though they were divorced, Ray and I still went fishing when he came off the road. He took me to Cedar Point and Niagara Falls, showed up at my high school football games whenever he was in town. He was a great father but he was a mess as a husband."

"There's that marriage thing again. See?"

He smiled. "Thinking back, Pops was a lot like your Benny. Never met a female he didn't want to know better."

Max nodded her understanding. That was definitely Benny's problem. She wondered how Kaitlin was faring, then shook her head because she already knew how it would play out. "Neither of your parents remarried."

"Nope. They won't admit it but they're still in love with each other."

"You think so?"

"I know so. They've been doing the tango around each other for twenty years, but Mama's a lot like you—doesn't want her heart broken again."

"Smart woman."

"Way too smart for Pops. He actually thought she was going to put up with him catting around because all his other women had."

"But she wasn't like his other women."

"Bingo."

Max wondered if she'd ever get to meet Black America's favorite divorced sweethearts.

The dogs were lying in the sun soaking up the warmth of the concrete patio, and as the conversation between Max and Adam slowed, Ruby trotted over and gave Max a little bark. To which Max replied, "Okay. Let me take these dishes inside and we'll go."

Adam looked up at Max as she gathered her plate and silverware. "What's she want?"

"To go play. Ossie, grab the Frisbees."

The two Frisbees were stacked faceup on the patio near the steps, so Ossie walked over, picked up the two yellow discs with his teeth, and waited.

Adam was amazed.

Max saw his reaction and said, "Doc, you're a scientist. You of all people should know how incredibly smart some dogs are. I don't know why you keep acting so surprised."

"You're right, but truthfully, after what happened to me, I didn't care to know a thing about dogs, let alone whether they were smart or not. This is the longest I've been around canines in my life."

"And you seem to be doing okay."

He shrugged. "We'll see."

"Hand me your plate, I'll take it in with mine." She then gave her sore back a few tentative twists. The meds had kicked in but she wasn't sure she was ready for an extended workout. "I don't know if my back is going to like tossing Frisbees."

Just then Benny stepped out onto the patio. "Hey babe."

Max was surprised to see him. "Hey. Did you find a place?"

"Yeah. What time do you want me here in the morning? We didn't talk about that before I left."

"Nine A.M."

He smiled that dark angel smile. "Okay."

"Do me a favor before you go?"

"Sure."

"I hurt my back yesterday and the dogs want to play Frisbee. Can you give them about thirty minutes?"

"No problem." He removed his jean jacket and asked Ossie, "You ready, my brother? Let me take the Frisbees." Ossie brought them over. Benny tossed one vertically, caught it, and asked Ruby, "Ready, baby girl?"

Ruby barked.

Max grinned.

Adam looked on silently.

Benny and the dogs set off toward the steps.

Max said, "I owe you, Benny."

"Hey, no problem. That's what we Black Knights are for."

"I'll come down and watch in a minute."

"Okay."

When Max went inside to take in the dishes, Adam again noted the easy relationship she seemed to have with her ex, and it made him wonder if she was really as cured as she claimed. Benny, on the other hand, hadn't even blinked when she'd asked the favor; in fact, he seemed glad to please her. Adam imagined that most men would. Was Benny still in love with her? Adam didn't like where his thoughts were taking him. Granted, he was determined not to make any moves on Max, but the idea that he might have to watch her and Benny getting back together didn't sit well. Of course, he had no say in the matter, and they certainly wouldn't consult him beforehand, but he had been enjoying his time with her, and a part of him resented Benny's presence. He was also honest enough with himself to envy Benny's relationships with the dogs because it was something he would never have. Her dogs meant a lot to Max, and any man trying to get next to her had to hook up with the canines, too, or keep stepping. That said, he had no idea why he was even out here thinking about her when he could be in the lab working on what really mattered in his life.

When Max returned, she told Adam, "I'm going down to watch the dogs and Benny. You're welcome to come along."

He shook his head. "I need to get back to work. Thanks for dinner, though."

"No problem."

They stood together in the silence for a moment and unspoken words rose between them once more. Max said, "If you come up for air later, I'll make you a banana split."

"That's tempting."

"I try."

Adam wanted to trace his finger down the soft golden cheek and then over the beguiling curves of her mouth.

For her part, Max's attraction to him was growing as well. "If I don't see you anymore today, what do you want for breakfast in the morning?" she asked.

"Eggs, bacon, toast."

"All yours."

Adam wished she were. The look in her eyes and the tone of her voice made him take a deep mental breath to calm himself. Blame it on his celibacy, blame it on her, blame it on whatever, but he was hard as a rock. "How's your back?"

"Much better."

"Where are you sleeping tonight?"

"In the bed I had delivered this afternoon."

Adam was disappointed, and as if she'd read his mind, she gave him a siren smile. "See you later, Doc."

With that, she moved to the stairs and headed down to the beach.

Wanting her and not afraid to admit it to himself, Adam watched her for a few moments as she made her descent, then went back inside.

On the way to the basement he saw an angry-looking Kaitlin come in the front door.

She asked, "Where's Benny?"

"Down on the beach with Max and the dogs."

"Did he forget I was waiting in the car?"

Adam shrugged. "No idea. Maybe you should ask him."

"Maybe I will." And she stomped away.

Adam shook his head. He wondered what her daddy was going to say when he found out Kaitlin was chasing after Benny instead of him. Up to her weave, indeed. Smiling to himself, he moved on.

Max watched the dogs jumping and twisting in the air to retrieve the Frisbees. They were having a good time chasing the ones Benny sailed out over the water and the ones he zoomed down the beach. Max was glad he was here. No way would her back have held up under the stress of the game, and the dogs needed to play.

Benny spun a high one to Ruby who jumped in the air and whirled like a gymnast to catch it.

Max clapped.

Benny grinned and called out, "Good girl, Rube." Then he shouted, "Here's one for you, Os!"

Ossie ran under it, then propelled his powerful body up into the air and snatched it down.

The four of them were having such a good time, no one noticed Kaitlin's presence until she gritted out, "Benny? Weren't we supposed to be going to dinner?"

He looked her way. "Hey. Yep. Soon as I get done here. Max hurt her back and the dogs need their exercise."

Kaitlin turned a glare at Max, who shrugged in silent response.

Kaitlin asked, "How much longer are you going to be?"

"Ten, fifteen minutes. If you have something else to do, I understand."

"I don't," and she said it so quickly, Max had to turn away to keep Kaitlin from seeing her smile.

Kaitlin folded her arms impatiently while Benny and the dogs took off for a run.

"They'll be back in a minute," Max assured her.

"Whatever."

Max turned. "What is wrong with you? Your weave too tight, what?"

"This isn't a weave."

"Whatever," Max echoed.

"I see why he divorced you."

"Little girl, you couldn't see a Bradley tank on a sunny day." Chuckling sarcastically, Max started toward the steps, then tossed back over her shoulder, "Have a good time with Benny. And watch out for those tanks."

Back inside the house, Max cleaned up the kitchen. She loaded the dishwasher and put the leftovers in the fridge. Kaitlin was a silly fool, and if the young woman had a better attitude, she might have warned her about Benny, but since Kaitlin apparently knew all, she wasn't telling her a damn thing.

Once the dishwasher was running and everything was back in its place, Max went out to see if Benny and the dogs were back. They were. Max collected the dogs, gave Benny a hug of thanks, then he and the disgruntled Kaitlin went on their way.

Seven

After Benny's black Explorer drove off, Max let the dogs out the front door and left them to their own devices. They'd spend the time sniffing for squirrels and chipmunks, exploring the vast fenced-in complex, then come back to the house when they were done. Max didn't mind the roaming. She wanted them to know each and every inch of the property because the knowledge might come in handy somewhere down the road.

Max sat on the floor of the empty living room and opened her laptop. She sent a message to her friend, Techno Queen Portia, to ask if anything had come back on the e-mail Adam had received. Done, Max checked her mail. Seeing nothing needing her immediate attention, she signed off and closed the laptop.

Downstairs in his lab, Adam sighed with frustration. The solution to his problem continued to elude him. He'd tried everything he could think of to get the prototype to produce heat for longer periods. He'd altered the bath components, fiddled with the metal housing's chemical composition, and even heated the inner works artificially, but the results were always the same. Nothing.

He checked his watch. A couple of hours had passed since dinner. He stretched his tired arms and shoulders and decided to take a break. *Maybe a banana split might help.* The thought brought on a smile. In reality, taking her up on the offer was nothing more than an opportunity for him to spend time with her, but he had no shame, he'd take what he could get.

Out on the patio, Max set her book aside and looked at her watch. Seven-thirty. The sun had lost most of its heat and the air had cooled, but because of the state's northerly position there was at least another hour or so of daylight. She hadn't seen Adam, and admitted to herself that she was disappointed that the good doctor hadn't come up out of his hole and taken advantage of her dessert offer, because she wanted to spend more time with him. On the other hand, she knew she had no business wanting his company. After all, she was here to do a job. But hey, a girl could dream.

She heard the patio door opening. To her delight, Adam stepped out. "Hey," she said softly. "How's tricks?"

He shook his head. "Still giving me fits. I decided to take a break. Is it too late for that banana split?"

"Nope." She got up, and as she did heard the dogs barking out front. The angry timbre of the sounds made her grab up her BlackBerry and start punching in codes. The dogs had small cameras and a bunch of other electronic gadgets in their collars. She impatiently waited the few seconds while the picture downloaded, and then stared. "Oh, shit!"

"What's wrong?"

Max ran. "The dogs have some guy treed. Get inside! Lock the door!"

Adam didn't, of course. He took off right behind her.

Max tore through the house and out to the Honda. She threw open the hatch, snatched out the wheel well cover, and pulled out her Glock. She primed it, her face grim. Noticing Adam behind her, she said, "Didn't I tell you to stay inside?"

"Yeah, but—"

"But nothing!" she snapped. "When I tell you something, you damn well better do it!"

"Hey!" he said, offended.

"I'm supposed to be protecting you, remember? I can't do that if you don't cooperate. Now, come on! I'll deal with you later."

Adam followed, not sure whether to laugh or be mad.

Sure enough, Ruby and Ossie had a man up a tree. He was hanging from a large branch that put him just out of reach of the snarling dogs. They were growling, jumping and trying to grab hold so they could bring him down. He was screaming.

When Max walked up, she saw a handgun on the ground that he must have dropped. The dogs stopped their jumping at the sight of her but continued to circle beneath their prey and growl menacingly.

The thin man finally noticed Max and Adam and he gushed in an Eastern European accent, "Oh thank the saints. Are these animals yours?"

"Who are you?" Max asked.

"Sergei Robinski. Please call the dogs."

"Do you know this is private property?"

A mad Ruby jumped again. Robinski screeched and hastily pulled his legs up out of the way just in time to avoid her sharp teeth. With one eye on the dogs and the other on Max's Glock, he answered, "No. I mean yes, but I'm just a poor salesman looking for new customer for my cousin's business."

Max picked up the gun. "Which is?"

"Computer repair."

"You always carry a gun when you make sales calls, Mr. Robinski?"

"This is a dangerous country, sometimes. Please, take the dogs away so that I may come down," he pleaded.

Max could see him eyeing Adam. "Sorry. Can't do that. You're going to have to stay up there until the police come."

"The police?"

"Yep. You're trespassing." Max didn't believe a word of his story. Ignoring him for the moment, she told the dogs, "Good job, you two."

Max pulled out her phone and placed a call. When she was done, she snapped the phone closed and stuck it back on her belt. "Police will be here shortly. Nice meeting you, Mr. Robinski."

She then looked at the tight-faced Adam. "Let's go."

Robinski called out, "Wait!"

Max tossed back. "You can tell your story to the police."

"Please!"

"The dogs will keep you company."

On the way back to the house she asked Adam, "How many people around here know who you are and what you do?"

"Around here? I'm not sure."

"Do people in the scientific community know you work here?"

"Some do. Why?"

"Because if whomever sent Robinski wasn't sure you lived here, they're real sure now after seeing your face." She looked his way and said seriously, "Next time, do as I ask."

Adam stopped, but she kept walking. He watched her stride off, feeling like a kid who'd just been to the principal's office. She was right, of course, but he was male, and taking orders from a female in a potentially dangerous situation was hard to do. Society raised men to stand and fight, not to hide behind locked doors. This was not going to be easy, he realized, and she was really really mad.

Yes, she was. Pacing in the living room, Max wondered why she had to fight this battle every time she was assigned to a man. Invariably she had to yell at them for not taking her seriously. Usually after she pointed out that if they could protect themselves she wouldn't have been hired, they got it, but it was still maddening. She was the one with the training, she was the one with the gun, not them. It came to her then that she should calm down. What's done was done. Her call hadn't been to the police but to the FBI. If Robinski was something besides a computer salesman—and she was sure he was—the agents from the Bureau would sort it out. Once they made their report, she'd know more about what she might be potentially facing and plan accordingly so she could keep Dr. Dummy out of harm's way.

In response to Max's call, the Bureau agents—two women—arrived within the hour and took the very angry Sergei Robinski into custody. The dogs had terrified him so much that he'd soiled himself trying to get away from them. The agents had to drape a tarp over the backseat of their car before they allowed him to get in. Max had located a car down by the gate that she assumed to be his. The agents made a call to have it towed to their office so they could comb through it.

Watching them drive away, Max said to Adam, "They'll find out who he really is." She turned his way and said sincerely, "You have to follow my directions."

"I know, and my apologies. Hard for a man to take orders."

"Believe me, you're not the first man to tell me that."

"Men give you a hard time."

"Always."

Their eyes held and their mutual attraction rose and singed away the tension like sunlight burning off the fog. Max looked away first. "Um, I want to check out the video from the dogs' collars. I'll get my laptop."

A few minutes later Max and Adam were at the patio table, using the laptop to watch a replay of the video from Ossie's camera. She was seated and Adam was standing close, leaning over the screen. The dogs were lying on the patio, chilling.

The picture that came up was a bit jumpy. Max assumed it was because the dogs had been running after the screaming Robinski. She said, "I'll have to let Portia know that the camera's stabilizer still needs a tweak."

"That's awesome clarity."

Max could feel the warmth of his body bathing her gently. "Yeah, girlfriend is the diva. Her little toys are getting better and better."

"She built the camera?"

Max smiled, watching Robinski on the monitor

hauling ass up the tree. "Yep, she has all types of good-
ies in her pipeline, not to mention the dog breeding
she's into." Max studied the dogs' vertical leaps. "Look
at the way Ruby is springing off that other tree in order
to get a better angle. She is so smart."

The sight and sounds of the angry dogs chasing
down and then treeing Robinski forced Adam to take
in a deep breath. That was how he'd been run down,
and all of a sudden his head was filled with the sounds
and the pain and his own screams. He was twelve
again, rolling and screaming and trying to escape the
big teeth that were tearing open his face, and his hands
were bloody—

"Adam!"

Max called again, "Adam!" He was ashen, gray.
Gone. Somewhere.

He seemed to shake himself free and his eyes met
hers. In the background she could hear Ossie and Ruby
snarling and barking on the video and she knew. "Oh
lord. I'm sorry." She quickly muted the volume then
closed the program. Stricken, she searched his grimly
set face. "I'm so sorry."

"Damn," he whispered. "I'm shaking." He held out
his hand and the palsy was evident. "Haven't had one
of those in years."

The therapist Adam had seen after the attack called
the frightening episodes waking nightmares. They'd
occurred more frequently back then and would take
him over at a moment's notice. Those, coupled with
the real nightmares that terrorized him at night, left
him too scared to sleep and too scared to be awake for
months. Now, like most men, he was angry at and
embarrassed by his weakness before a woman. He

could only imagine what she must be thinking. "I have to go," he said.

Max wanted to smack herself for being so unfeeling, even though that hadn't been her intent. Watching him walk to the door, she longed to call him back and say she was sorry, again, and that it was okay if he had issues with the dogs, but she'd spent most of her adult life working with men. She knew how prideful they could be. Anything she said might be construed as pity, so she remained silent and watched him disappear inside the house.

The dogs were lying a few feet away, and they watched his exit, too. When Adam closed the door behind him, Ossie lifted his head and let out a series of mournful barks. Max walked over and knelt beside him. She stroked his neck and said softly, "I know, babe. I know. But he's going to have to work this through on his own."

Adam didn't go to the lab. Instead he found himself upstairs in his room, staring at his reflection in the mirror. What would people think if they knew that the man *Time* magazine called "one of the brightest minds of the future" could be turned into a quivering mass of protoplasm by a couple of canines? Granted, he had good reason. The attack on him had been no joke, and left him physically scarred for life. But he was a grown man now and he needed to come to grips with the experience so he could shake free of the demons that remained hidden in his psyche. But how, was the question.

He turned away from the mirror and walked over to the windows. He could see her down on the beach walking with the dogs. He wondered what she'd thought of him and his fit. No man wanted to let a woman see him under such circumstances, mainly because it elicited pity, and that was the last thing he wanted from the tall beauty outside. Had she not called his name, there was no telling how far he might have sunk into that memory. He was glad she had, though, and wondered if she'd ever call him by his given name again. Even though she'd yelled it, the remembrance touched him.

Max decided to let the dogs sleep in the car. She put their bedding on the floor of the hatch but left the hatch open just in case they needed to get out for whatever reason, and also because they were her first line of defense. She stroked each dog in parting. "Keep an eye on things out here, okay?"

They settled in and she went back into the house.

Upstairs in her bedroom, Max looked around at the white-primed walls. The room would be purple with indigo accents once the final paint was rolled on. The adjoining bathroom's ugly cabbage rose wallpaper had been removed and in its place was more white primer.

As she undressed for her shower she thought about Adam. She knew he hadn't wanted her to see him so vulnerable, but the episode was not something she would ever hold over his head or joke about with someone else. The fact that the attack still haunted him spoke to how much it had affected him.

The hot shower felt good on her still healing back. Afterward, she put on her favorite Dallas Cowboys nightshirt jersey and stuck her feet back into her boots.

Grabbing a few items, she went down the hall to check out Kaitlin's room. There was too much at stake not to take a good look around.

Just like Adam said, there was an elaborately scrolled wooden *K* on the door to Kaitlin's room. Max tried the knob. Locked. No problem. She opened up her small packet of burglary tools and picked the lock. She assumed Benny would keep Kaitlin occupied until morning, so she had little fear of being caught. She flicked on the light switch beside her and stared around in wonder at the pink and white fairyland. The foo-foo canopied bed, the ruffles, the lace, froze Max in place. The room looked like it had been decorated by Laura Ashley on steroids. It was a marked contrast to the rest of the tumbledown house. Max wondered who'd paid for it all. Her father, possibly? She couldn't see Adam doing it.

She had come in to take a peek at Kaitlin's computer, which she now saw sitting on a small table covered by a cutesy pink gingham tablecloth. Wondering how anybody could be in this sugar sweet room and not go into a diabetic shock, she pulled out the white French provincial chair with its pink flowered cushion and sat down in front of the monitor.

The computer booted up with no problem. Max clicked on AOL and hoped Kaitlin was one of those lazy folks who kept their password stored on the computer. As the sign-on dialog box appeared, Max smiled. Sure enough, the password was stored. All she had to do was hit Enter, and AOL did the rest.

Because the government was paying her to be nosy, she felt not an ounce of guilt reading the young woman's sent e-mails. Especially when she read one in particular:

> **Father. How are you. Well I hope. FYI. Adam has hired a housekeeper to replace Mrs. Wagner. She's some tall ugly woman named Max Blake. She has turned the house upside down and is throwing herself at him by running around wearing nothing but a towel. This is disrupting Adam's work so much that he is snapping at me and being mean. Can you come up and talk to him about replacing her? K**

Max shook her head and said aloud, "Miss Kaitlin, I got over being called tall and ugly a long time ago." For a moment she let herself remember the hell that had been middle school, where the boys and many of the girls called her everything from Geoffrey the Toys 'R' Us Giraffe to Andre the Giant.

Brushing aside the memories of those haters, she scanned all of Kaitlin's recently sent and received mail, but none of the other messages pertained to her, nor did she see anything that might link Kaitlin to the e-mail Adam had received about his mother or the appearance of Robinski. Satisfied for now, but still no closer to any answers as to who the men threatening Adam might be, she signed off, then shut down the computer.

Max put everything back the way she'd found it, hit the light switch, locked the door, and returned to her own room. After removing her boots and turning off her own light, she climbed into the new bed and snuggled beneath the crisp, new, lilac-colored bedding. It was only ten-thirty, early for her to be turning in, but she was tired and glad to be finally sleeping in a bed again.

It took her a while to doze off, though, because Adam Gary kept floating across her mind. His parents were relatively well off financially, so she assumed he'd received some kind of counseling after the terrible attack. Having been trained in intelligence, she knew that the mind could be a tricky entity, especially in response to trauma. She just hoped he'd find a way to see himself clear because he needed light to quell the darkness encasing him.

Jan Kruger was furious. Not only had Vlad Oskar not gone to Michigan as he'd been assigned, but he'd sent an underling in his place, an underling who'd not been properly screened and apparently could no longer be found. According to the heavily sweating Oskar, it had been six hours since he last made contact, and repeated attempts to rouse the agent via his mobile phone had been unsuccessful. "So where do you think he is?" Jan asked, turning cold blue eyes on the short, brown-eyed Oskar staring back at him from the monitor on his laptop. Jan was in a hotel suite in Chicago, and Oskar was in his car in Miami.

"I don't know," Oskar said tightly.

"Did he arrive?"

"Yes. I spoke with him as he drove up to the house's gate. After that, nothing."

"You were supposed to go personally."

"I know," he said, and took a moment to wipe at the moisture gathering above his thin upper lip. "But the woman selling the plane components we need said I had to do the deal today or she'd sell to another customer.

I had no choice but to send someone to Michigan in my place."

Jan didn't respond. He knew the components were necessary for reprogramming the computers in the planes he'd purchased in Copenhagen. Finding someone on the black market who dealt in quality merchandise like the female dealer in Miami had not been easy. However, the understanding didn't diminish the danger they all might be facing if Oskar's man was in the hands of the police. "Keep trying to contact him, and stay in touch."

"I will," Oskar promised, then quickly signed off.

Jan stared distastefully at the blank monitor screen. Oskar might have been telling the truth about the components, but Jan was convinced he hadn't gone to Michigan because he'd been afraid. Oskar had been recruited and brought on board by one of the old Afrikaners, named Rand, whose money was helping to finance the operation. Jan had had misgivings from the very beginning about Oskar's suitability, but kept his mouth shut because technically Rand and his wealthy fellows, all of whom had been prominent members of the Nationalist Party before the collapse of the old ways, were in charge. As a result, they were at their homes in Durban and outside of Pretoria while he was here cleaning up Oskar's mess.

Jan made a few calls to his moles in an attempt to find out if the missing man had been taken into custody, as he suspected. He was promised an answer as soon as possible, but in the meantime was left to wonder if their plan was already starting to unravel. He placed one more call, to a person who boasted of being a member of Adam Gary's inner circle. The contact had promised to deliver the prototype—for a price, of course—but

Jan trusted him about as much as he trusted Oskar. Jan was a man of discipline and order, but he could feel the reins slipping from his fingers. To counter that he'd have to move up the schedule because he refused to allow all the work they'd put into this be for naught. He checked his watch. He'd come to Chicago on behalf of the South African government to attend a United Nations fund-raiser, and he needed to get dressed. After he returned, he'd place a call to Oskar and hope the sweaty little man had better news.

Adam awakened to the smell of bacon frying. He remembered Max saying something about breakfast this morning, so he got up. Usually he'd be out jogging by now, but the anticipation of food and Max's company overrode all else.

When he entered the kitchen, she was spooning fat yellow scrambled eggs into a bowl. The kitchen smelled amazingly like his mama's kitchen when he was growing up. "Smells good in here."

"Morning," she said, smiling. She was wearing a Dallas Stars T-shirt, shorts, and sandals. "Toast will be up in a second. Do you want orange juice?"

Adam looked over at her and wondered if Benny had any idea how lucky he'd been to wake up to her every morning. "Orange juice is fine. But I can get it." He went to the big new fridge and opened the door. It was filled with everything from butter to apples. Shaking his head, he grabbed the juice carton and closed the door. "There's a lot of stuff in there."

"You can't be the next Lewis Latimer on an empty stomach. Gotta keep you fed." The toast popped out of the new four-slot toaster nice and brown. She put the four slices on a plate, slapped some butter on them, and came to the table.

Intrigued by her reference to Latimer and the sway of her walk as she moved around the kitchen, he asked, "What do you know about Lewis Latimer."

"Other than he perfected the filament in Edison's original lightbulbs?"

He grinned and took a seat at the table. "Yeah."

"That he doesn't get the credit he deserves."

"Bingo."

She inclined her head royally and sat.

Enjoying her, he filled his plate with the eggs, grits, bacon, and toast. After waiting politely for her to do the same, he dug in. Just like yesterday's dinner, the food was great. "You're a good cook. Not many women cook anymore."

"I enjoy it, but my mama thought my sister and I would never learn."

"There's another one of you?"

She grinned. "Yes, I have a sister named JT."

"Which stands for?"

"Jessi Theresa."

"She do security work, too?"

"No, she's a sports agent. Basketball clients, mostly."

Adam stopped and stared. "Really?"

Max smiled. "No conventional women's work for the Blake girls. My mama thinks it's genetic."

"How so?"

"Both of my great-great-great-grandmothers were pistols. One, Grace Atwood Blake, organized a wagon train of mail order brides and took them to Kansas City back in the late 1800s. She was also one of the first African American lady bankers."

"Wow," he said. Savoring his grits, he wondered how he was going to convince her to stay and cook for him for the rest of his life. "What about your other grandmother?"

"Granny Loreli was a gambler."

"You're kidding."

"Nope, and family history says she was real good at it. She and my grandmother Grace were close friends and eventually two of their children married each other. That's where I get my green eyes. Supposedly, Granny Loreli had green ones, and they've been popping up every other generation or so since."

He checked out those compelling eyes. A man could drown in them, he realized, and to keep from doing so, he shifted his attention down to his plate. "So what did their husbands do?"

"Loreli's husband, Jake, was a pig farmer, and Grace's husband, Jackson, was a Texas lawman. I guess being with the police is in my blood, too."

Adam was impressed by her stories. There were many African American families who could relate the proud facts of their ancestral history, but unfortunately his wasn't one of them. His mother Lauren was adopted, and his biological father, Craig McDonald, killed in 'Nam, had been abandoned at birth on the streets of Chicago and grew up in foster care. But apparently Max Blake was a descendant of some remarkable women. No wonder she was so vivid.

Max watched him discreetly while she ate. In spite of their on and off head butting, she still thought he was gorgeous. The sexy angles of the thin moustache curving down his mouth to merge with the close-clipped hair that rode up his chin to the razor-cut sideburns enhanced his features. His lips were fine, he was fine, and he was watching her. She let him look, and the power in his dark eyes touched her in much the same way the heat of his body had teased her yesterday on the patio. She could feel the temp rising in the quiet kitchen. Every once in a blue moon she ran across a man whose presence was impossible to ignore, and Adam Gary appeared to be one. But in her line of work, playing midnight twister with the client was not only highly unethical, it could be dangerous.

"Can you pass me that marmalade, please?" she asked.

He handed her the small jar. Their fingers brushed and the current crackled.

Max wanted nothing more than to roll all over the floor with this man; find out if that mouth was as wonderful as it appeared, run her hands up and down those strong arms and play Shakespeare's two-backed beast until neither of them could walk, but, Adam Gary was a client; Chandler had sent her to protect the doctor, not to play doctor. "So, do you have any idea who Robinski might be?" She thought turning her mind back to the job was way safer than letting it go in the direction it was headed.

Adam observed her over his cup of coffee. Seeing her delicately suck some of the marmalade off the tip of her finger after slathering the sweetness on her toast made his manhood harden like a pipe. "No idea," he replied in a calm voice. "I had a couple Eastern European countries that wanted to send some of their graduates over to observe."

"What did you tell them?"

"I was knee deep into the prototype at the time and

didn't need the distractions, so I told them, no."

"How'd they contact you? Snail mall, cell, e-mail?"

He watched the tip of her tongue catch a stray piece of marmalade from the corner of her bottom lip. "E-mail."

"Did they know you were working out of this house?"

"I don't think so. I'd just published the first article with my preliminary findings about the prototype, and the journal listed my e-mail address. They contacted me a few days after that."

"Who else have you had contact with? Foreign contacts."

"The Saudis, the Russians. The Israelis, the Japanese, and the Chinese."

"Popular man," she said. "They all want the same thing?"

"Yep. Me and my lab."

She poured herself more juice. "When was the last time you heard from any of them?"

"A few days before the conference in Madrid. Got a call from a man who wouldn't tell me his name, but he said he could arrange for me to go straight from there to a lab in a secret location. Offered me stupid money."

"Accent?"

"Yeah. Australia? New Zealand?"

She looked surprised. "Good grief, how many dogs are in this hunt?"

"I don't want to know."

"Any luck on fixing the problem with the prototype?"

"Nope. Not yet."

"Well, keep me posted."

"Will do."

Eight

They concentrated on finishing breakfast but in reality were back to silently checking each other out again. The cracks in Adam's celibacy vow were widening like fissures in thin ice. Although he knew he shouldn't, he wanted to smell the perfume on her skin again and wondered what it would feel like to trace his finger over the soft curves of her luscious mouth. How would she react if he placed slow, heated kisses along that elegant neck then down to the hollow of her throat? He knew firsthand that her breasts were small, the way he liked, and thinking about pleasuring them set off more cracks and fissures.

Seemingly unaware of how she was affecting him, she pushed her chair back and stood. His eyes followed her as she moved away to pour more coffee. Over his own coffee cup, he savored the way she walked and the lean, lithe lioness air she exuded. Lioness was a good description, he reflected, because he was hard as a lion in heat.

Max was very aware of Adam, so much so that she wanted to fan herself. Standing at the sink, she looked

over her shoulder and saw him still watching her with
such cool intensity the heat of it forced her to turn away
and close her eyes until the ripples passed. *Lord!* She
was going to have to rethink that whole ice water thing.
The voice in her head said: *All right, Blake. He's a
man, nothing more, and you've been dealing with men
all of your life. Pull it together, girl!* She drew in a deep
breath, released the death grip she had on the edge of
the sink, and turned back to face him with her refilled
cup in her hand. He had the nerve to be smiling.

"Something funny?" she asked.

"No ma'am," he replied with eyes that lied. "Just enjoying the morning."

The idea that this tough cookie of a woman could be
flustered by him was as surprising as it was fascinating.
He was certain she'd felt the temperature rising in the
room just as he had, and the fact that she'd turned away
so quickly spoke volumes. He studied her for a few more
silent moments, then stood. "Thanks for breakfast."

Max shook off the fantasy of him taking her naked
on the tablecloth, and asked, "What do you want for
dinner?"

"Whatever you cook will be fine, but I am a carni-
vore, so no vegan stuff."

"Understood."

In the silence that followed, what they both felt remained unspoken, so he said, "I'll see you later, Ms.
Blake."

She nodded. "Later."

When he left the kitchen, Max realized her heart
was racing.

The rest of the morning was a whirlwind of hammers,

saws, ladders, and paint as the workmen arrived and began their day.

Benny arrived promptly at nine. He strolled in with a starry-eyed, sleepy-looking Kaitlin. Max wondered if the girl knew the buttons on her blouse were askew. Kaitlin's fingers waggled a good-bye at Benny then she floated up the stairs to her room.

Benny watched her departure then gave Max a smile of welcome while he took in all of the activity. "Looks like a three-ring circus," he shouted over the noise.

"I know. Are you ready to get to work?"

He yelled back, "Lead me to it. You want to play poker tonight?"

Max grinned. "Yeah."

Outside, they spent a few moments discussing the logistics of the operation. The property stretched a mile and a half in each direction, so Benny had his work cut out for him, but he promised that when he finished installing the motion detectors with their halogen lights and mini video cameras, Max would be able to access real-time pictures of every inch of the place from either her handheld or laptop.

Pleased, she left him to do his thing, with the dogs tagging along. She took out her phone and put in a call to the Bureau office in Grand Rapids. When the agent picked up, she was told that Robinski's fingerprints belonged not to a computer repair salesman but to a former KGB operative now working for an Eastern European energy cartel.

The female agent said, "The only thing on his person besides a fake driver's license and the gun was a picture phone."

Max was confused. "So, he was just here to take pictures?"

"No clue. We're going to hold onto him for a while and see if he tells us anything. He is on the no fly list, though, so he'll probably end up being kicked over to Immigration, then deported. If you need additional bodies out there, just let us know. That property has enough trees where we could easily hide a couple of agents in a car for a few days."

"I'm hoping that won't be necessary but it's good to know I have backup if I need it."

"The county sheriff's a good guy, too. Call him. If anything jumps off, he'd be able to get his people there faster than we would."

"Okay."

She and the agent spent a few more moments talking, then Max ended the call and went back inside. So Robinski was here to just take pictures? Of what? Whom? Adam undoubtedly. She was glad Benny was on the case, because something told her things were getting ready to heat up.

Speaking of heat, she spent the rest of the morning thinking about Adam even though it seemed that a woman like her had no business being attracted to a brother with an IQ in the stratosphere. His client status notwithstanding, she had a GED diploma and a two-year police academy degree; that was it. Everything she'd learned over and above that had been up close and personal in the school of life: Marines, Homicide, black ops for various government agencies, and now Myk Chandler's group, NIA. A Texas girl with her "around the way" background rarely crossed paths with the Brainiac Brothers of America, let alone be around one fine enough to want to hitch herself to his rocket and ride it to Saturn. But she did, and anybody with a lick of sense knew that was a real bad idea.

At noon everybody broke for lunch. Benny and Kaitlin drove into town for burgers and fries, while the workers ate in their trucks or relaxed down on the beach. Alone in the kitchen, Max put together two ham and cheese sandwiches bulging with tomatoes and lettuce. One would be for herself and the other for the Man in the Basement.

With his sandwich, some chips, and a glass of lime Kool-Aid chilling on the tray she was balancing, Max rapped on the lab door and called out, "Lunch, Doc."

To her surprise, he didn't yell back about being left alone, he simply opened the door. His presence rolled over her like the warmth of a June day. "Lunch," she said again, all the while wondering if there was something she could ingest to quell her growing attraction to him.

He took the tray. "Thanks."

"I forgot to ask you about food allergies. Do you have any?" Max was hoping idle chitchat would keep her from thinking about what happened at breakfast.

"Not that I know of."

"Just checking. Don't want to feed you something I shouldn't." The chitchat didn't help; she found herself staring at his mouth longer than she should have, then caught herself and raised her eyes to his amused ones.

He said, "Appreciate the concern."

Max couldn't remember a man ever making her dizzy, but looking up at him made her feel just that. "All righty, then. I'm going to leave you to your lunch. I'll see you later." Waving good-bye as she walked off, she called back, "Dinner's at six."

Adam watched the sweet rhythm of her retreat, felt more fissures open up, then shaking his head, quietly closed himself in again.

Dinner that evening made Adam sure he'd died and gone to heaven. The barbecued chicken, coleslaw, and baked beans were as good as any he'd ever tasted. He'd spent the afternoon closeted in the lab, and having dinner on the patio made him feel like a prisoner given early release. His enjoyment was increased by having her seated across the table from him. "Another great meal."

Max saluted him with her glass of lime Kool-Aid. "Thanks."

"You have a thing for green Kool-Aid, don't you?"

"I do, and it's a love that reaches all the way back to my childhood. My sister JT is a grape girl. I prefer this."

"Who's the oldest?"

"She is by about fifteen months."

"Is she as fierce as you?"

Max studied him. "In her own way, yes."

"You two must have been rough on the brothers growing up."

Her smile was bittersweet. "Not really. We were both as tall in high school as we are now, so there weren't any dates. Boys preferred the petite cheerleader types."

He nodded his understanding. "The tall girls at my high school didn't get asked out much, either."

"Which did you date? The giraffes or the poodles?"

He dropped his head. "Poodles."

"Pitiful," she chuckled softly. "The story of my life."

"It wouldn't be poodles now, though."

"Yeah right."

"No," he laughed. "I've learned. Tall ladies have their own special élan."

"Oh, now you speak French, too?"

"French, Italian, Portuguese."

Max sat back. His eyes were working overtime. "You are lying."

He grinned. "You're right. The Italian part is a lie."

Her amused eyes met his. "Braniacs aren't supposed to be charmers."

He drew on his drink. "No?"

"No. You're supposed to be this schlump of a brother with taped Coke-bottle glasses and a pocket protector."

"But I'm not," he stated.

"No, you aren't," she said more quietly than she'd intended.

The vibe they'd set in motion at breakfast kicked in again, big-time.

He told her, "You are the most fascinating woman I've met in a while."

"Like maybe you get out a lot."

He threw back his head and laughed.

Max liked the rich sound of his laugh. He didn't do it enough for her, though. Grinning, she said, "Sorry. Were you being serious?"

"I was."

Their shared grins filled them both.

Max said, "You're pretty fascinating too, Doc."

"Good. Glad I'm making some kind of impression."

"Oh, you are. Believe me." In order to keep from jumping across the table on him, Max turned her head and looked out toward the lake's calming water and reminded herself that playing footsie with the client was a no-no.

Adam studied her elegant profile and wondered how much longer he was going to be able to keep his desire for her to himself. The celibacy vow was gone, blown away, leaving in its wake a stirring need, not just for any woman, but for this one. He had always prided himself on his discipline and work ethic, but for the first time in his life, neither attribute ruled. The unconventional Max Blake had reduced or elevated him, depending on one's point of view, to just a regular everyday brother trying to get next to a sister who made him ache at the sight of her. Adam found the realization startling and humbling. Wanting to hear her sigh when he kissed her, wanting to feel the softness of her skin beneath the soft slide of his hands, was suddenly as important as finding a solution to the problem plaguing his prototype. By all rights, the prototype should be the only thing on his mind, but his well-ordered life had been tossed out of the window the moment she showed up in his doorway wearing a Stetson and those green snakeskin boots.

As if she could feel his thoughts, she turned her head and met his eyes, saying, "This is the part where I ask what you're thinking about, but I already know."

"Do you?"

She nodded. "And it's a bad idea to mix business with pleasure, especially in a situation like this."

"So, the answer is no?"

She allowed a small smile to show. "Let's just say I'm going to hold out for as long as I can."

"Good plan, but a flawed one."

"Oh really?" she asked, amused. "Why so?"

"Because there's nothing a man enjoys more than a challenge."

"And that's what you think I am?"

"I know that's what you are."

"A woman likes a challenge, too," she tossed back, "especially one determined not to succumb. Better bring your A game."

"Oh, I will. Don't worry."

Max was certain the umbrella over their heads was smoldering. The confident way in which he was studying her made her ask, "Got a little bit of playa in you, do you?"

"Enough."

"Who'd've thought?"

"You just watch out."

Max's nipples tightened shamelessly. Even though she was sure her discipline would carry the day, in reality all she could think about was how he'd feel against her in bed. "Oh, I plan to."

They assessed each other for a few silent moments longer, then she said, "I'm going to take the plates back inside, then the dogs and I are heading for the beach. Care to join us?"

Adam's eyes shifted to the dogs lying quietly on the edge of the large patio. As he had mused earlier, he knew he was going to have to come to terms with his issues surrounding them. "I—"

"Hey Doc?" Benny called from the doorway. "You mind if we play poker here tonight?"

Adam turned. "Nope."

Benny grinned. "Good. Game'll start around eight." He disappeared.

Max checked her watch—six-thirty—then looked down into the eyes of the man who'd stated his intention to seduce her and to whom she had given a tacit okay to do so. "Are you going to play?"

"Probably not. You?"

She shrugged. "Maybe. We'll see." She began gathering up the paper plates and cups, telling herself that resisting Dr. Gary the Mack would be easy. "What did you decide about the beach?"

"I'll take a rain check."

"Okay." She studied him.

He studied her.

She finally said, "See you later."

He nodded, and she took the dinner leavings into the house.

When she returned, she called the dogs and the three of them left to hit the beach.

Adam sat and watched her toss the Frisbees while his need to know absolutely everything about Max Blake grew stronger. He had no idea why this particular woman should move him in ways others had not, but she had, to the point of distraction.

Around seven-thirty that evening Benny's poker players began arriving, bearing chips, salsa, beer, and all the other munchies associated with such a gathering. Most of the men invited were from the contractors working on the house, and Max greeted them with a smile. Benny's date for the evening, a tall blonde with blue eyes, was introduced as Gretchen. Max wondered if Kaitlin knew that Benny had moved on. The answer became apparent when Kaitlin showed up downstairs dressed in a killer red dress and shoes.

While Max and the others sat at the table and pretended invisibility, Benny introduced Gretchen to Kaitlin, and Kaitlin stiffened like a piece of wood. "This is the waitress from the place we had dinner at last night," she said.

Gretchen didn't look the least bit ashamed, and Max saw no reason for her to. "Nice seeing you again," Gretchen said to Kaitlin with a smile.

Kaitlin obviously felt differently. Seething, she gave Benny a stony look then stormed out to the patio. If Benny felt any remorse, he didn't show it. Instead he cracked open the new deck and the game began.

An hour later Max looked at the useless cards in her hand and cracked, "You know, if my grandmother Loreli were here, she'd be kicking your butts."

Benny tossed back, "Well, until your granny rises from the dead, we'll just keep kicking yours."

The other men around the table chuckled good-naturedly.

Max stuck out her tongue at her ex, then decided she'd lost enough money for one night. She put down her hand. "I'm out. I'll settle up later."

Benny grinned. "You sure?"

"Yes, Ben, I'm sure. Only thing I have left are the dogs, and you are not getting my babies."

While the men set up for another hand, Max left them and went out to the patio to check on the dogs and to get some air.

She was surprised to see Kaitlin seated at the table. She assumed the young woman would be in her frothy pink room sending her daddy poison e-mails about Benny. The dogs were lying in their spot by the edge of the patio.

"You come to gloat?" Kaitlin asked her.

Max took up a position with her back against the patio railing. "Nope. I usually don't kick other women when they're down."

Kaitlin stared out at the water for a few silent moments then turned back to say, "This is that tank you were trying to warn me about, isn't it?"

"Yeah," Max replied softly, "it is."

Kaitlin sighed.

Max told her, "At least you didn't marry him."

"Was it bad?"

"For me, yeah, because I got tired of smelling perfume that wasn't mine, seeing lipstick that wasn't mine, and hearing him yell out names that weren't mine when we were making love."

"I really thought he liked me."

"He probably still does. His problem is he's never met a woman he didn't like."

For a moment there was silence.

Kaitlin said, "My father wants me to marry Adam."

Max fought to keep her voice neutral. "Really? Why?"

"He thinks we'd be the perfect couple."

"What do you think?"

"I don't think Adam's feeling it, and my father isn't going to understand that it's not going to happen."

Max studied Kaitlin's face. "I'm sure once you explain—"

"No. My father thinks whatever he wants he should have, even if it means pimping his daughter to get it."

Max was surprised by the bitterness of her tone. "Sounds like you and your father need to do some serious talking."

"I wish." She sighed again, then slowly got to her feet. "I'm going to my room. Thanks for listening."

"Any time."

She went back into the house.

Max looked over at the dogs and said, "Stay tuned."

Ruby barked.

If Max found her encounter with Kaitlin surprising, what she found upon entering the kitchen startled her even more. Seated at the table with the poker players was Adam Gary. The stack of chips in front of him was high enough to build the Empire State Building, and the cigar he had stuck in his teeth was fat and lit. Max stared.

Benny grumbled, "Next time, remind me not to invite Rain Man here to the table."

Max chuckled and flashed the pleased-looking Adam a smile. "You losing, Ben?"

Benny studied his cards. "I don't want to talk about it."

Adam spread yet another winning hand on the tablecloth. "Read 'em and weep, gentlemen."

Howls of disbelief filled the kitchen, then they threw in their cards.

In the end it was the last hand. The clock showed it to be past ten, and the contractors needed to get home. Benny walked them to the door, then he and Gretchen left in his car to spend the rest of the evening together. Max was left to clean up the kitchen.

To her delight, Adam pitched in without being asked, and it made the work go faster. Once they were done, Max turned from the sink and said, "Thanks."

"You're welcome."

"You weren't lying when you said you could play poker."

"Don't tell Benny, but I hustled my way through undergrad playing poker."

"He's going to want to play again. He hates losing."

"If I have the time."

Max flicked off the kitchen lights and plunged the room into darkness. As if they'd talked about it, the two walked through the silent house and outside to the patio. Night had fallen. The lake sparkled like ink under the pale rays of the moonlight, and the breeze was soft and refreshing.

"Are the dogs put down for the night?" he asked.

She nodded. "They're out in the car. The carpenters promised to start the pen tomorrow."

"They don't have to."

Max searched his face in the moonlight. "Excuse me?"

"I know that isn't what I said before, but penning them up isn't going to solve my problem."

Max waited for him to explain.

"I need to face this head-on."

"So what's that mean?"

"Not sure, but I think I want to take them with me when I do my run in the morning."

"Really?"

"Yeah. My version of immersion therapy."

Max remembered his reaction to the video, and she wasn't sure if this idea was good or not. "Okay," she said, hoping to keep the skepticism out of her voice. "Just tell them where you're going running and they'll follow."

Adam looked out over the water. He wasn't sure if he could approach the dogs so directly, and yes, the thought of doing it kicked up his anxiety, but he refused to spend the rest of his life cowering in a corner every time a dog crossed his path, so this had to be done.

"You're really going to do this?" Max asked, looking up at him.

"I'm going to give it my best shot."

In spite of her misgivings, Max admired anyone with the guts to take on their inner fears. "Then you go, Doc. If there's any way I can help, just holla."

He smiled. "Will do."

The silence rose between them once again. They were as aware of each other's presence as they were of the night breeze flowing in off the lake.

He finally said, "There is something you can do for me."

"And that is?"

He reached out and very slowly and gently traced a finger over the curve of her lips. "This . . ." he whispered. Slowly lowering his head, he touched his mouth to hers, brushing his warm lips over hers. ". . . if that's okay."

Max knew this was a bad idea, but she whispered in turn, "It's okay. . . ."

Then she was in his arms and learning firsthand that his kisses were as gloriously intense as he, and that, lord, the man could kiss. He kissed her as if she were treasure, precious; as if the only reason he drew breath was to hear her sigh, make her feel. Desire began to creep into her blood like the heated aftermath of an expensive cognac, and she wanted more.

Adam met that need. He wanted her to remember these opening notes, wanted her to remember him above all others, so he ran his palm up and down her pliant back and placed kisses against the edges of her mouth. He tasted the soft skin behind her ear and took in deep draws of the faint scent of her perfume clinging to her throat. It had been some time since he'd made love to a woman, but it wasn't something a man forgot, so he continued in his quest to make the night memorable by cupping her small breast and feeling the hard nipple burn like a brand against his palm. He dropped his head and bit her gently, savoring the groan she gave up and the way she trembled so sensually.

Without a word he worked the thin strap of her green halter top down her arm, exposing her breast to his eyes, his worshipping finger, and to the moonlight.

Looking down into her eyes, he played slowly; circling, lingering. The heat now claiming Max was so sweet she had to close her eyes. Almost instinctively, she knew that if she didn't get away from the man, she might never be whole again, but she couldn't move, didn't want to; not with him enticing her this way.

Adam couldn't resist. When she closed her eyes, his desire climbed. Bending his head to the nipple he'd prepared so thoroughly, he slid his tongue over the point then took her into his mouth.

Max groaned aloud. The sensations vibrated through her like a harp. There was something about trysting outside in the dark that had always turned Max on, but adding him to the equation seemed to make it that much hotter.

Max had no memory of her shirt being tugged all the way down, but it was somehow around her waist and she was nude to her neck. He was taking full sensual advantage, too, slowly teasing his tongue around her breasts, sucking on her nipples like erotic pieces of hard candy, and all she could do was let her head fall back and stand there on shaking legs that were being caressed by his strong possessive hands.

He recaptured her mouth and filled his palms with her hips. Pulling her forward so she could feel how much he wanted her, he let his heat say all.

Max understood each and every word, and when he blissfully moved the crinkly fabric of her long cotton skirt over the skin of her behind and then up and down the backs of her thighs, she knew she was in the hands of a master. And when that masterful touch slid her skirt to her waist and found its way to her thong, she was pulsing, wet and well on her way to orgasm.

It took all Adam had not to throw her down on the cement and take her like a caveman. Not having had a woman in such a long time, coupled with the hot wet beauty pulsating beneath his touch, was a recipe for disaster, especially since all of his condoms were upstairs in his room, but he held on. She deserved better than the patio. He promised himself that next time he'd make sure they were near his bed. That in mind, the pleasure tonight would be all hers. His could wait; he'd waited this long.

So he slid to his knees and kissed his way to the heat between her thighs. Max spread her legs without shame, relishing his tribute, and because he was so good, a minute later the orgasm crackled through her like lightning and she let the world know with a hoarse, night-piercing shout of joy.

She came back to herself holding her skirt up and leaning against the table for support. He kissed her mouth, mumbled something about seeing her in the morning, and was gone.

Alone now, she slowly dropped her skirt, fell into

one of the chairs and put her head on the tabletop. Nothing in Adam Gary's file had prepared her for what just happened. Nothing. With the echoes of her orgasm pulsating like a faint drumbeat, and her breathing still uneven, Max Blake realized that even though this was only his opening volley, he had the touch of a man who could make a woman crave that pleasure for the rest of her life, and that admission scared her to death.

Nine

Max awoke to the sound of the dogs barking. Concerned that they'd treed another intruder, she tossed off the sheet, stuck her feet into her green boots, reached for her Glock lying on the nightstand and hurried to investigate. Ossie and Ruby only barked for good reason. She remembered Adam talking about taking them running with him this morning, but the barks she heard didn't sound like fun.

This time there was no treed Robinski but an irate older Black man yelling at the dogs from inside his late model BMW. "Get the hell out of here!"

Max could only wonder who he was and why he was here at such an ungodly hour. The sun was just coming up. Ossie and Ruby were prowling around the car, making sure he stayed inside. Shaking off the fuzziness of sleep, she called out to the dogs, "Okay, you two, I'll take it from here."

Gun raised, Max told the man, "You can get out of the car, sir, but keep your hands in sight."

He stared at her. "Who are you?" he asked.

"Step out of the car."

He did as he was told, but demanded brusquely, "Where is Dr. Gary?"

"Right here."

Max turned. Seeing him made her wonder how many times she'd have to tell tell him to keep his butt in the house during situations like this one before he obeyed.

He seemed to interpret her thoughts. "He's harmless. He's Kaitlin's father."

Max lowered the gun. So this was Daddy. Dr. Sylvester Kent was bald, about five-foot-seven inches tall, and slightly built. He was wearing an expensive-looking blue and white jogging suit. His large head and thin build reminded Max of a cricket. Jiminy Cricket to be exact.

Kent asked Adam, "Who the hell is this?"

Adam was enjoying Kent's pompous rage, but he was enjoying Max's surprising attire even more. She was quite a sight for this early in the morning in her thigh-high Cowboys jersey and green boots. The golden legs seemed to go on forever, and he could see the nipples of her small breasts pressing against the jersey's fabric. When he thought back on how she'd responded to his pleasuring those same nipples last night, he decided to put his mind on something safer. "Max Blake. Sylvester Kent."

Max nodded a greeting, but noticed that Kent didn't respond. She assumed it stemmed from his daughter's e-mail and from the fact that politeness didn't seem to run in the family.

Adam explained, "Ms. Blake is just being careful. We had an uninvited guest the other day."

"Who?"

Adam shrugged. "Some man claiming to be a computer repairman. FBI took him away." He had no intention of telling Sylvester the full story.

Kent turned a withering eye on Max. "Do you have a permit for that thing?"

"Yep." Then ignoring him, she called out, "Ossie and Ruby, go play on the beach, I'll be there in a minute." They took off.

She turned to Adam. "Thought you were going to run this morning."

"Hard night, so I slept in."

His eyes said it all. Memories of last night rolled over her, and she shook her head. Still ignoring the glaring Kent, she said to Adam, "Let me put on some clothes and I'll get your breakfast."

"Okay," he replied, trying not to ogle those gorgeous bare legs.

"How do you want your eggs?"

"Bare—I mean scrambled."

Max gave him an odd look, then said, "It'll be ready in a bit."

She shot Kent a glance over her shoulder then walked off. Adam watched the sway of her hips and the way the motion played with the edges of her thigh-high jersey. *Damn!*

"Adam, who is she, really?"

He cleared his mind of the vision that had him so entranced and the recurring memories of last night. "She's my new housekeeper. I'm sure Kaitlin e-mailed you about her."

Kent hemmed and hawed as if he didn't want to reveal the truth. "I thought you didn't like dogs?"

"I don't, but Ruby and Ossie are a unique breed."

"They're a menace," Kent corrected, and ran a hand over his bald head. "Vicious dogs like those shouldn't be running loose."

Adam saw that Kent was sweating. "Naw. They're okay." Smiling to himself, he thought maybe the dogs weren't such a bad addition to the household after all.

When the men entered the house, Kent looked around and the first thing he said was, "What have you done to the place?"

"Decided to make it a home," Adam lied. "Max has been in charge, and she's doing a good job. Kaitlin's helped out, too."

"So Kaitlin is proving her value, just as I predicted."

"If you mean with my mail, yes."

Kent walked around, looking displeased at the mess. "You know I'm hoping you and Kaitlin will still hit it off."

"I know you do, but I told you a year ago it wasn't going to happen, and you sending her here to play secretary won't change things."

"She'd make you a perfect wife, Adam. She's poised. She knows how to entertain."

"Even if I was looking, which I'm not, Kaitlin wouldn't be it. She's too young and she's not my type."

"I still say she'd be perfect."

"You have your opinion, and I have mine."

They were at an impasse, but Adam knew Sly would keep pressing his case, no matter what. In the beginning of Sly's academic career such single-mindedness had been necessary to propel him to the top of his field. Back then Dr. Sylvester Kent was one of the most highly sought after researchers in the country. But when hubris took over and he began to believe his own press clippings, his world started to unravel. Scandal replaced scholarship. Colleagues became witnesses for the prosecution in cases involving malfeasance, questionable use of university funds, and child support. He lost his tenure, then his job, then his fame. For the past eighteen months he'd been teaching an intro physics class at one of the state's community colleges, and instead of being grateful to be working at all, he had nothing but contempt for the students, the other members of the faculty, and for the everyday, ordinary life he was now forced to lead. Adam didn't feel sorry for him. "What brings you by?"

Kent shrugged. "Just wanted to see how you and Kaitlin were doing."

Adam watched Max cut through on her way to the kitchen. She had on a pair of snug red capris and a thin black halter top. Her flip-flops showed off purple toenails. The male in him preferred the short jersey.

Kent's voice interrupted Adam's reverie. "Where'd you find her?"

He turned his attention back to Kent. "She was recommended by a friend."

"Woman like that could distract a man from his work."

Adam didn't reply.

Kent added hastily, "I'm not insinuating anything, of course. I know how serious you are about the prototype." He then cast a glance around at the remodeling. "Who's paying for all this?"

"The DOD."

"Really?"

"Have you had breakfast?"

"No. I drove straight through." He lived in Grand Rapids, the state's second largest city.

"Then join us."

"I'd like that."

Adam knew he would.

"Good morning, everyone," Kaitlin called out cheerily as she sat down. No pearls this morning. She had on an old pair of green sweats and sneaker mules on her feet.

Her father apparently wasn't feeling the sweats, because he said, "Morning, Kait. I trust you are usually better dressed most mornings."

"I am, Father. It's pretty early. I haven't had time to get it together." She helped herself to the carafe of OJ on the table and poured herself a glass. After taking a dainty sip, she set down the glass and gave her father a fake-looking smile.

"The early bird always gets the worm," he said with amused solemnity. "Isn't that right, Adam?"

Adam toasted him with his cup of coffee but didn't reply.

Max was in the process of putting eggs, grits, and the rest of breakfast on the table when Kent said, "I prefer my eggs sunny side up."

Max looked at the bowl of scrambled eggs and said, "I'm sorry. You must have this place confused with a restaurant."

That said, she went back to the fridge, pulled out butter and orange marmalade for her toast, then took her own seat. "Adam, will you pass me the eggs, please."

With amusement on his face, he picked up the bowl, and on that note breakfast began.

Over the course of the meal, Max didn't say much. In fact no one said much because the pompous Sylvester Kent apparently loved the sound of his own voice. When he wasn't chastising Kaitlin about her posture and correcting the way she handled her silverware, he was berating everybody and everything, from the President to the janitors who swept his classrooms after hours. "Laziest bunch of misfits I've ever had the displeasure of meeting."

Max wondered whether he'd been born with all that arrogance or if he had grown into it over his lifetime. She'd heard her share of windbags, but this cricket-looking character took the cake.

He then asked Adam, "So how's the prototype coming?"

"It's coming."

"I'd like to look at it. I hear you're having problems. Maybe I can help."

Adam shook his head. "You don't have the clearance anymore, remember."

Kent leaned back and waved a well manicured hand dismissively. "Oh, who cares about that. I won't tell if you won't."

"DOD cares, so, no."

Kent leaned forward and stated, "Surely a quick peek isn't going to compromise national security. You're taking this entirely too seriously."

"Yes, I am," Adam replied over his raised coffee cup.

Max saw Kaitlin's eyes flash with quiet satisfaction. The girl seemed pleased that her father was not getting his way on the issue.

Kent then declared pompously, "Well, maybe I'll just have to sneak in and find out what's going on on my own."

Max drawled, "I wouldn't do that if I were you. My dogs don't like folks sneaking around."

He tossed back, "If those dogs come anywhere near me, they'll be in the pound."

"If they catch you sneaking around, there isn't going to be enough of you left to call the pound."

He began to sputter.

In no mood for a discussion, Max picked up her plate, walked it the short distance to the sink, then went outside to play with the dogs.

She was tossing them pieces of driftwood when Adam came down to the beach about thirty minutes later.

He said, "You okay?"

"Just fine."

The sky above was gray, and the sun was hiding behind the clouds. Max had all kinds of emotions flailing around inside her, the least being her unabated attraction to yon tall, dark, and handsome scientist. She'd hoped that a bite of the dog would mellow her out and free her to concentrate on something else besides jumping his bones, but it hadn't quite worked out that way. The man's hands were magical, and any woman in her right mind would want more. "Is Kent always so pompous?"

"Always."

"How long is he staying?"

Adam shrugged. "No clue. Depends on what he's after, and he is after something. He always is."

"Interesting man."

"I almost choked when you told him you weren't running a restaurant."

"The help probably don't speak wherever he comes from."

"And that would be Gary, Indiana."

Max was surprised. "How long has he been using that faky jakey supposed-to-be British accent?"

"He's talked that way the whole ten years I've known him."

Max shook her head. "Well, keep him away from me."

"Do my best."

Adam wanted to kiss her good morning but he was sure Kent was up in the window watching, so he had to content himself with just looking at her; studying the bones in her face, watching the way the wind ruffled her short spiky hair, looking down into her eyes.

"You know," Max said softly, and she had to force herself not to touch his bearded cheek and feel the warmth of his skin, "that was very good last night."

He smiled a smile that had probably been breaking hearts since the sixth grade. "Glad you enjoyed it."

"I didn't hold out very long, did I?"

"I wasn't going to bring that up."

"Such a gentleman."

"My mama raised me well."

Chuckling, she bent to take the stick from Ruby's mouth then handed it wordlessly to Adam.

He looked down into Ruby's intelligent eyes, then back at Max. He tossed the wood a short distance down the beach and Ruby took off like the athlete Max knew she'd truly be in time. She was just over two years old now.

"They love to play," Max told him. "If they had their way, they'd do nothing but this all day every day."

Picking up a nearby Frisbee, she sailed it down the beach in Ossie's direction. He leapt into the air and brought it down. "This and swim."

Ossie brought Max the Frisbee, and she sailed it again so he could go after it. Ruby trotted back with the stick in her teeth and waited for Adam to free it and throw it.

Adam hesitated. Throwing a stick was one thing, but he wasn't sure he was ready to get near Ruby's teeth just yet. The dog waited patiently. Adam could see Max watching him from where she stood a few feet away, but she didn't say anything. Steeling himself, he reached down and gave the wood a gentle tug. Ruby released it and took off. Grinning, Adam threw it as far as he could, and she chased it excitedly. When Adam looked Max's way, he saw that she was smiling, too. She nodded her approval, and a pleased Adam waited for Ruby to race back so he could throw it to her again.

The workmen began arriving at nine and effectively put an end to the morning's playtime. The quietness of the beach was replaced by a cacophony of whining saws, pounding hammers, and the footsteps of men and women going in and out of the house. To Max's displeasure, Kent announced he would be spending the day, ostensibly to catch up on things with Kaitlin, but she was convinced he was hanging around just to be nosy. Adam, on the other hand, planned on working all day.

"Coward," Max accused him playfully as she walked with him down to his lab. "You're trying to duck Kent."

"Bingo."

"Don't leave me with that man," Max warned teasingly.

He chuckled. They were now by the lab door and alone.

"How's your back?" Adam asked, fishing for a way to make her stay as long as he could.

"Almost good as new."

"Thanks for helping fix up the house."

"No problem."

Max had no idea why she'd followed him down here. That neither of them seemed capable of doing anything but staring at each other and asking inane questions was apparent. He circled his arms around her waist and peered down into her face. "This okay?" he asked.

"Quite."

"Don't want to be pushy."

"I'll let you know if that happens."

"Want to kiss you."

"Want to be kissed."

He grinned and slowly lowered his head to fit action to words. His mouth was warm, the electricity instant, total, numbing. Max eased herself closer and the kiss deepened, filling them both with the sweet opening notes of desire they'd experienced last night in the moonlight.

Adam wondered if he'd ever get used to how perfectly her tall lean body fit flush against his own, or cease to be amazed by how soft and silky the skin of her arms and back felt under his exploring palms.

"Oh wow. Sorry, you two."

They broke the embrace and saw an embarrassed-looking Benny standing a few feet away.

"Didn't mean to interrupt."

Max asked, "What's the problem, Ben?"

"Who is that crazy man upstairs? He's about to make your painters quit."

Max gave a soft curse. Sighing, she asked Adam, "Permission to shoot Kent?"

"Permission granted. Just have the dogs drag the corpse out into the lake."

She grinned. "You go to work. I'll see you later."

Benny nodded at Adam. "'Bye, Doc."

Adam nodded, and entered the lab smiling. Sylvester Kent had no idea who he was dealing with, but he was sure Max would have that fixed by lunchtime.

Max found Kent upstairs on the second floor. The painters were standing around looking mutinous while he was elaborately explaining the deficiencies of their work. "Look at that corner," he was saying when Max and Benny walked up. "I've seen baboons wield a brush better."

Max folded her arms and growled, "Kent!"

He spun. Seeing her standing there, he said dismissively, "Oh, it's you. I was just telling these men that the ceiling will have to be redone."

"Oh really."

"Anyone with an eye can see that."

Max glanced around at the angry painters and said to one of the young apprentices, "Jason, you and Dr. Kent are about the same size. Would you take off your whites and hand them here, please."

Jason began shaking himself out of his white overalls. Once he had them off, he handed them over.

She said, "Thanks," turned to Kent and held them out. "Put these on."

Confused, he took a step back, "Whatever for?"

"Apparently, baboons can do a better job, so I want to see if it's true."

The painters snickered and Benny just flat out laughed.

Max stood there waiting.

"How dare you insinuate—"

"It was okay when you were insinuating."

He looked livid.

Max said, "Stay out the way, or I'll have you put out."

"You wouldn't dare."

"Oh I'll dare. In fact, I'll put you out personally." She handed the smiling Jason back his overalls. "Thanks."

"You're welcome," he said.

Max announced for all to hear, "If Dr. Kent even looks at you, I want to know."

The men smiled and resumed working.

Max looked at Kent, said, "Have a nice day," and stalked off.

She didn't see Kent for the rest of the morning. She assumed he was hiding out in Kaitlin's room but didn't care, she just needed him to stay out of her way.

After lunch she was down on the beach playing fetch with Ossie and Ruby when she looked up to see Kent making his way down the stairs. Not happy, she ignored him until he got close enough to say, "Ms. Blake?"

She noted the change in his tone. He sounded conciliatory. She wasn't buying it, though. "Dr. Kent." She sent the Frisbee down the beach for Ossie.

"I've come to apologize."

Max stopped and studied the fake smile on his face. "Oh really? Figured out where the power is around here, have you?"

He coughed in response.

"That's okay, Dr. Kent. Takes a big man to recognize the woman behind the throne."

He stared.

Ruby trotted over to Max's side, and she patted her neck affectionately.

Kent asked, "Who are you really?"

"I'm the housekeeper." She tossed the Frisbee for Ruby this time. "And my job is to make sure Dr. Gary isn't bothered." She held his eyes boldly.

"I have Adam's best interest at heart, too."

"Is that why you're trying to force your daughter down his throat?"

His eyes widened.

"I don't pull punches Dr. Kent, especially when I'm wading in somebody else's bullshit. With you, I'm guessing I'll be needing my waders."

He drew himself up. "Do you know who I am?"

"Nope, and I don't care." It was her experience that men like Kent hated it when women refused to be intimidated or impressed. She took the Frisbee from the waiting Ossie and sent it hurtling down the beach.

Kent answered his own question. "I am so far above you both academically and socially—"

"And that counts, where? Maybe in a university cafeteria, but not anyplace else."

He looked at her as if she'd just grown another head.

Max had had enough. Smiling, she said, "Thanks for the apology. I'll see you later."

She called the dogs to her side and the three of them jogged away from him and up the beach. She could feel his eyes burning her back, but it didn't bother her at all.

Ten

The knock on Adam's door wasn't a familiar one. He called out, "Yeah?"

"It's Benny."

Curious as to what Max's ex wanted, Adam went to the door.

When he opened it, Benny smiled and said, "Sorry to bother you, Doc. Just wanted to give you your own copy of these." He handed over a set of drawings and some photos.

Adam gave them a quick glance. "What are they?"

"Specs for the surveillance setups—motion detectors, cameras. Tells you where each unit is placed. Not sure if General Sherman would give you your own, so . . ." He shrugged as if that were explanation enough.

Adam chuckled. "General Sherman?"

Benny nodded and grinned. "Yeah. Cleopatra, Queen Makeda, Hannibal. Everybody who knows her has a different name for her. Woman is one of a kind."

Adam shook his head.

Benny added, "Got a lot of Napoleon in her, too, but then if I knew how to kill a man twenty-five different ways, I'd be a bit arrogant, too."

Adam stared.

"Yeah. Don't let those gorgeous legs fool you. Girl-friend majored in extermination for a while."

Adam swallowed. "Why are you telling me this?"

"So you'll know who you're dealing with up front. Me, I didn't value her or treat her right, and now I regret every morning I wake up and she's not beside me." Benny held Adam's eyes, then added, "Just so you'll know."

Adam wasn't surprised to hear that Benny still loved his ex-wife. Max seemed to be the kind of woman who cultivated memories a man would take to his grave. *Assassin!* He turned his mind away from that. "Thanks, man."

"You're welcome. I got a few more details to handle outside, then I should be out of your way for good."

"Okay."

Benny started to walk away, and turned back, "Oh, and Doc?"

"Yeah."

"I know better than to stick my nose in Max's love life, so you'll get no drama from me."

"Good to know."

Benny disappeared and Max closed the door. *An assassin!* Had Benny been telling the truth or just messing with his head? He had no way of knowing. Would his knowledge of who she'd been impact the attraction he had for the person she was now? He had no way of knowing that, either. The only thing he was certain of was that he needed some answers.

* * *

At five that afternoon the workmen began packing up. They were done. Since it was Friday, everyone was looking forward to the weekend. Standing in the newly plastered and painted expanse of the living room, Max looked around, pleased. Proudly sporting new colors, light fixtures, and wall plates, the grand old house seemed to be smiling, too.

When Adam strolled in, she gestured around the room. "Do you like it?"

"I do. Never thought a cleaning and some paint could make this old girl shine."

"She does look good."

"Yes, she does. Thanks for doing this," he said sincerely. "If it weren't for you, I'd still be living with dust balls and cobwebs."

"True dat." She chuckled.

Benny walked in. He was carrying a couple of tool boxes. "My work here is done, Your Majesty. I'm heading home."

She smiled. "Okay, Benny. Thanks a lot."

"You're welcome. Take care, Doc. Next time I'm up this way I'll be looking to win some of my money back."

Adam grinned. "Any time."

Benny departed with a wave.

Adam could see Max watching Benny long after he left the room. It made him wonder again how she really felt about her ex.

As if having read his mind, she said, "You know, it would be nice if Benny fell in love so hard he couldn't walk. Preferably with a woman who won't give him the time of day."

Adam chuckled. "Women are so vengeful."

"Yep, and I'd buy VIP front row seats just to watch."

"Thought you liked your ex."

"I do, but if there is a goddess, and she is just, somewhere on the planet is a woman who will make him eat his socks before she says yes."

"I'm not going to have to eat mine, am I?"

Max smiled. "Oh, I don't know. Are you partial to cotton or manmade fibers?"

"Whatever is cheap."

Max shook her head. She felt her phone vibrating, and freeing it from her belt, said to Adam, "Excuse me a minute." Into the phone, she said, "Yeah?"

It was Portia calling to give her an update on the mysterious e-mail sent to Adam a few days ago. They talked for a few moments, then Max replaced the phone. "Portia traced that e-mail to a server in Russia. Apparently, the perps are pretty good at hiding themselves because she's run into a dead end. She'll keep trying, though."

Adam nodded.

"You haven't received anything else?"

"Nope."

"Okay."

In spite of Adam's good mood, he continued to be haunted by Benny's startling revelation. Was she really as deadly as he'd claimed? Were the hits government sanctioned or was she a freelancer for hire? Adam thought he might have seen too many movies because his imagination was running wild. He needed answers and had no idea how to approach her about getting to the truth. For a moment he contemplated what to do, then said, *To hell with it.* "Did you really kill people for a living?"

Max stiffened. Her green eyes became distant, emotionless, and she tossed back, "If you're asking, you already know the answer, and since Chandler would never breach a confidence, you must've been talking to Benny."

Adam didn't reply. The chill now emanating from her made him wish he'd kept his damn mouth shut. Benny, too.

"That's not something I talk about. Maybe some other time." Then she added coolly, "I'm sure you want to get back to work. I'll let you know when dinner's ready." And she walked away.

Adam wanted to bang his head against the wall.

Max went into the kitchen and hoped rattling some pots and pans would bring down her temper. As she cut up a whole chicken into fryable parts, she wanted to gut Benny. *How dare he!* She knew without a doubt that he'd done it on purpose. He'd probably wigged out when he saw them kissing, and this was his way of sabotaging whatever might be happening between her and the doc. She slammed the knife down on the joint that separated the leg from the thigh wishing it were Benny's neck instead. *Damn him!* And he wondered why she'd divorced him. She severed the second leg joint with the same emotion.

From behind her, she heard Kaitlin ask, "Who're you mad at?"

Max turned on her like Linda Blair.

Kaitlin took a wary step back. "Whoa. That mad, huh?"

"Madder. What can I do for you, Kaitlin?" Max set

the skillet on the eye of the stove and angrily slapped in large spoonfuls of Crisco.

"Just wanted to find out what you said to my father that sent him running back to Grand Rapids."

"Why? Are you mad, too?"

"Oh, no. I wanted to say thanks."

"When did he leave?"

"Right after I saw you two talking down on the beach. He was hot when he came inside. Told me he'd see me in a few days, and roared off in his car."

"Good."

"But what did you say?"

"Apparently nothing he wanted to hear."

Max got out the flour canister and dumped a cup of the contents into a large Ziploc bag then added seasonings. She could feel Kaitlin's eyes on her back, but went on about what she was doing. Whatever the young woman had come to say, she was going to have to say it. Max was in no mood to play What Are You Thinking? with a girl with a crazy daddy. *I'm going to geld Benny!*

Kaitlin asked, "Is it okay if I eat with you all?"

Max shook her head with bittersweet amusement. "Sure. There's plenty. Anything else?"

"No," Kaitlin said softly. "I'll—talk to you later."

Max didn't turn to watch her go.

But once she was alone again and the chicken was frying, she paused and replayed the conversation with Adam. He didn't impress her as the type of person who condoned political assassination, and now that she had some years on herself she didn't either, but back then she'd been twenty-five, full of herself, the government's power, and looking for adventure. Yes, she'd done some things that she saw as morally repugnant, which is why she'd gotten out of the business, but she had no more idea how to explain that to him than she had the ability to change her past. *Guess that's that.* Whatever had been trying to bloom between them was probably history now. Men like Adam didn't bring home former assassins to meet the folks—not that she was after all that, but . . . She sighed. She sensed they could have had a good time because she liked him; even the geeky parts of him were sweet. Now he probably wanted nothing to do with her, and she couldn't fault him. With that in mind, her assignment to him went back to being just that—an assignment—and when it was completed she and the dogs would be moving on.

Down in the lab, Adam could smell the chicken frying, but all he could see was the look in Max's eyes when she walked off. Instead of working on the prototype, he needed to be working on a twenty-first century version of Mr. Peabody's Way-Back Machine so he could go back in time and slap a hand over his own stupid mouth. She'd looked so devastated and angry, he'd wanted to immediately pull her into his arms and whisper how sorry he was for even bringing up such a personal question. *Too late.* He dropped his head into his hands. For all of his off-the-chain IQ, he felt dumb as a box of rocks, and he had no idea how to fix this, or even if it could be.

He heard what sounded like scratching on the door and looked up. Then he heard the bark. *Ossie?* He went to the door, opened it, and sure enough, there stood the big male. He was carrying a small folded piece of paper in his mouth. Adam's wariness of the dog's teeth kicked in again, but his curiosity was stronger, so he reached down and gently tugged the paper free. Opening it, he read the one word. *Dinner.* When he looked up, Ossie was walking away.

To Adam's disappointment when he entered the kitchen, she wasn't there. The piping hot food was set out on the table so he could help himself, and there was a full place setting along with a big glass of green Kool-Aid, but no Max. He left the kitchen, walked to the patio door and looked out. He spotted her seated down on the beach with the dogs. The three of them were watching the waves and the gray sky day fade into evening. The wind had picked up and was buffeting the thin red windbreaker she wore. He sensed her pensiveness and wondered about the myriad feelings churning inside himself. *This is the reason you can't have women in your life,* the voice in his head pointed out. *Especially a woman so far beyond your reach you have no business even talking to her, let alone wanting her the way you do.*

Turning away, Adam went back to the kitchen, fixed himself a plate, picked up his Kool-Aid and silently carried them down to the lab.

Max didn't see much of Adam over the next few days. She assumed he was knee deep in his work. His absence suited her just fine but she did miss their interaction.

One night, unable to sleep, she drifted out onto the balcony of her freshly painted, newly furnished bedroom and looked out over the inky lake. The warm breeze ruffled her long nightshirt as she silently stood in front of the wrought-iron railing. She had seen many moons shining down on many bodies of water all over the world. Rio, San Francisco, Sydney, Hong Kong. Each location had its own special feel but all seemed to draw her. She was a creature of the night; always had been. Even growing up, many a night her mother had found her sitting outside on their porch in the dark, gazing up at the stars, while everyone else in their small town outside of Austin was asleep.

"Girl, it's three-thirty in the morning. What are you doing out here?"

"Looking at the stars. Do you think the ones here are the same ones people see in China?"

"I don't know but you can go to the library and find out. For now, get in the bed! You got school in the morning!"

Max smiled at the memory. Her mama had been wearing that ratty old pink chenille bathrobe she and JT hated so much, and she'd had those fat, old school, pink foam curlers in her hair. Max had gone to bed, and to the library the next day, but the facts and pictures only seemed to spawn more dreaming. Hopes of seeing the world was one of the reasons she'd joined the Corps; that and the juvenile court judge who gave the then eighteen-year-old Max the choice of signing up for the military or being incarcerated until she turned twenty-one for stealing her third car in six months.

She'd chosen the military, of course, and by doing so, got to see firsthand what the stars in Asia looked like. She'd also gotten the opportunity to grow up, something her poor mama had been praying for. Through it all though, she continued to be drawn to nights like these.

Max had turned to go back inside when she spotted movement down on the beach. It was Adam, and he was jogging with the dogs. She looked at the lighted face of her watch. Four A.M. She wondered if he'd been having trouble sleeping, too, or if the run was a way to clear his mind. Either way, she was glad that he was dealing with the dogs head-on, and that they seemed to have taken to him. Other than that, she told herself that Adam Gary's personal issues weren't her concern. She was here to protect him, and if she had to shoot someone to keep him safe, she hoped he wouldn't mind.

Max had taken to bringing him meals on a tray and leaving it in front of his door. She'd then knock to let him know he had food and head back upstairs. Later in the day she'd venture back down to pick up the tray and replace it with whatever meal was next. This morning, just as she was coming down the stairs, he opened the door. Three days had passed since seeing him on the beach, and he looked like Jim Beckworth, the famous Black mountain man. His beard had grown out, there were dark circles under his eyes, and the unwashed smell of him was enough to make her take a step back.

"Hey," he said tiredly.

"Hey," she responded. "You okay?"

"Just tired."

"Breakfast?"

"Maybe later. Need to walk, clear my head."

"Okay."

And he was gone.

For the next week, Max spent her days making sure he stayed fed, ordered a bunch of books online so she could catch up on her reading, and played with the dogs to keep them sharp and in shape. Nobody heard from Dr. Sylvester Kent, and Max and Kaitlin settled into an odd sort of truce.

"So, what is your degree in?" Max asked as they lay out on the patio's chaise loungers while the dogs played in the surf and the sunshine.

"Marketing."

"Then what are you doing here? Besides your daddy, of course."

"I got laid off six months ago. Daddy said Adam needed a secretary, and since I was having trouble finding something on my own, I said okay." Then she added, "The other stuff, the marriage and all that, well, that was daddy's idea, too."

She turned so she could see Max's face. "He was Adam's graduate advisor, and back then Adam used to come to the house a lot for dinner and help with his work and stuff. I've had a crush on him since I was probably fourteen."

Max was surprised by the girl's honesty, if that's what it was. "And your father knew?"

"Of course. He always told me that when I got older, Adam would marry me."

Max was floored. "And you believed him?"

Kaitlin came to her own defense. "I was fourteen. Daddy was God, and besides, Adam was always nice. Yeah, he was older but he never treated me like a little kid, until I moved in here and started throwing myself at him."

Max simply shook her head. "Well, there isn't a woman alive who hasn't done something stupid because of a man, so don't beat yourself up. Tell me this, though: What brought abut this change in your attitude?"

"Benny."

Max scanned her eyes. "Benny," she echoed doubtfully.

"When he came in here with that waitress, I felt hurt and cheap, like maybe I had been nothing more than a booty call. Then when I sat out here, I admitted to myself that that's all I was for him."

"That's Benny." Max had her own beef to settle with Mr. Watson. She wondered if she'd be able to restrain herself and act like an adult the next time they crossed paths, or if she'd shoot him on sight. She leaned toward the latter. "Made you grow up a little bit?" Max asked quietly.

Kaitlin nodded, saying, "Yeah. I thought about my life while I was out here that night and realized I'm twenty-five and I don't have one. There's stuff I want to do, and see, and maybe be, but none of it has to do with being here shilling for Daddy because he wants his fame back."

Max was impressed. "You've been thinking about this?"

"I have."

"So what are you going to do?"

She shrugged. "Look for a job, and in the meantime try and be a real secretary to Adam. Have you seen how much mail he gets?"

"No."

"Some of it is related to his work but most is from the women who saw him in *Time* magazine last year."

Max was confused. "These are fan letters?"

"No, marriage proposals."

Max grinned, "You're lying."

Kaitlin shook her head. "Nope, there were almost a thousand last time I counted."

Max found that amazing. "Has he written any of the women back?"

"No."

That didn't surprise Max. Something similar had happened to Chandler's brother, Drake Randolph, now the mayor of Detroit. Drake had also appeared in a magazine spread, but unlike Adam, Drake reportedly answered each and every one of the thousands of letters he received. "I can't see him taking the time to do all that."

"Me, either, which is why I suggested he let me send them a form letter thank-you note."

"What did he say?"

"Nothing."

Max was amazed. Yes, Adam Gary was a cutie, but marriage proposals? She understood his reluctance to get involved with the letters, though. The only way she would marry again was if somebody put a gun to her head.

"Max, are you mad at Adam about something?"

"Nope," she answered nonchalantly. "Why'd you ask?"

She shrugged. "Because he's not hanging around anymore."

"That's not unusual, is it?"

"No, but you two seemed . . ." Kaitlin shook her head. "Never mind."

Max met her eyes for a moment, then picked up one of the books beside her and began reading.

The pounding on the door woke Max up. "Max! Wake up! I found it!"

Asleep but moving, she threw back the covers, saw the clock read four A.M., and groaned. "What do you want, dammit!"

The door was flung open and there he stood, beaming. "I did it! I fixed it. It works!"

Max gave him a half smile then fell back on the bed. "This is the prototype?"

He ran to her side. "Yes! It works! It'll hold heat for as long as I need it to."

Still smiling, she said, "Congratulations."

"I have to make some calls!" That said, he tore out of the room like a madman and disappeared.

Max chuckled and got back into bed. Then she jumped up, screaming his name, "Adam!"

She caught him on the way to the lab.

"What's the matter?"

"I know how happy you are," she said, "but hold off on telling anyone just yet. Let's keep this on the down low until we see how the DOD wants to handle this. Okay?"

He looked so disappointed, Max had to force her smile not to show.

He finally said, "Okay."

"Good. Congratulations again."

Their eyes met. The lure in him slid straight through to Max's bones, and she had to remind herself that she and he were not to be. "See you later."

In spite of Max's disappointing directive, Adam was still the happiest scientist on the planet. Finally! He'd found the solution almost by accident. It had just been a matter of tweaking the ratios in the metal's tensile strength, and when he did that, voilà! The grid was able to hold a constant temperature. He'd been running it at sixty-seven degrees for the last twenty-four hours and it hadn't varied more than two degrees up or down. He wanted to climb on the roof and shout the news to the world. He'd done it. Adam Gary's lifelong quest for an energy source that people everywhere could use and afford had been fulfilled!

When Jan Kruger got the call saying Dr. Gary had perfected the prototype, he smiled. Now they could move. So far, Oskar's man had not resurfaced, but since the FBI had not come knocking on Jan's door, he felt free to go ahead with his plan. The first order of business would be to gather his troops and bring Gary on board. Apparently, the kidnap attempt and the e-mail threatening his mother had frightened him enough to want in. According to the contact, Gary had agreed to the price Jan had offered for the prototype and would work with his people to develop more.

Having Gary on board willingly was infinitely wiser than the earlier plan. Kidnapping him when he'd been just an obscure scientist working on a project that might or might not be successful had been feasible a few weeks ago, but now, with Gary enjoying such overnight prominence, taking that tack had become problematic. The world now knew Gary's name, and to have him disappear at the height of this media frenzy would only serve to bring the world's law enforcement agencies down on the kidnappers' heads. Jan didn't need that. The media would know his name and the names of his associates soon enough.

So for the moment things were going well. Back home in South Africa, disgruntled soldiers still loyal to the old Nationalist Party regime were being secretly recruited to their army. Jan hoped to have five thousand troops under his command when it became time to launch the offensive. He knew thousands more soldiers would be needed eventually, especially if the battle was a prolonged one, but he was counting on the ranks to swell every day as White South Africans joined to aid the cause.

Until then he was content knowing that in a few days he'd have Dr. Gary and the prototype in his possession. Soon, he thought, he and his forces would be ready to take their place in history.

Eleven

The house phone began ringing at seven A.M. The global wire services and news organizations had somehow gotten wind of Adam's accomplishment and were clamoring for interviews and information. Max instructed Kaitlin to tell the callers they'd dialed the wrong number. Kaitlin tried that, but the volume continued to mount, so Max just unplugged the phone. That put a stop to it, and Max went looking for Adam.

Outside, she picked up the binoculars from the tabletop and scanned the area. She spotted him about a half mile down the beach jogging with the dogs. The trio were in perfect rhythm, the dogs on either side of him. The thin white tank top he was wearing showed off the toned brown muscles in his arms and shoulders, while his red track shorts did the same for the well-formed legs. He was distracting, to say the least, especially to a woman sworn to professionalism. She allowed herself a few more seconds of ogling, then put the binoculars back down on the patio chair to wait.

When the three came back up to the house, the dogs

went for their water while he went through his cool-down routine.

"Mornin'" he said to her in a winded voice. Hands on his knees, he bent at the waist, took in some deep breaths and checked his watch.

Max nodded. "Morning."

Their eyes met. Neither of them addressed the newest tension between them.

Max asked instead, "Did you call somebody last night?"

He wiped his face on the towel in his hands. "Nope. Why?"

"The newspeople are blowing up the phone."

"Wasn't me. Have you talked to Kaitlin? She's the only other person I told besides you."

Max cursed inwardly. "Okay. Thanks." She went back inside. Sure enough, Kaitlin was the culprit.

"I called Daddy right after Adam told me." At the terse set of Max's features, she explained, "I didn't know I wasn't supposed to. I know Daddy's crazy but I thought he'd be happy for Adam."

"It's okay. It's my fault," Max said. "I should have said something about keeping this on the low low."

Adam entered, and when Max explained the situation to him, he asked Kaitlin, "Do you think he called the media?"

Kaitlin shrugged.

"Get him on the phone for me, would you, please. Use the house phone so we can put him on the speaker."

A few moments later, Kent's voice came over the line. "Hello?"

"Sly. It's me, Adam."

"Adam. Congratulations. I heard the exciting news. Outstanding."

"Thanks a lot. Any idea how the media found out? Phone's been ringing off the hook."

Kent laughed. "Ah, they're calling, are they? Good. I figured you'd be too exhausted to do anything today but sleep, so I've taken the liberty of declaring myself your agent."

Max stared at Adam in surprise.

"My agent?" Adam thundered.

"Yes. I've already contacted most of the media and the pertinent journals. All contacts are to go through me. Has Kaitlin been keeping a log of who's called there so that I—"

"Listen to me," Adam said grimly. "You call them and tell them you made a mistake. We don't have an agreement of any kind."

"Adam, there are people lined up to pay you millions for that prototype. All you have to do is let me—"

"Have access to something that's not yours to sell. I know."

Kent took immediate offense. "Had it not been for me, you'd be stuck in some obscure lab working for peanuts! You owe me, Adam Gary!"

"Just make the calls!" Adam snapped, then reached over and ended the connection. His angry eyes met Max's, and she couldn't recall ever seeing him so furious.

Kaitlin appeared on the verge of tears. "Adam, I'm so sorry."

"It's okay. I'm mad at him, not you. Do you know anything about these deals?"

"Not really. When he was here, he said something

about needing you to sign some kind of paper, and that he—Daddy—would get a mil and a half if you did." Then she confessed, "That's what I was really doing up in your room that time. I was looking for something with your signature on it. Daddy said he needed it. I didn't find anything, though."

Adam's lips thinned. "Did he say who this deal was with?"

She shook her head. "No."

Max wondered what this all meant. Kent sounded furious to be booted out of his so-called position. Had he already been paid? If he had, Max hoped he hadn't blown his wad on cheap women and toupees because once the unknown partner learned that he didn't represent anybody but himself, they were going to want that money back.

Kaitlin said again, "Adam, I'm really sorry."

He shook his head. "Don't worry about it."

Max said, "Kaitlin, do me a favor. Bring me all of the mail that's lying around."

Kaitlin looked confused by the request, but agreed. While she went to get it, Max glanced at Adam and saw that his anger hadn't dissipated.

He said, "No telling who Kent's been talking to."

"Or what he told them, but it'll all come out. Don't worry."

"Why do you want the mail?"

"Just to see what's in it."

Kaitlin returned with a handful of envelopes of all sizes. "This is the most recent stuff."

Max took the pile from her. "Thanks."

"You still want me to run to the store?" Kaitlin asked.

"Yes, please. I left the list on the table along with

some cash. Make sure you get only that brand of dog food. Ruby and Ossie won't eat anything else."

"Gotcha. I'll see you later."

Once she was gone, Max handed the mail to Adam. "So that I don't get hit with a felony, you open it."

They went out to the patio and Adam spent a few silent moments opening the envelopes and scanning the contents. To protect his privacy he'd been using a post office box forwarding service down in central Ohio. When his mail arrived there, the service sent it on to him in Michigan. This batch held no surprises. Some were journal articles and letters from colleagues. There were also a few more responses to *Time* magazine letters, one of which included a picture of the Jamaican writer and her four kids. He tossed the pile on the table and sat back.

Max could tell he was still mad, and she thought he had good reason. Kent had bigger balls than she had initially given him credit for. To actually try and gangster your way into someone else's life said a lot about who Kent thought himself to be.

She studied Adam's face. During the days leading up to his success with the prototype, he hadn't shaved, bathed, or slept. She also remembered how bad he'd smelled. This morning he was back to being clean and handsome. He'd cut his hair, and the beard surrounding his chin and lips was once again trimmed down to a seductive shadow. The brown eyes still looked tired, though, but that was to be expected. She was sure it had been weeks since he'd had a full night's sleep.

Adam decided there was nothing he could do about Kent right now. As Max had said, everything would come out in the end, but as he glanced her way, he wondered how his situation with her would end. For now, it was still unresolved, and in spite of her congratulations on his achievement, she remained distant and professional, so much so that out here under the 65 degree morning, there was an icy breeze between them. He didn't know how to talk to her about the elephant in the room, and she sure didn't look like she was going to bring it up. "What were you hoping to find in the mail?" he asked.

"Maybe something related to Kent's supposed deal. A letter of inquiry, or one of introduction to you from whoever he's been talking with."

Adam said, "If he's really been talking to somebody."

"We know he talked to the media and the pertinent journals," she said in a voice that mimicked Kent's pretentious tones.

He let a small smile show. It had been a while since they'd spoken more than a few words to each other, and Adam realized how much longer it had been since he'd seen her smile. "Max, about the last time you and I talked—"

"When you asked me if I really killed people for a living?"

He winced inwardly. "Yes. I just wanted to say I was wrong to drop that on you out of the blue."

"No kidding."

Adam pushed down his temper. "Are you going to let me apologize?"

"I'm not sure."

He looked to the sky for strength.

Max turned her attention to the beach, where the

waves were breaking softly against the shore. "How about I accept your apology and we just not talk about it again?" she asked quietly.

It was not what Adam wanted; he wanted to *know*, maybe to understand, but he could only take what she offered, so he said, "Deal."

"And from now on this is strictly professional. No more kissing, no more—more."

He was wearing a soft smile. "Yes, ma'am."

Max didn't think he was giving the conversation the levity it deserved. "I'm serious."

"I can see that," he replied.

She turned away from his potent eyes and wondered when she'd lost control of the situation, because it certainly felt like she had. "And no flirting allowed, either."

"That's no fun."

"There isn't going to be any *fun*."

"I understand that. No kisses unless you ask."

Max stared at him across the table.

With a knowing smile on his handsome face, he slowly got to his feet. The yawn and stretch that followed spoke to how exhausted he was. "I need to go to bed, been up all night. That run took the last of my energy. Maybe now I can sleep."

Because of all the morning drama, Max had yet to start breakfast. "Do you want to eat first?"

He shook his head. "No, but definitely later." He stared down at her and wondered if he'd hold her in his arms again. "Wake me up if something jumps off."

"Will do. Go get some rest."

He didn't have to be told twice.

After he disappeared inside the house, Max softly

bounced her forehead against the tabletop. *Professional. You have to stay professional.* Surely she wasn't going to lose her mind a second time. Giving in to her desire was as bad an idea as it had been before, but the man was as tempting as a fat piece of her mama's chocolate cake.

A short while later, Kaitlin returned bearing groceries and news. "There are TV trucks down by the gate."

Max turned from the bacon she was frying. "What?"

Kaitlin put the bags on the table. "TV trucks. Bunch of cables all over the road. I already called Sheriff Ramos."

"Good. How many trucks?"

"Five."

Max stared.

Kaitlin began to empty the bags. "One from Detroit, two from Grand Rapids, and one each from Kalamazoo and Muskegon."

Max didn't like it at all. This was supposed to be a *secret* operation. Apparently, she needed to start handing out dictionaries.

"I hid my face as best I could when I passed them."

"Good girl."

"So what do we do about them?"

"For now, nothing. I'm hoping the sheriff will give them the bum's rush. If not, we'll have Adam call Washington when he wakes up and find out what they want him to do."

In Max's ideal world they would be packing up and moving out. With all the potential media coverage, the people who'd sent the threatening e-mail and whoever Kent was purportedly dealing with would undoubtedly be able to determine Adam's location before dinnertime. Add them to the perps who'd tried to kidnap him in Madrid, and it became a mix that could be a problem for a one-woman, two-dog operation. DOD had billed this assignment as a simple one because he was supposedly working in secrecy. She'd been hired to keep an eye on things until the prototype was perfected, then hand him and it over to his Washington handlers. No one had taken Kent into account, however. Thanks to him, the world was now sitting outside the gate, and if the people in Washington had any sense they'd move Adam and his operation to a secured government facility as soon as possible.

But with no clear directive, they had to stay put. Meanwhile, she planned to put in a call to Myk for ideas. "Thanks for going to the store."

Kaitlin said, "No problem. Can I eat?"

Max smiled. "Yep."

While Kaitlin grabbed a plate, Max went outside to the patio to check on and feed the dogs.

While they ate, she again surveyed the surroundings with an eye toward security. Because of where the house sat, a well-equipped group of defenders could hold the line for some time if the bad guys tried an assault from the lake, but she and the dogs didn't constitute a group. If a team came with more than four or five men, it could get dicey, especially if they had a lot of firepower. Her toys were locked away in the hold of the car and she was armed for bear, but were the choice hers, they'd all be getting the hell out of Dodge because her posse wasn't big enough to do a remake of *Shootout at the OK Corral*.

Kaitlin stuck her head around the door and said, "Max, the sheriff's here."

Sheriff Marco Ramos was tall, handsome, and Hispanic.

"Ms. Blake?"

Max shook his hand.

He said, "We moved the press out to the public road. Legally, we can't make them go away."

"I understand," Max said. The public road was a pretty good piece away, so that news pleased her.

"A deputy will cruise by periodically to make sure nothing's going on, so if you need us, just give us a call." He handed her his business card.

"Thank you."

As Max was walking him back to the front door, he stopped and asked, "So, is Dr. Gary's invention really going to do all the things the newspeople are saying?"

She shrugged. "Who knows? I'm just the housekeeper, and I don't have a clue to what the doc's been doing down in that lab."

He smiled. "I understand. Well, tell him congratulations."

"I will."

He touched his hat and stepped back out into the sunshine.

When Max closed the door, Kaitlin was standing there and she gushed, "Now that was some serious eye candy."

Max grinned. "Oh, yeah!"

Both women laughed.

Adam slept away the day. With the phone unplugged and the sheriff on patrol outside, Max's afternoon was an uneventful one until she heard the dogs barking out front. With her Glock strapped to her thigh and hidden beneath her ankle-length T-shirt dress, she hurried to the door. Ruby and Ossie were barking ferociously at a three-man camera crew standing in the gravel driveway in a tableau that could only be described as Frozen Fear. All three looked too scared to even breathe, and the dogs were making sure they stayed that way.

Max walked out and called them off. Ruby and Ossie heeled but their brows remained furrowed, their eyes keen. "This is private property, gentlemen," she told them. "Please leave if you don't want to be interviewing the sheriff."

"Uh, and your name is?" one of the men asked in a shaky voice. He kept shooting wary glances at the dogs.

"In five seconds you are going to be racing the dogs back to wherever your vehicle is parked, so I suggest you get a head start. One!"

They stared.

"Two!"

Ruby and Ossie stood up, bared their teeth and began to growl. The eyes of the newsies widened and the men began backing away.

"Three!"

They were now running as fast as they could while carrying all their equipment, and Max fought to keep a straight face. "Four!" she yelled.

She heard one of the men wail, and saw them run faster and disappear around the bend in the drive. "Five!"

She gave the dogs the command to go and they took off at lightning speed. In the distance she heard fear-fed screams and then car doors slamming, followed by the sound of screeching tires and a vehicle taking off down the road.

A few moments later the dogs came trotting back into view, and Max said with affection. "I think Kaitlin brought back some doggie treats just for you two." And she gave each an affectionate scratch behind their ears. "These people must think we're playing with them."

Ruby barked.

Max said, "I don't think so, either, girlfriend."

Adam awakened around eight that evening. Groggy but feeling better, he got out of bed and padded to the windows that looked out onto the lake. The sun was going down in its signature blaze of oranges and reds, tinting the surface of the water with the same vivid hues. He stretched and yawned. Yesterday he'd still been searching for a solution to the prototype's problems, but now, he couldn't suppress his grin. Picking up the remote, he clicked on the television and punched up one of the cable news channels. He wanted to see what, if anything, they were saying about him. He didn't have long to wait. A beat later he saw a picture of his face flash onto the screen, and turned up the volume.

> *"Dr. Adam Gary, an African American scientist* Time *magazine picked as one of this country's brightest minds, has reportedly invented a revolutionary energy device that may wipe out our dependence on foreign oil forever. Rumors of the invention's potential sent oil stocks plummeting to record lows. In other news, Vice President—"*

Adam clicked off the TV and went to the shower.

Downstairs in the kitchen, he found his dinner warming in the stove, but didn't see Max. Too hungry to do anything but eat, he sat down and filled himself with a salmon fillet glazed with lemon pepper sauce, coleslaw, and a foil-wrapped baked potato. The ubiquitous green Kool-Aid was in a pitcher in the fridge, and he poured himself a brimming glass to wash it all down. When he was done eating, and feeling fat and satisfied, he put his empty dishes in the sink and went in search of Max.

She was seated under the umbrella, working on her laptop in the fading light. At his approach she looked up. "Did you sleep?"

"Yes." He liked the thin sleeveless T-shirt dress she had on. The yellow color showed off the burnished beauty of her neck, shoulders, and arms. His desire for her kept rising and there didn't seem to be a way to make it stop.

She went back to pecking on the keyboard. "You're are all over the net and the TV."

"I saw one of the CNN reports. Supposedly, oil stocks dropped."

"Big-time. I talked to Myk. He said he'll try to get the media to go away and has a call in to the Defense Department about moving you to a more secure location. He said it may take a couple of days. He also said not to give any interviews, and to say congratulations."

"That brother is on it."

"Amen. I'm glad he's on our side."

"What are you up to?" he asked, taking a seat and indicating her laptop.

"Downloading some new Portia toys."

"Ah." Adam wondered if he'd ever have the opportunity to meet the techno talented Portia. He asked, "What kind of software is it?"

Max shrugged. "No idea. Portia says it's a surprise."

In response to a prompt, Max keyed in the required actions then watched the program come to an end. A picture of Jesse and James, siblings of Ruby and Ossie, came on the screen. Their faces represented Portia's trademark. Max shut down the OS and closed the top.

"I haven't seen Kaitlin," Adam said. "Is she here?"

"No, she went to Lansing to hang out with her girls. She'll be back tomorrow night sometime. She said she knew another way to the highway, so getting past the TV trucks wasn't going to be a problem."

"What TV trucks?"

"I didn't tell you?"

"No."

So she told him about the trucks, the sheriff, and the TV crew the dogs had chased away.

"Wow. I didn't think it would blow up like this."

"I don't think anyone else did, either. Except maybe Kaitlin's daddy."

"She hear anything else from him?"

"Not that I know of."

It seemed they had run out of things to talk about because silence fell between them and then grew. When she glanced his way, he was watching her, and Max hastily but smoothly glanced away again, even as she mentally chided herself for still wanting more of his magic kisses.

Twelve

Hoping that putting some distance between herself and him would bolster her weakening resolve, Max stood and walked over to the railing. The moon was rising in the darkening sky. Against the silence, the rhythmic sound of the waves was like a sonata composed by Mother Nature. When he rose silently and came to stand next to her, she could feel his presence as well as she could feel her own heart beating.

"We need to resolve this," he said softly.

Max knew he was right. The barrier she'd tried to erect around her desire didn't seem to be working. If anything, it was making her want him all the more. Last time they'd come together he'd given her only a taste of his wizardry and she'd been left panting, pulsing and wet. Would a full dose of his loving cure her craving? Would it satisfy her so that in the morning she could shower, dress, and go back to concentrating on doing her job? Max had no idea, but knew of only one way to find out.

She turned her head his way and was again struck by how fine he was, even in the gloom. Whoever thought she'd be wanting to do the wild thing with a brother who spoke chemical equations as a second language? Feeling mesmerized, she lightly traced her finger down the long thin stripe of his moustache to where it merged into the hair dusting his lower jaw. The skin was warm beneath her touch, and she could hear him taking in slow measured breaths. Her finger rounded his chin, then slowed as it encountered the ridges and irregularities where his skin had been repaired after the mauling. An odd sadness tightened her heart. Leaning up, she kissed the spot, wanting passion to replace the painful memories. She flicked her tongue against it softly, then pressed her lips against the spot. In response, he pulled her roughly into his arms, and the kiss that followed made her soar. He was such a master. He seemed to know exactly how long to place his lips against hers to ignite the flame, and how to fit his body ardently against her own. The feel of his lips moving over hers infected her with his heat, and as the kiss deepened and her hands began to move over the strength in his arms, she wondered if he'd taken a course in a school somewhere that showed him the perfect way to mate his tongue with hers.

She had no answers, however. She was too busy melting under the lips now moving slowly up her jaw to her ear, and ripening under the hot hand weaving spells over her back in the thin T-shirt dress.

Adam's long celibate manhood was demanding to be satisfied. Now. It wanted to take this sweet-tasting woman. Now. But he forced himself to go slow; she was too beautiful to treat badly, too fiery not to want to linger over and savor. He sampled the soft skin beneath her ear and knew he hadn't gotten enough of her last time and sensed that she felt the same, so he planned to make up for it tonight, even if it took him until sunrise.

Recapturing her lush mouth, he moved a hand over her tempting breasts, plying the nipples until they hardened, teasing them until she moaned. The knowledge that he could make her respond this way pleased him, fueled him. Wanting more, he lowered his head and loved the buds through the fabric of her dress.

Max was on fire. His hot mouth had her nipples pleading for mercy. He sucked and nibbled and plucked until she was breathless and shimmering. She let him play a bit longer then stepped back. With her body pulsing wantonly and her passion-lidded eyes holding his, she reached down and slowly pulled her dress up and off. Tossing it aside, she stood there in the moonlight wearing nothing but her black transparent bra, black thong, and short-heeled sandals.

As the moonlight illuminated her lean form, he whispered, "God, you're beautiful. . . ."

Entranced, he lightly circled an expert finger around her bursting nipple. Treating its twin to the same silent stroking, he continued until the sensations made her head fall back and her lips part in response. As before, he knew just how to touch her, how to make her moan. His tongue wantonly entered the fray then, and she gasped sensually. He played her with his mouth, fingers, and tongue, filling her with pleasure until she was brimming with desire and her tissue thin bra was damp from his loving. She was damp, too. His hand wandering over her hips and between her thighs wantonly confirmed it, and she scandalously parted her legs for more.

Like most men, Adam thought thongs the sexiest bits of froth ever invented. Something about the thin strips of lace running between a woman's thighs and then teasingly outlining her hips made him want to touch, slide, and fondle; made him want to ease the lace aside, drop to his knees and kiss his way to paradise. Fitting thought to action, he did just that.

Max just knew she was going to die. She was no prude, she'd been loved like this before, but he was good. His technique staggered her, and when he parted her and slid a bold finger inside, the orgasm buckled her, shattered her, then became all the more intense because he didn't stop. He kept up the carnal conquering, pleasuring her erotically, making her widen her stance so she could feel him everywhere, and as he bit her passionately, Maxine Loreli Blake came again with a strangled cry.

Then the dogs were beside them barking furiously. They'd been summoned by her screams and had come racing from their beds in the car to aid her, only to find her standing with her thong in tatters, her legs spread, and Adam on his knees. "Go away!" she commanded in a voice that held no authority at all. "I'm fine."

Ruby and Ossie were still barking, though. A chuckling Adam kissed her navel and stood. A month ago, the dogs appearing out of thin air would have scared him to death, but now he told them affectionately. "Your mama is fine, go back to bed."

Every cell in Max's body was vibrating sensually. The idea of the dogs coming to her rescue was amusing, and she appreciated their devotion, but four was a crowd. "We need to be behind locked doors," she said to Adam. "Your bed or mine?"

"Definitely mine."

The sureness of his tone made Max's desire rebloom.

Already anticipating the slide of his body against her own, she said, "I'll take them back and meet you upstairs."

"You might want to grab your dress."

Max shook her head. He'd made her so brainless she'd paid no attention to her nearly nude state. It took her a moment to find it under the moonlight, but once she did, she slipped it on and escorted the dogs away.

Upstairs, Adam was so engorged he could hardly move, yet somehow managed to drag fresh sheets on the beds before she arrived. When she entered, he was seated against the headboard, needing her like an oasis needed rain. Under the dim light of the far side of the room, she peeled off her dress again and joined him on the bed.

"The dogs shouldn't bother us now," she told him.

Adam's eyes glowed at the sight of her golden nudity. He was nude, too, and had no way of hiding how much he wanted her.

"You look real glad to see me," she said with quiet amusement.

"That's what happens when a man's been celibate for two years." He reached up and grazed a bent knuckle over the soft skin of her cheek. "I'm apologizing in advance if I get a little wild."

"Sometimes wild is good."

Grinning, he eased her in against him, and then his mood turned serious as he looked down into her beautiful face. His opening kiss was tender, gentle. This was going to be their first real time together, and even though he was hard and hurting, he wanted to relish her, taste her, and hear her sigh as he made her his.

They slid down to the sheet and he left her sweet

mouth so he could adore his way over her silken form with lingering, humid kisses. The small breasts drew him like a moth to flame, and he spent an inordinate amount of time coaxing the cinnamon brown nipples to ripen just the way he liked. As she arched temptingly in response, he kept up the play until each bud was hard and damp.

Max groaned with pleasure. She definitely took back the crack about his loving being cold as ice water. He had her at a low boil. Dr. Adam Gary could make love to her until Christmas and she'd greedily want more. To that end, she rose up and began to work her way over his body in much the same way he'd done her. Treating him to kisses, licks, and passionate nibbles, she slowly and deliberately toured her way down his planes and angles to the mahogany prize that made him male. No shame in her game, she flicked her tongue over the soft velvety head and heard him draw in a loud measured breath. Max knew a thing or two about pleasing a man, so using her hands and mouth, she showed him just how much.

Adam was sure he'd died and gone to heaven. Max Blake was scandalous and he was glad as hell that she was. He could think of no better way to end his celibacy than to be with a woman who enjoyed giving pleasure as much as she did receiving, but after a few more minutes of glory he growled deep in his throat and backed away to keep himself from exploding.

Pleased, Max licked her lips like a contented lioness and whispered heatedly, "Let's put you out of your misery, then we can enjoy ourselves."

She rolled on the condom he handed her, then straddled him. A delighted Adam put his hands on her waist and eased his way into paradise. The sheer sensations made his eyes close, the heat of her enfolding him almost more than he could stand. The tight warmth threatened to push him over the edge, and he wanted to thrust his way to completion then and there, but held on. *Lord, she felt good.* She then leaned forward and gifted him with kisses so enticing he began to move inside her with a rhythm as old as time, and she answered with ancient female response. Soon they were casting shadows on the wall that erotically mirrored their movements. His hands guided her hips in the cadence of his loving and she rode him in tune. Because of his celibacy, it didn't take long for the orgasm to grab him, and when it did, his body exploded and he began to thrust as if his life were hanging in the balance. Out of control, he let his body have its head while he shouted and roared and shouted some more.

Caught up in his storm, the bursting Max came a heartbeat later, and she hoarsely screamed her joy into his shoulder so that the dogs wouldn't kick in the door.

They moved their lust fest to the shower, where Adam, relieved by their first coupling, worshipped her, adored her, and impaled her under the stream of water. Max came with her long legs wrapped around his waist and her back arched, supported by his strong hands. She was limp by the time they returned to the bed, and he dried her so slowly and deliciously, it wasn't long before they began again; exploring, kissing, licking, loving. After two years of celibacy Adam had a wealth of passion to bestow, and Max was glad to be his beneficiary.

Eventually they had to stop because neither of them could move, so Adam clicked off the lamp, snuggled up against her beautiful warm body, and they slept.

* * *

The next morning Adam awoke alone. Concerned, he sat up and looked around, but when the smell of bacon frying drifted to his nose, he fell back on the bed. The memories of last night came back with the sharp clarity of a DVD, and he found himself grinning like a twelve-year-old kid waking up at Disney World. *Wow!* He didn't need a graduate course to know that women like Max Blake were rare, and that few men were lucky enough to have such a jewel cross their paths. In the bed, in the shower; lying down, standing up; turned this way, leaning that way, they'd sexually explored each other to the limits of their endurance, and Adam considered himself the luckiest brother in the world.

Downstairs, she had her back turned when he entered the kitchen. The CD player was bumping Anthony Hamilton. Adam stood in the doorway for a moment checking out her loose-fitting white halter and short denim skirt that showcased her legs. The memories of those fine brown limbs wrapped around his waist made him as hard as he'd been last night.

Finally noticing him, she stopped and smiled. "Mornin'."

"Mornin'."

"Feeling better now that you got that celibacy monkey off your back?"

"Oh, yeah," he replied, grinning, then asked, "Where are the dogs?"

"Out front eating. Why?"

"Don't want them blocking my morning kiss."

Max put the steaming scrambled eggs in a bowl, turned to him and asked playfully, "Who said I'm giving out kisses this morning?"

Chuckling, he walked over to where she stood by the counter and looked down into her sparkling eyes. He traced a finger over the divine curves of her mouth, then slowly leaned down to taste it.

After a few moments of silent bliss, Max whispered, "I guess I am. . . ." Her arms slid up his back and he pulled her closer to increase the intensity of his greeting. They got so hung up they didn't care that the eggs were getting cold or that the now done toast was waiting in the toaster; the kisses and exploring hands were the only nourishment they craved.

Max had promised herself that she was only going to make love to this man one time. Once. But after last night, seemingly all he had to do was walk in the room and she went hot and damp. Like now. The lips moving over her shoulder, the hands peeling down her straps so he could say good morning to her breasts, left her tingling and breathless. He flicked his tongue against her straining nipples and made her croon when he took her in fully, then played, dallied, and lingered. "Oh, lord . . ."

He paid her pleading no mind. Slipping his hands beneath her short skirt, he continued his morning salutation to her breasts while he explored the damp hidden treasure bisected by her thong. Wanting to know what color she was wearing, he moved the denim aside so he could see. Red. Hot. He toured a hand over the flat plane of her dark hair and savored the feel of the thin fabric and the humid heat of her skin. He boldly moved his finger lower, teasing, plucking, and when she groaned and spread her legs so lusciously, he once again hardened like a pipe.

Throbbing with lust, Adam watched her rise and fall

to his sweet manipulations. With his other hand he made sure her breasts weren't neglected, then leaned down and bit them blissfully. Raising his head, his dewed fingers continuing to play between her red-thonged thighs, he husked out against her ear, "Come for me. . . ."

Max mewled in shuddering response. Last night's loving had given her the stamina to stave off a quick orgasm, but his rich-voiced invitation set her on the brink.

"Maybe this will help. . . ." and he slid in two long-boned fingers.

She gasped. Her body greedily rode the sensations of being filled. The fingers began their lazy sensual assault and her hips rode the rhythm until the heat became so overwhelming she splintered like glass, shouting hoarsely and hoping it would never end.

It did, of course, but only long enough for him to replace his fingers with something harder and far more substantial. He was big, and Max loved it. Having been an Amazon all of her life, finding a man capable of supporting her weight and stroking her back and forth while she held on with her legs wrapped around his waist was priceless. The expert hands guided her lustily on his condom-sheathed manhood until sensations became their world.

He climaxed first, pumping like a man gone wild, and she followed, crooning and mindless as wave after body-shattering wave rolled over them and swept them out to sea.

After a shower and breakfast, a smiling Adam was working in the lab and reflecting on the pleasurable morning when his cell phone rang. Pulling it from his hip, he checked the number, but there was nothing on the display. Puzzled, he raised it to his ear. "Yeah."

"Dr. Gary?" The accented voice wasn't a familiar one.

"Yes."

"Good morning. I'm calling on behalf of friends."

He went still. He instantly knew who he was talking to. "Which friends?"

"Your Madrid friends."

"Ah, the cowards that threatened my mother. What the hell do you want?"

"I'm sorry if our methods were unorthodox, but I'm glad to hear your are going to join us."

"Join you?"

Adam looked over at Ossie lying in the doorway, then said to the caller, "Can you hold for a moment, please." He muted the phone and said to Ossie, "Ossie, go get Max. Quick."

Ossie took off.

Adam went back to his call. "I'm sorry. Now, you were saying?"

"My friends would like to make the exchange as soon as possible."

"Well, since I have no idea what you're talking about, that might be problematic."

The man didn't respond for a moment, then said, "Are you trying to up the price?"

"No."

"Are you not Adam Gary?"

"I am."

"Then why the riddles? You signed a contract."

"I've signed nothing."

The voice became insistent. "Dr. Kent assured us everything was in order."

Adam's lips thinned. "Then there's the problem. Dr. Kent doesn't represent me."

Again the other end of the line went silent, then the man gritted out, "We have paid you and we expect to take possession."

Adam saw the concerned-looking Max standing in the doorway with the dogs. "You may have paid Kent, but he isn't authorized to speak for me. I suggest you talk to him."

"We will not be shoved aside so that you can raise the price."

"Look, man, I'm not going to argue with you about it, so talk to Kent. 'Bye!" and he closed the phone.

Max asked, "What was that?"

"It seems Kaitlin's daddy has arranged to sell my prototype and they want me to hand it over."

"Who are they?"

He shrugged. "My friends from Madrid." Adam was furious that Kent had tied himself to men who thought that threatening the life of his mother was no big deal. Adam couldn't wait to see Kent again so he could beat the hell out of him. He opened his phone and angrily punched in Kent's number. It rang, then transferred him to the voice mail. Adam left a terse profane message then hung up.

Max was thinking. "The folks in Washington need to know about this. How long would it take you to download all of your work and wipe your hard drives clean?"

Adam looked confused. "Why?"

"Because I don't like the sound of that call. How long?"

"Couple hours."

"Get started."

He stared.

"Please, Adam. Call Washington and then do the computers. If nothing jumps off, fine, but if we have to bug out of here on the run, I don't want your work found."

Adam agreed with her. "I'm on it."

"Good. I'm going to make some calls, then I'll be back."

Upstairs, Max put in a call to Chandler. When he answered, she ran the situation by him.

Myk said, "Sounds like somebody needs to whip Kent's ass. If you don't hear anything from Washington by this evening, I want you to get Adam out of there as quickly and as quietly as possible. Is the media still there?"

"No idea, but supposedly there's a way out that by-passes them."

"Good. We don't need them in the mix, too. Bring him down here and we'll go from there."

"Okay."

"And Max?"

"Yeah?"

"Be careful."

"Most definitely. I'll keep you posted."

She ended the call.

Adam spent the rest of the morning downloading his work onto small portable drives, shredding papers and thinking about the mysterious call. What had Kent done and how much had he been paid? Kaitlin mentioned something about half a million dollars. Had Kent pocketed that much? If he had, Adam understood why the caller wasn't happy. Would they be pissed off enough to try and take the prototype by force? Apparently Max thought so, and so did he, otherwise he wouldn't be down here doing what he was doing.

The man called Adam back around noon. "My friends want their property, Dr. Gary, and if we have to retrieve it in person we will. I will call you back in one hour."

The transmission ended.

Adam left the lab to let Max know about the call when his phone went off again. The number was Kaitlin's. "Yeah?"

She was screaming and crying and he couldn't understand a word. "Kaitlin! Kaitlin! Slow down! I can't understand you, slow down!"

He got her to calm down long enough to explain. What she told him was staggering. Dr. Sylvester Kent was dead. He'd been shot in the head gangland style, and according to Kaitlin, whoever murdered him had also cut out his tongue.

He consoled her as best he could on the phone. She promised to call him later, after the police did their preliminary investigation, and then hung up.

A now grim Adam placed a call to Washington. His contact was a man named Jeffries. A secretary answered. Jeffries was in a meeting with his boss, Adam was told. "Is there any way I can reach him? This is an emergency."

"I'm sorry, sir, but Mr. Jeffries will be unavailable until the end of the day. I'll let him know you called."

"But—"

Click. She was gone.

Frustrated, Adam closed the phone.

Jan Kruger thought Kent deserved to die for his perfidy. After receiving Kent's assurances that the deal was done, he had expected the exchange to go smoothly. Instead he would have to spend the day putting together a team to try and take Gary and the prototype by force. *Damn Kent!* He should have known better than to trust someone of his race. It was bad enough that Jan and his friends were staking their future on the invention of a Black, but they had no other choice. Once they were confident in their ability to reproduce the prototype, Gary would no longer be necessary. Now, however, he was very necessary, and Jan planned to oversee the operation to snare him personally. He wanted no more screw-ups. Killing Kent might have been a mistake, but he had no time for second thoughts or remorse.

Thirteen

When Max heard the news about Kent, all she could do was shake her head. He'd been a tremendous pain in the butt but no one deserved to be murdered in cold blood. Without firm evidence, Max knew the authorities wouldn't be able to tie Kent's death to the men wanting Adam's prototype, but she didn't believe in coincidences. "Did Kaitlin say how long he'd been dead?"

"Coroner told her two, maybe three hours."

"So it happened sometime this morning."

Adam nodded, then told her about the second call he'd received from the man claiming ownership of the prototype.

Max said, "I'll touch base with Portia and the Bureau to see if there's a way to find out who he is and where he's calling from. How are you coming with the downloads?"

"Nearly done. Most of the paper has been shredded, too."

"Good. Finish up as soon as you can. We're out of here first thing in the morning if your man Jeffries doesn't call this evening."

"Where to?"

"Detroit, first. We'll figure out where next when we get there."

"Sounds good."

Max mined her brain for any other information she might need to know. "Can the prototype travel?"

"Yes."

"Safely?"

"Without question."

"How big is it?"

"Not very. Want to see it?"

Max was surprised by the offer. "Yeah."

It was the first time she had been in his inner sanctum. She looked around at all the computers, the stuffed bookshelves, and the large chalkboard filled with equations. The all-white room with its countertops reminded her of her high school chem lab.

To Max, the prototype looked like one of the tubes you put your check into at the bank drive-up. It was made of a transparent material that felt light yet strong in her hand. There were two dark metal caps on each end, and sealed inside was a gently roiling substance that looked liked liquid black pearls. Grays and blacks merged and separated in a dance that was mesmerizing. She looked up at him. "What is this stuff?"

"Mostly chemicals. Carbon for one." He went on to explain the science behind his discovery.

Max followed the explanation just fine until he slipped into his second language and began talking chemical equationese. Chuckling, she held up her hand. "Whoa, Doc. Whoa. You're making me dizzy, here. I'm just a country girl, remember."

"Sorry," he said with an embarrassed smile.

"No need to apologize. This is something you're passionate about. I like that Einstein mind."

"Never been wanted for my mind before."

"Oh, it's not just your mind, believe me."

He laughed. "Are the rest of the women in your family as real as you are?"

Max shrugged. "I suppose. My mama raised JT and me to mean what we say and say what we mean. My job is in the mix, too, though. I've worked beside a lot of men, and they respect a woman who's up front. Cuts out a lot of the bullshit."

Adam agreed. He'd met few women who appreciated his love for science, which is why his two fiancées never worked out. As for being up front with him, both women would say whatever they thought he wanted to hear. Beautiful and brainless, the both of them. Being around Max proved that he'd saved himself and his fiancées a lot of grief by calling the engagements to a halt.

Max was still studying his fascinating invention. "So how will this work?"

"It fits inside of a receptacle that will hopefully be standard in all future homes. The receptacle is made out of a material that reacts with the casing and distributes the heat."

Max was impressed. "And it won't explode or anything like that if it gets knocked around?"

Adam gestured for the tube. When she handed it over, he smacked it against the edge of the lab's counter. It didn't break. The chemicals inside sped up their roll for a second or two, but nothing else happened.

"I am too scared of you," she declared with amused awe. *All that brain and fabulous in bed, too! Lord, have mercy.* Forcing herself to keep her mind on the problem at hand, she said to him, "Okay. Let me see what Portia can do about our caller, and you finish up down here. When you're done, pack a bag and put it in my car. Only the essentials. We don't have a lot of room."

He nodded his understanding.

She leaned up, gave him a quick kiss and said, "See you later."

Jan Kruger was ready to begin the assault on Gary's residence. He was done calling Gary and trying to do this like gentlemen. According to Kent, the only resistance they were liable to encounter was the housekeeper and her two dogs. Kruger was sure such a laughable security force would be no problem at all.

The man claiming to have paid for the prototype didn't call back, and a sense of foreboding dropped down on Max like a heavy winter coat. As the day lengthened, she became so convinced something bad was about to go down, she got out her handheld. Using Benny's software, she scanned the perimeter for lurkers. Seeing nothing, she and the dogs went out to the car.

Keeping an eye open for trouble, she popped the gate on the back of the Honda and lifted the well cover. Inside was her weapons locker and the bag holding the dogs' protective gear. Hoisting the heavy footlocker out of the car, she grabbed the bag with her other hand then carried it all back into the house.

Out on the patio, she removed the collars Ruby and Ossie were wearing and replaced them with the ones she fished out of the bag. Portia called them war collars. Each was made of a lightweight fabric that was virtually indestructible in order to protect all the nanotechnology inside. Max had tried the collars out for the first time during an art theft investigation in Greece she and the dogs had been hired for a few months back, and she thought the collars were Portia's best work by far. Inside were digital cameras Max could access, and Portia could access from her farm down in Ohio as well. There was also GPS technology that enabled a satellite to pinpoint the dogs' locations anywhere on the planet, and a few other magic gadgets that helped Max stay one step ahead.

Once the collars were secured, she strapped on their vests and secured the Velcro fasteners on their backs and beneath their bellies. Made out of the same bullet-proof materials used by human law enforcement agencies, the vests, like the collars, had been customized for protection and ease of wear. Satisfied that her babies were outfitted for whatever might jump off, she turned her attention to her weapons. The twenty-first century version of the AK-47 she began putting together was part rifle, part machine gun. The German weapons manufacturer who'd asked her to test-drive it called it a hybrid. It was sleek, lightweight, and deadly. She'd trained on it extensively but hadn't had cause to put it to use. In reality, she hoped she wouldn't have to. Having been a Girl Scout, however, Max knew better than to be unprepared.

She glanced up and saw Adam standing by the door watching her. His face was unreadable but his eyes were on the gun.

"Computers all set?" she asked, keeping her tone light and going back to her task. While he looked on silently, she added the last piece, then raised the large weapon to check the sight.

He moved closer. She met his eyes and said, "If you have something to say, now's the time."

Adam didn't know what to say. The big gun brought home the fact that Max Blake was no ordinary woman. Most of the ladies he knew were content to carry handbags filled with makeup, but this one earned a weapon that looked like something out of *The Terminator*. "Not sure what to say."

Max shrugged. "Think of it as an insurance policy."

Adam gave her a smile. "Okay."

Max appreciated his smile because she wanted him to understand who she was. "I'm security, Adam. Can't fight the bad guys with a curling iron."

He smiled. "Guess not." Then he added, "That's a big gun."

She let a small smile peep out. "It is indeed." She explained its pedigree, and when she was done she asked, "Ever fired a weapon?"

"No. I'm real good with a fishing pole, though."

She grinned. "It's a good skill to have in your repertoire, Doc. Never know when it may come in handy. You might want to get some training once this adventure is over."

Adam wasn't sure whether it was something he wanted to do in the future, but it was something to consider. He glanced over at the dogs outfitted in their gear. "Whoa. They look serious."

"Don't want them to be hurt. Portia designed the vests and the collars."

Adam walked over to take a closer look. Although he and the dogs had come to a truce of sorts, he was still hesitant about touching them. He noted the new collars. "What's the deal on these?" he asked.

Max explained how the collars functioned.

Adam appeared impressed. "GPS?"

"Along with a few other bells and whistles. We're doing a year-long field test. If they work out, Portia will put them on the market."

"So they're prototypes?"

"Basically, yes."

"This Portia is someone I'd like to meet."

"She'd probably like to meet you, too. You two can compare brains." Max noted that he seemed more comfortable now than he'd been when he first stepped out to join her, and she was glad. "Is your bag in the car?"

"Yes, ma'am. I'm ready to roll whenever you are."

"Good. Anything from Washington?"

He shook his head.

Max wondered what was going on with that. DOD was supposed to be doing oversight on Adam's project; now they were nowhere to be found. Was something else in the mix impacting their getting in touch? The phone's landline was still unplugged, but they had his cell number. "Not hearing back from Jeffries bothers me. I don't understand."

"Me, either, but the government bureaucracy sings their own tune."

"I know that, but still—"

There were two jet skis out on the lake moving at a pretty good clip toward the beach. The noisy machines were common on the rest of the big lake, but with this being private property, riders seldom ventured this close to the shore. Max picked up her binoculars to check out the skiers, and when she saw the black wet suits and the hoods, she said to Adam, "Inside, please, Adam. I don't like the looks of them." She brought the glasses down. "Please, quickly."

He looked grim as she picked up the weapon.

"Now, Adam," she growled, then trained her attention on the approaching jet skis. The dogs came over and stood by her side, their faces turned to the beach.

Adam's jaw tightened and he reluctantly disappeared inside.

What with all the plants surrounding the patio railing, Max was sure the riders couldn't see her weapon, so she waited. Once they reached the beach, one man got off, but the other stayed in the water and held on to the empty ski.

Max stood so she could be seen, then called down, "You're on private property."

The man stopped and looked up. "I wish to speak with Dr. Gary." The accent was not one she could pinpoint with any accuracy.

"There's no Dr. Gary here. Try down the beach."

The first bullet hit the glass door behind her, shattering it and making her scramble. Another shot rang out, followed by two more, but by then, angry, she was firing back. She sprayed the hill, churning up sand and vegetation and forcing him to run for his life. Their automatic rifles were no match for the power in her well-trained hands and she let them know it. Running toward the stairs, Max tried her best to blow the skis out of the water, but the terrified men were already aboard and hauling ass back to a big boat sitting ominously on the horizon. Snatching her phone free, she held it up and took as many pics of the boat and the skis as she could. The big boat was a ways out, but she hoped a zoom

during the printing process would show some details
Myk and Portia could use it to track it down. By now the
jet skis were too far away for her weapon to reach, so she
headed back up the steps. On the patio stood Adam and
the dogs. He looked grave, the dogs alert.

When she reached the top, she met his eyes and said,
"Guess the party's on."

Max put in a call to Chandler and to the Bureau
agent in Grand Rapids. Both promised to get in touch
with their Fed contacts and call her back as soon as
possible to let her know how to proceed. She also put
in a call to the Coast Guard. She was pleased to hear
that the Bureau had already contacted them and that a
cutter was on its way, but she wasn't planning on
waiting around for them to show up. She knew the
perps would be back, and if they had any sense, they'd
come with more peeps and more firepower. It was
time to leave.

Because she had been preparing for this all day, it
didn't take long for them to get ready. She took a moment to activate the collars on the dogs. The signal
would engage the satellite and alert Portia that they
were on the move. On a quick last run through the
house to lock it down and make certain nothing important had been left behind, Max saw a line of jet skis
making their way back toward the house. She cursed
and took off toward the front door. Adam and the dogs
were already in the Honda. She scrambled under the
wheel and started the engine. "The jet skis are coming
and they brought friends."

Her adrenaline running, Max hit the accelerator and
headed down the drive. Looking into the rearview mirror at the dogs, she said, "I'm sorry Ossie."

Seeing Adam's confused face, she explained, "He gets car sick. I may have to knock him out before this is over."

As the car sped toward the gate, Max tensed at the sight of an SUV and two armed men waiting there. She cursed inwardly but didn't slow. She had no idea who they were or why they were there, but she didn't think they were friends. She yelled to her passengers, "Get down and hold on!"

She stomped on the accelerator and the Honda roared toward the gate. The men's eyes widened and they scrambled out of the way. She crashed through the gate to the sound of weapons fire. Max could hear the pings and thuds of bullets hitting the body of the car as she broke free but she didn't slow. The bumpy unpaved road tossed them around like a ride at the state fair, and she could hear Ossie's whimpers of distress but she kept driving.

Adam had never experienced anything like this. A quick look in the busted mirror on his side showed the SUV barreling after them. "They're coming!" he called out.

"I see them. Hold on!"

She took the curve on what had to be two wheels, and Adam felt his seat belt snap him back against the seat. He was glad to have it on. The Honda was far enough ahead that the guns being fired at it were having trouble finding the mark, but the SUV was gaining.

Max told Adam, "Grab my phone off my belt. Hit the red button on the face, then the green one."

Adam fumbled for her clip. He freed it, and when he opened it saw that the phone's face was unlike any he'd ever seen before. The wheels of the Honda hit a particularly large crater and the force almost made him drop the phone. Once he recovered, he quickly punched the buttons. A second later a female voice came over the phone's speaker. "What's up, sis?"

Max hollered back, "Portia! I'm rolling and I'm hot!"

A bullet shattered the back window and covered the backseat and the dogs with shards of glass. Max cursed.

Portia asked, "Is that gunfire?"

"Yes, ma'am!"

Max steered around a crater the size of the Grand Canyon and kept her attention on the road ahead. They were coming up to the county road that led back to the highway, and she had no clue what she'd find at the junction.

Portia said, "Okay, Max, I have you and the babies on screen. I have your perps, too. Is Dr. Gary with you?"

"Yeah. He's holding the phone."

"Okay, we'll do intros later. Where are you heading?"

"Big Bad Wolf. I may need to hide in the sunflowers, though."

"No problem."

"Thanks, babe!"

"In case your phone is being monitored, use the new software you downloaded to keep me posted. It's safer."

"Will do. I'll check in once I get to the Wolf's den."

"Okay. I'm still trying to ID your caller. Good luck!"

"'Bye," Max said. "Thanks, Adam."

Adam was so dazed by all that was happening he

didn't know what to think. The people behind them were actually shooting. He felt like he was in a movie, but this was real.

Max came up to the junction and her eyes widened at the sight of all the trailers, cars, and cameras parked on both sides of the road. The media. She'd forgotten about them. She hoped they had their cameras rolling because things were about to get wild.

With the SUV hot on her tail, Max blew through the junction, took the curve at an incredible speed and charged onto the county road. She could see the surprise on the faces as she flew by. In the rearview mirror she watched them running like ants for their cameras while others ran for their cars. When the SUV thundered by them a second or two later, all hell broke loose as many of them scrambled out of the way. Max was grim. Knowing the media, she was certain some of the reporters were going to try and join the chase, and that was the last thing she needed.

Adam jumped when Max's phone rang. "Should I answer?"

"Yes!"

Max was rolling at a good ninety miles an hour down a road with a posted speed of fifty-five. In a few minutes she'd be coming up on a residential area. Small towns didn't usually have high-speed chases so she hoped no one would be hurt. From the speaker phone she heard, "Max, this is Gadget!"

If Max hadn't been so busy dodging minivans and sedate, sedan-driving townies, she would have smiled hearing the voice of her good friend. "Where are you?"

"With Hannibal."

"Why the hell hasn't DOD contacted us?"

"Got a couple rogue Pentagon elephants in the mix. Hannibal wants you to bring the doc to him."

"I've got armed bogeys on my ass, and the media! How am I supposed to swing that?"

"The media?"

"Yeah!"

"You're Cleopatra Jones, I have faith in you. The Wolf has a new whip ready to go. Once you grab it, meet me where the sunflowers grow and I'll take it from there."

Wheels screaming, Max passed a pokey motor scooter.

"I'll see if we can't get those cockroaches on your tail some Raid. Stay safe."

"Will do!"

And he was gone.

Adam stared. "Who was that?"

"Myk Chandler's brother." Max passed a school bus and swerved to miss hitting an elderly driver making a slow exit out of McDonald's. "I'll explain later!"

She cast an eye to the back and the dogs. Ruby was staring out of the shattered hatch window and barking angrily at the SUV, but Ossie was lying down. Max had some meds on board that would let him sleep through the long road trip they were facing, but she didn't know when she'd be able to stop so she could administer it. Grim because she knew how uncomfortable he must be, she had to put him out of her mind for now and try and make it to Detroit in one piece.

Suddenly, Max saw two brown cruisers from the county sheriff roar up behind the SUV and turn on their lights. She yelled a triumphant, "Yes!"

At first she didn't think the SUV was going to stop,

but the driver must have come to his senses because as she pulled away the perps fell farther and farther back. Her last view was of the deputies with their guns drawn, approaching the vehicle. However, the media was still coming. She could see a white van struggling to catch her, but because she knew they weren't going to be shooting at her no matter the outcome, she slowed a bit, blew out a breath, and concentrated on finding a posted sign that would lead them to the highway.

Jan Kruger was grim. Gary had gotten away! According to the two men he'd sent in to scout, the house-keeper or whoever the woman was claiming to be had fired on them with a weapon powerful enough to make them run for their lives. So much for the laughable security. He cursed Kent again and tried to figure out what to do next. After the disastrous assault attempt, they'd abandoned the big boat and were now on a smaller one speeding away from the scene as fast as the engine would go. He assumed the Coast Guard would be showing up soon to investigate, and he wanted to put as much distance as possible between him and the now empty big boat. He glanced over at Oskar. The man was sweating and looked a bit green. Apparently, water travel didn't suit him, but that was the least of Jan's worries.

Once they docked, Jan, Oskar, and the two merce-naries with them jumped out and the operator of the boat roared away. There was supposed to be a car wait-ing for them. Just as Kruger grabbed up his phone to find out where it was, a Hummer and a pickup truck drove up. Jan ignored them for a moment. "Where's Gary now?" he demanded of Oskar.

The short squat Oskar took out his laptop and punched in a few numbers. He studied the screen. "He still has his cell phone on. They're heading east."

"Good."

The driver of the Hummer—a member of a South African family now living in Grand Rapids—handed Jan the keys then got into the pickup and was driven away. Jan and the others piled into the Hummer and followed the narrow country roads to the highway.

Fourteen

Merging onto the interstate, Max took the Honda's speed up to seventy-five, then hit the cruise. Pulling her foot off of the accelerator, she relaxed and steered. Now that they'd seemingly shaken all of their tails, Ossie was her chief concern. She looked up at the mirror. "Ossie?"

Ruby put her head up instead and barked a couple of times as if to relay Ossie's poor state.

"I know, baby," Max responded sympathetically. "I'm going to stop first chance I get." She watched Ruby resume her position close to her brother's side and her heart swelled. Max looked Adam's way. "How you holding up?"

"I'm blown away, but I'm fine. Never been shot at before."

Max nodded her understanding. "Nothing like a bunch of bullets to get your attention."

"Got that right." He then asked, "What was all that talk about Big Bad Wolves and elephants and Hannibal? I'm guessing they're code names?"

"Yes. Big Bad Wolf is Mykal Chandler."

Adam smiled. "Okay."

"I guess his wife gave him the name."

"Gadget?"

"A friend named Saint, and like I said earlier, he's Chandler's brother. Half brother, if you want to get technical. Only man I know who can enter and exit a locked room. He has almost as many toys as Portia."

"Hannibal?"

"The President."

Adam stared. "Of the United States?"

"Yeah."

"I'm going to see the President?"

"Apparently."

A stunned Adam sat back against the seat. "Why?"

"For your safety, I assume. Things must be real ugly if he's taking you in."

Adam thought about that. "This is serious, isn't it?"

"As a heart attack," she replied gravely. "And it's all connected to your prototype. Any idea why?"

"No. The thing heats homes, that's all."

"Saint mentioned rogue elephants in the Pentagon. I wonder how that ties in?"

Adam shrugged.

"Maybe Chandler will know more."

Adam hoped so, because right now he was having trouble telling up from down. While she drove, he tried to make sense of his new, upside down world. *The President!* He had always wanted to meet the nation's first African American chief of state. The former five-star general and ambassador to the United Nations had taken the oath of office three years ago and was leading the nation in an unprecedented renaissance of technology, education, and public works. Had Adam been told a few months back that he'd be meeting the President courtesy of a woman with a big gun and two dogs with GPS capabilities, he'd have asked if the person had been doing crack, yet here he was, on his way to the White House—to be protected, no less, from what or whom he didn't know.

He looked over at Max. Her face was serious and her jaw set tight. After watching her sweep the beach with her Terminator and experiencing the way she drove to escape that SUV, he made a promise to himself never to cross her. Girlfriend did not play. However, being male, Adam wasn't sure how he felt about having to hide behind her skirts, so to speak. He had no problem with a law enforcement officer being female if he needed rescuing from a mugging or something else requiring that type of assistance, but this situation with her being the alpha individual was different.

Or was it? He had been raised by a strong female who also didn't play, and because of her he'd always prided himself on being all for gender equality. But this? Being told to go hide inside while she whipped on the bad guys wasn't doing it for him, on any level. Would he feel differently if the command had come from a man? Probably. So his problem, he had to admit, was him. Was he man enough to step back and let the lady do her job? That was the question. He wasn't sure, but he hoped that his indecision didn't get him killed.

It was seven in the evening when they pulled into a gas station outside of Grand Rapids. Max, dressed in a dark brown shirt, shorts, brown hikers, and socks, looked like a park ranger instead of who she really was—a woman packing weapons of mass destruction in the well of her Honda. She swiped her credit card through the slot and pumped the gas while discreetly keeping an eye out for trouble. The station had eight pumps. Five were occupied. There was a teenage boy in a turned around baseball cap. Across from him stood a young mother fueling a green minivan holding the requisite 2.2 kids. Beside and behind Max were three seniors, one of whom was a woman. The shot-up Honda with a cracked window was drawing attention, so Max turned her back on the curious eyes and mentally willed the pump to hurry up. Adam had gone inside the convenience store to buy water and snacks. As he came back out with his purchases, she was pleased to see that he hadn't been inside messing around. The sooner they got back on the road, the sooner they'd get to Detroit.

With the car fueled up, she grabbed the receipt from the pump, climbed back in under the wheel and said to Adam, "I wanted to give Ossie his med, but time to go. Too many eyes on us right now."

The station was a lot busier than it had been when they first pulled up, and all of the people going in and out of the store were slowing down to take a look at the car. Max couldn't blame them. The Honda's right front was heavily damaged. The busted headlight and crumpled hood were the result of the collision with the fence. There were bullet holes in the doors and on the tailgate. The shards of glass all over the backseat were going to be a hazard to the dogs when it got dark because they wouldn't be able to see them, so she would to have to stop somewhere and clean it up before then. As she steered the Honda away from the gas station and back toward the highway, she kept her eyes on the mirrors to make sure they weren't being followed and hoped they could find a rest stop nearby so she could see to her dogs.

She found a spot thirty miles down the road. It took her all of ten minutes to do what she had to do, then she and her crew were rolling again.

They were now heading east, and the sun was setting behind them in all its blazing glory. The drive to Detroit would take nearly three hours, but Ossie was asleep, the Honda's gas tank was full, and so far no one was on their tail. Max hoped for an uneventful ride.

It was not to be. As they passed through Grand Ledge, a suburb west of Lansing, the state capital, a Hummer sporting camouflage paint suddenly appeared in Max's rear mirror. The hulking vehicle was a little ways back, but it looked to be rolling, so Max moved into the right lane to let it pass. When it came up beside her, she glanced over. Leaning out of the passenger window was a soldier with a gun. She stomped on the brake. Her quick reaction saved them because the Honda slowed just enough for the Hummer to pass it and mess up the gun man's aim. The big gun gave off a boom that probably killed a tree or two along the roadside, but Max and her crew were in one piece.

Alarmed, she left the road and tore down the shoulder to pass the slow-moving traffic in front of her. The ride was bumpy and she prayed they didn't run over something that would slash the tires, or hit a concrete bridge abutment. When she saw an opening in the traffic ahead, she powered back onto the pavement, floored the accelerator and took the Honda up to a smooth sailing ninety. The Hummer was trying to keep up, but it was boxy, slow, and big, no match for her smaller, nimbler vehicle.

She turned to check out Adam. He looked stunned. "You okay?" she asked him. She kept an eye on her mirror to make sure the Hummer wasn't gaining.

"I don't know," he confessed. "Was that the Army?"

Max was stunned, too. "It sure looked like it."

Adam turned around to gauge the Hummer's progress and saw that it was falling farther behind. "They could have killed us!"

"I think that was their intent."

"What in the hell is going on?"

"Wish I knew," Max said. "Why would the U.S. Army try and take us out?"

"Didn't your friend say something about the Pentagon?"

"Yeah. Rogue elephants. I wonder if somebody's gone off the farm?"

She looked over at Adam, who replied, "You mean like somebody operating outside the lines?"

"Yeah. It wouldn't be the first time."

"Really?"

Max knew that the stories of generals running amok were highly classified, which was why few people were aware of the four-star busted two years ago for providing weapons to a militia group in Washington State, or of another quietly tried and jailed six months ago for heading up an international trafficking ring that specialized in young Russian boys. Why would someone in the Army be after Adam's prototype, though? The device had to hold some kind of serious value for all this drama to be happening. She wished she knew the answer because the question was nagging at her like a bad tooth.

Night had fallen as they sped from Lansing to Detroit. Neither she nor Adam had spoken in a while. Both were deep in thought, searching for clues to the riddle threatening their lives.

Max was glad it was dark. Checking her mirrors like clockwork for bogeys, she hoped the night would hide them until they reached Myk's place.

She picked up the next bogey just outside of the city limits. She was heading south on the Lodge Expressway, glad to be only a few minutes from their destination, when a sleek silver sedan rolled up on her in the sparse evening traffic and tried to ram her from behind. Fighting to right the wheel, she managed to gain control, only to be bumped again with so much force the Honda was sent spinning like a break dancer on his head, across the two empty left lanes and directly toward the concrete highway divider. Cursing, Max turned the wheel in the direction of the spin, hoping they wouldn't hit the divider head on. At the last second the steering caught and the tail end hit the wall instead. The impact slammed them. Pieces of plastic, shattered headlight housing, and sections of the bumper flew into the air, but she was already maneuvering the battered Honda back on the road.

The other car gave chase. No lumbering Hummer this time. The opposition was in something fast—faster than the Honda—but Max planned to give them a run for their money. In truth, what she really wanted to do was stop the car, grab her gun out of the back, and blow them to hell, but she doubted they'd be polite enough to wait for her to do that, so driving was all she had. Luckily, she was good at it.

She stomped the Honda up to ninety-five and dared them to keep up. Under the overhead lights illuminating the road, she did the next few miles weaving in and out of the traffic so fast the other cars she passed might as well have been standing still. On the long empty stretches she was rolling at a hundred, then 110. She flashed past a sign indicating construction up ahead, but pressed on with the sedan glued to her tail. She paid no attention to the next construction sign, which reminded her she was only a half mile from the construction and hoped the sedan would too. Max roared around a Greyhound bus poking along in front of her. Swinging the Honda back into the left lane, she saw the sedan appear from behind the bus then zoom up behind her. Her mirror showed the bus merging to the right in anticipation of the upcoming construction zone, then she focused her attention on driving. Less than thirty feet ahead stood huge concrete blocks cutting off the lane. Because of the Honda's high profile, she was pretty sure the sedan couldn't see around it and at the speed they were traveling, she was also sure they were counting on her to alert them to hazards. Wrong. As she neared the construction barrier it seemed to grow larger and larger. Max waited until the last possible moment to swing over, and as she zipped out, the sedan slammed into the concrete and went up in flames.

"Yeah!" Adam yelled, pumping a triumphant fist.

Max looked over at him and grinned. Ruby was barking in the backseat.

Adam said sagely, "I think I may need a new pair of drawers, but that was some hellified driving." He looked back and saw the fire. It sobered him for a moment. "That could have been us."

Max disagreed. "Not with me driving."

Adam chuckled and sat back to enjoy the rest of the ride.

A short while later they were exiting the highway

because the Honda was done. Having taken bullets, fences, rammings, and bounces off highway dividers it barely rolled. Max managed to coax it up the ramp and onto the street, but she sensed once she cut the ignition it wouldn't start again.

Adam looked around at the stark, dark surroundings and didn't have to be told that this was not one of the city's better areas. "Where are we?"

"West side."

Max considered her options. She could call Mykal, but Portia had warned her not to use her phone, and for good reason. Cells were notoriously insecure, and calling him might send the unwanted guests to his door. She thought about using the software on the laptop but dropped that idea, too. Nighttime brought out all kinds of predators and carnivores, and she didn't want to wind up shooting some dummy bent on jacking her computer while she was sitting in the car using it. She peered around. For now they were on their own, and not knowing if the friends of the men in the Hummer or sedan were close by, waiting for another opportunity to pounce, she thought it best to find a hidey hole ASAP.

Jan and the others had been tracking the silver car and the Honda on Oskar's computer. The camera mounted on the car's dashboard had been able to give a real time view of the chase. The woman's amazingly adept driving left Jan looking forward to meeting her face-to-face. She impressed him as being a remarkable individual and he wanted to know all about her. He'd silently cheered as the Honda was rammed and sent spinning across the road, but minutes later when a brilliant flash of light filled the screen just before it went dark, he demanded, "What's happened?"

Oskar punched in codes and numbers. "Looks like the car crashed."

"What!"

"I'm getting nothing from the sensors inside. Can't tell if the drivers got out in time but it doesn't appear as if they did."

Sevi Crane, one of the young mercenaries, asked, "Are they dead?"

"Possibly."

Jan cursed. He didn't know the men in the car well enough to mourn, but he did mourn the fact that Gary continued to slip through his fingers. Detroit was a Black enclave he would normally have avoided given a choice, due to the crime and the races of the people who lived there, but necessity dictated he go in after the prey. The Hummer they were in was less than thirty minutes away. He and his men were now wearing the uniforms of the United States Army. Jan planned to use the ruse to do whatever it took to get Gary. A few well-placed calls from his Washington contacts would keep the local law enforcement agencies from interfering, and that was all the help he would need.

"Find the Honda's last known location. With all the damage to it, it couldn't have gotten far. We'll begin our search there when we arrive."

Ossie was stirring in the backseat, which meant the med was wearing off. Good, Max thought. She didn't want to have to carry him. She looked over at Adam. He'd been a trooper so far. Not once had he told her how to drive or second-guessed any of the choices she'd made since leaving his place. She appreciated it, too. First chance she got, she planned to give him his just reward; not that she knew when that would be, because they were a little busy at the moment, but it would be ripe and ready when the time came. "I'm going to give Ossie a few more minutes to come off the drugs then we'll head out."

A skeptical Adam looked around. "Where?"

"Friend's place. About six blocks. We'll hole up there until morning."

After all they'd been through, if she had told him they were waiting for the biblical pillar of cloud to lead them to safety, he would have been okay with it. Max Blake knew her job. She was fierce, beautiful, and deadly, and he was glad she was on his side.

Max and Adam spent the next few minutes preparing to abandon the Honda. She figured by morning the vehicle would either be stolen or stripped within an inch of its life. Either way, she hoped that anyone looking for Adam would lose the trail.

When they were ready, they got out with the dogs and started walking up the street. He had the prototype and his clothes stashed in the big duffel that had been resting on the backseat. Max was shouldering another duffel that held her laptop, a few personal necessities, and her toys.

It was a warm night. There was minimal traffic going up and down the small street and even less people. The area looked to be a forgotten place. The stores that had once been a viable and necessary part of the community were boarded up, and stood like aging hulks in the darkness. On the corner coming up was a mom-and-pop liquor store. Its lights flashed like a multicolored beacon.

A small group of men were hanging in front of the place, laughing and signifying, but when Max, Adam, and the dogs walked out of the darkness and into the store's garish light, not a sound could be heard. The men seemed to sense the aura of danger surrounding Max as she passed by; Adam certainly did. No one moved or said a word.

A few blocks up, Max led Adam and the dogs around to the back of an old brick building that looked as abandoned as its neighbors. He could see boards over the windows and a few derelict cars languishing in what had once served as the parking lot. She walked up to a metal door and beat on it with the edge of her closed fist. When no one answered, she pounded again. A few seconds later a small panel in the upper portion of the door slid open and a pair of eyes filled the space. "Yeah?"

The voice came through a speaker but the dark made it impossible for Adam to determine its location.

Max said, "Tell Sweetness that Jinga's here."

The eyes studied Max and then Adam and the dogs. The panel closed just as noiselessly as it had opened. He looked over at Max but she was too busy scanning their surroundings to notice. A few minutes later the door was opened and they all went inside.

It took Adam's eyes a moment to adjust to the dim light. They were standing in what looked to be a bank lobby. He could see the teller stations and the counters along the walls, but everything, including the floors, was covered in dust, making the place look as abandoned on the inside as it appeared to be on the outside. The man who'd let them in, a buffed-up brother wearing a black suit and black turtleneck, was also armed. "This way," he said.

Adam looked over at Max. She winked, but he could see the weariness in her eyes.

Their host ushered them onto an elevator whose walls were encased in the quilted padding usually reserved for freight elevators. The ride up took only a few minutes. According to the display panel, they were on the sixth floor when the doors opened again. They stepped out into a hallway of another world. The soft blue paint and the framed art lining the walls could have been the intro to any fancy penthouse apartment in New York or L.A. As they followed their guide, rooms to the right and left offered fleeting glimpses of expensive modern furniture, lavish drapes, and gleaming curio cabinets holding crystal.

Where are we? an amazed Adam wanted to know. Who'd created this slice of heaven in the middle of the struggling streets outside, and why?

The answer came in the form of a huge, bald, light-skinned man dressed in a gray silk turtleneck and dark pants. He stepped out of a room at the end of the hall and, at the sight of Max, spread open his long muscular arms like wings and said in a voice filled with knowing and affection, "Jinga."

Adam watched Max step up to the hug and return it with equal affection. "How are you, Sweetness?"

"Always glad to entertain a queen. How have you been?"

The man smiled down at Ruby and Ossie. "Hey, you two. You been keeping your mama out of trouble?" He scratched their necks.

Only then did the man train his golden assessing eyes on Adam. "And this is?"

Adam said, "Adam Gary."

Sweetness paused, studied Adam for a moment, then asked, "*Dr.* Adam Gary?"

Adam was surprised by the recognition. "Yes."

"I read about you in *Time* magazine. Welcome to my home."

"Thanks for taking us in."

"The only time I see this lady lately is when she needs something," he said, but again the affection in his voice was easy to hear. "Come on in. You all hungry?"

"Starving." Max admitted.

"Good. The chef is here until midnight."

Adam had a hundred questions he wanted answered but decided to wait until he knew more about what was going on.

For dinner, they were given a choice of prime rib or orange glazed Cornish hens. Max chose the hens. Adam went with the beef. The main course, framed by savory veggies and still warm yeast rolls, was served in a dining room straight out of a decorator's magazine. The long table with its wine-red runner could easily sit twelve, so they congregated on one end while the dogs settled in on the far side of the room. Sweetness had sent one of his employees out to get food for Ruby and Ossie and they were patiently awaiting his return.

In the meantime, the three humans started in on their meals.

The food was fabulous, and Adam didn't realize just how hungry he was until he dug in. "Tell your chef thanks," a grateful Adam said to Sweetness.

Sweetness nodded. "I will."

Adam could see the man watching him discreetly, but he ignored the scrutiny for now in favor of satisfying his empty stomach. He couldn't ignore how tired Max appeared, however. Watching her raise the wine goblet to her lips, he noticed that her motions had slowed. She was still alert, but visibly less animated. Which was only to be expected when one spent the day kicking butt. *What a woman!* Shaking his head with amused awe, he went back to his plate.

After the meal, Sweetness said to Max, "So, tell me what's going on."

"You know I can't tell you everything."

"Understood."

"Here's the basics . . ." Max told him as much as she thought he needed to grasp the situation. She left out the part about her connection to Mykal Chandler and his shadowy organization, NIA. Mykal and his half brother, Drake Randolph, Detroit's mayor, formed the syndicate a few years back to battle crime by any means necessary. Sweetness didn't need to be in Myk's business, just like Myk didn't need to be in his.

Sweetness listened to the part about the Hummer. "The Army?" he asked, sounding concerned.

"The man was dressed in Army fatigues, Sweet."

"That's deep."

"No kidding."

Sweetness turned his hawk gold eyes on Adam, who met the gaze easily. He could see the man sizing him up.

Sweet finally asked, "What do you think all this is about, Dr. Gary?"

It was the sixty-four-thousand-dollar question, but

Adam had been mulling it over all day, and thought he had come up with the only answer that made sense. "Weapons. Somebody somewhere thinks my prototype can be turned into a weapon."

Sweetness, sitting in a high-back chair that could have come from Windsor Castle, held up his wine goblet, smiled and said, "Bingo!"

Fifteen

Max stared. It made perfect sense. "Can it be modified for that?"

"Theoretically anything that generates energy has the potential," came Adam's reply. And the more he thought about it, the more he was convinced he was on the right track. It angered him. He hadn't spent the last ten years trying to perfect a device designed to bring hope just so it could be jacked and morphed into something dark and deadly. He'd destroy it first.

Max asked Sweetness, "Where'd you place my bags?"

"In your room. Do you need them?"

"Just the laptop."

Adam had no idea how the signal was passed, but a few minutes later one of Sweetness's employees, a short burly man who looked like a miniature version of an African American sumo, set the laptop on the table in front of Max then exited silently.

Max lifted the top and booted up. Once the OS was ready, she keyed in the commands to access the software she'd downloaded from Portia. Nothing happened for a few seconds, and then to Max's surprise a wavering hologram of Portia appeared in the air above the laptop. "Wow!" she yelled.

Portia could be seen smiling as she asked, "How cool is this?"

Max looked at the men and they appeared just as stunned. "You have gone to the mountaintop on this one, girlfriend," Max crowed excitedly.

"Thanks. Something I've been playing with for a while. How are you?"

"Speechless."

Portia's image laughed. "Besides that?"

"In one piece, no thanks to the opposition, but we're with a friend."

"Glad to hear that. I've been worried."

Max then told Portia all that had happened since their last conversation. She also related Adam's theory.

Portia listened and at the end said, "Dr. Gary may be right. From the chatter I'm hearing, something is definitely whack at the Pentagon. I talked to Gadget a bit ago and he said Hannibal is sending in some undercover crews to fumigate the place, but a few of the rats got away. They may be too busy running to pay much attention to the prototype, but I wouldn't count on that." Then, as if thinking out loud, she added, "A weapon. Interesting."

Adam had a question. "Has there been anything else on the news about the prototype?"

"No, and that's been interesting, too. One minute you were all over the place, now, nothing. It's as if the story never existed."

Max was confused. "Nothing from the press?"

"Not a peep."

Max asked, "Do you think the government has put the info on lockdown or is this more magic from the Big Bad Wolf?"

"No idea. Oil prices climbed back to their usual numbers, though. It's as if the industry is no longer worried about the doc's baby impacting their profits."

"Maybe because they know something no one else does," Sweetness speculated. "Maybe they're confident the prototype won't reach the market."

Adam didn't like the sound of that.

Max didn't, either.

Portia said, "Best thing to do is get him to Hannibal. If he's taking Dr. Gary in, this situation is uglier than we know."

Max agreed. She searched her brain for any other issues needing Portia's attention. "Anything more on Robinski?"

"No. The Bureau slipped a beacon on him before they deported him, but it died a few minutes after he landed in Malaavia. They don't know if he found the bug or if it just malfunctioned. Either way, they lost track of him after that."

Max sighed. "Okay."

Portia asked, "Have you talked to the Wolf?"

"No. I don't want to compromise him or my friend. Would you let him know I'm in town, and that I'm safe? You have my coordinates. If he could send the new whip to me, that would be a better move. Just have him park it outside and I'll pick it up. We'll roll out soon as it arrives."

"Will do. I'll have him download this software so you won't have to use your phone. Definitely don't let the doc use his. In fact, ditch it. We know the perps already have his number and are probably monitoring it as we speak. You and the Wolf can talk once you reach the sunflowers."

Max nodded. "Okay, Portia. Thanks."

"No problem."

The hologram disappeared.

Sweetness said in awe, "Now, that was something. How much do you think she'd charge me to buy that software?"

Max responded, "Knowing Portia, more than all the gold in Switzerland." She was exhausted. The rigorous day had finally caught up with her, and she yawned behind her hand. "I need to go to bed."

Sweetness smiled, "Then come on."

It was past midnight. Their host led them through his home's vast spaces and to a red door beautifully carved in an African influenced motif. Inside the large room, the same air was reflected in the sumptuous linen drapes, the subtle animal prints, and the furniture made of teak. There were beaded floor pillows covered in reds and golds, and on the far side of the room, a kidney-shaped sunken tub with gold fixtures. Adam was impressed.

Sweetness said, "You should find everything you need, Jinga. If not, you know the routine."

Max nodded. The dogs found themselves a comfortable place and laid down.

Sweetness turned to Adam. "Dr. Gary, I've put you next door."

Adam hid his disappointment and said to Max, "Get some sleep and I'll see you in the morning."

She smiled sleepily. " 'Bye, Doc." Then turning her back, she stripped herself of the brown shirt and walked to the tub.

Adam's space next door was decorated along more masculine lines. The dark wood furniture, the shutters covering one whole wall, and the large ceiling fan gave off an island vibe. There was a sunken tub in this room, too, and he looked forward to a long chill.

Sweetness told him, "There's wine in the small fridge. Toiletries in that cabinet. If you need anything else, just pick up the phone and dial two."

Adam nodded. "Thanks." As the big man turned to leave, he said, "Can I ask you a question?"

"Sure."

"Why do you call her Jinga?"

"Do you know who Jinga was?" Sweetness asked.

Adam didn't.

"Angolan queen. Fought the Portuguese. Gave them fits."

Adam smiled. He understood now. "Thanks."

Sweetness nodded and left.

Alone, a relieved and weary Adam dropped into the nearest chair and held his head in his hands. Never in a million years would he have believed his life would turn into this. He was just a scientist trying to help the world, and now he was . . . he had no idea where he was, but he was safe and no one was shooting at him or trying to run them off the road. He walked over and turned on the water in the tub. While it ran, he undressed and turned on the CD player in the large entertainment unit. Soft jazz filled the room and he began to relax for what seemed like the first time that day. He looked at the wall separating his room from hers and wondered how she was doing. He hoped she was relaxing and not on her laptop working, but then again, her working on the lap-top was helping to keep him out of harm's way, so he couldn't be too mad at her if she was. Setting thoughts of Max aside, he went to check on the tub.

Later, he was lying in the bed, listening to the jazz by the light of a candle he'd lit, when he heard Max's voice come out of the shadows. "Doc? Are you sleep?"

Surprised, he sat up and looked around. "Where are you?"

"Over here."

And there she was, crossing the room by the faint illumination of the candle. She was wearing a T-shirt that hit her about mid-thigh. Her legs and feet were bare. As she crawled beneath the crisp cool sheet, he asked, "How'd you get in here?"

She snuggled back against him, and he placed an arm around her and kissed the top of her head. He could smell the fresh clean scent of her body. She felt good against him.

In a tired-sounding voice she answered, "The shutters are really a door."

Adam assumed she was referring to the wall-high shutters he'd assumed to be simply shutters. He'd have to check it out in the morning. In the meantime he was glad to have her near and pleased that she'd sought him out. "Tell me about Sweetness. Who is he? What's he do?"

But girlfriend was sleep. Gone. Adam chuckled softly. Guess his questions would have to wait. Content, he settled in and was soon asleep, too.

The next morning, it took Max a few moments to remember where she was. Once she did, she turned gently onto her stomach and watched him sleep. In the brief time they'd known each other, they'd gone from growling adversaries to lovers. She'd never had a man like him in her life before. In her world, the men lived on the edge, dangerous deadly men who didn't mind straddling the thin line between what was legal and what was not as long as the price was right. This gentle, sexy man of science was rooted in other things. She didn't think he had a dishonest bone in his body. He had no weapons experience and wouldn't know the first thing about covert operations, but she would remember him fondly once she delivered him to the President and they each went their separate ways.

The thought of moving on was disturbing, and because she wasn't the kind to do ties, she wondered why. She thought maybe it grew out of wanting to know more about him. In reality, she knew very little. Could he dance, sing? Was he AME? Who'd he hang out with in high school? Who was his first love? The answers hidden inside that extra large brain of his weren't destined for her, though. They would belong to some unknown woman in his future; a woman he'd wake up next to each morning, and who probably didn't roll with trained dogs and a grenade launcher. Thinking about that mythical woman didn't sit well, either, but because she didn't want to delve too deeply into her feelings, she left the bed as quietly as she could to begin the day.

Dressed and ready to rock and roll, Max and the dogs found Sweetness having his coffee in the dining room. He was reading the morning paper and eating from a large stack of pancakes.

At her entrance, he looked up and saluted her with his filled cup of coffee. "Morning, Jinga."

"Hey, Sweet. My whip arrive?"

"Yep. It's stashed in the garage downstairs."

He directed her to the coffee and to the various morning delights chilling under covers on the steam table. She put some bacon, toast, and fruit on her plate then sat down to join him.

He asked, "How'd you sleep?"

She thought about cuddling with Adam and smiled gently. "Okay." She took a sip of the coffee and let it flow into her still sleepy veins. "Thanks for the shelter."

"For you, the world."

She grinned and started in on her meal. She'd first met Sweet while working Homicide. Back then, he'd been consolidating his power, and the bodies of his rivals were showing up in Dumpsters and alleys all over town. A few had even been fished out of the river, but no charges ever came down because there'd been no solid evidence linking the deaths to anyone, least of all Sweetness. Tall, light-skinned, and movie star fine, he was the city's Mr. Big. Mayor Drake Randolph might rule above, but Eric Cole, aka Sweetness, ruled Detroit's underworld.

"Jinga, I can send some of my crew to ride with you, if you think that might help."

"Thanks, but if the government's involved, you should probably stay clear." She studied him for a few moments, then asked quietly, "When are you going to give up this life?"

He smiled softly. "Ah, my conscience."

"I'm serious, Sweet. I'd hate to read about your corpse being found in an alley somewhere, or worse, you get indicted. Even at your age you are still too pretty to do time."

Again that smile. "Hey, thirty-seven is not that old." Then he turned serious. "Truthfully, I have been thinking about it. Wondering what it would be like to just be plain ol' Eric. You know?"

She did. Sometimes she just wanted to be plain ol' Maxine Blake from small-town Texas. "I'll help any way I can."

"I know. Just not sure if I can walk away. The power, the money, the Life—it's in my blood." He shrugged. "We'll see."

Max knew this was his way of ending the conversation, and she respected that. The idea that he was even thinking about change made her hopeful, though. Had Sweetness lived in the fifteenth or sixteenth century, he would have been a prince, a doge. He was the consummate renaissance man—cultured, Harvard educated, and had traveled the world—but underneath all that refinement beat the heart of a gangsta. He considered himself a gentleman gangster, though, a throwback modeled on the suave and sophisticated Black kingpins who ruled Harlem in the thirties. Like them, he didn't deal drugs, but in spite of his other illegal dealings, he did his part for the community by donating to citywide charities and using his ties to trucking to provide fresh produce to many of the smaller food banks not funded by the large corporations. But in Max's mind, the good deeds didn't make him any less responsible for the crimes committed in his name. Which is why she wanted him to leave the Life. With his education, big heart, and smarts, she knew he could be so much more.

When Adam entered the dining room, he found Max and Sweetness bent over a map. She looked up and gave him a smile. "Mornin', Doc."

Sweetness nodded. "Good morning, Dr. Gary. I hope you slept well."

"I did. Thanks."

Sweetness directed him to the breakfast buffet. Adam fixed himself a plate then sat. Max said to him, "I'm trying to decide what route to take."

"Where are we going?"

"Central Ohio."

"Shortest distance between two points is always a straight line," he quoted around a bite of toast.

Max smiled and said, "Thank you, professor."

"Any time." The amused Adam felt no need to join the huddle around the map. He knew she didn't need his help, and he was okay with it.

A voice filled the air in the room. "Boss, we got problems."

Sweetness raised his head. "What kind?"

"The fucking Army."

Sweetness stared at Max. Adam froze.

Sweetness asked, "Where are they?"

"Half a block down. They're going door-to-door. Got a bunch of dogs with them."

"Okay. You know what to do."

Sweetness's eyes were hard. "Time for you to go, Jinga. We'll hold off the Portuguese for as long as we can."

She quickly motioned the dogs to her side, then leaned up and gave Sweetness a kiss on his golden cheek. "See you next time, Eric."

He smiled and nodded. "'Bye, Jinga." He added, "Nice meeting you, Doc. Hope you get the Nobel."

Adam grinned. "Thanks."

Adam and Max quickly ran back to the bedrooms for

their gear, then the four of them flew down a series of hallways to a door. It led to a ramp of sorts that funneled them down a flight of stairs, but because it was an incline, they could run faster. Max bolted through another door and they were underground. A few feet away sat a black Escalade with its engine running. They pulled open the doors and poured in.

Max strapped the dogs in, gave Ossie his pill, and stashed the duffels. She jumped in under the wheel and quickly adjusted the mirrors and seat. Snapping her seat belt into place, she put the car in gear and drive off. The dashboard was an unfamiliar one, but she didn't have time to check out the owner's manual, so it was going to have to be trial and error until she figured things out.

Max was glad Sweetness had had the vision to construct the tunnel. He'd given her a tour the last time she visited, so she knew it came out in a vacant lot about six blocks away. It was used almost exclusively at night, but now it was a little before nine in the morning. Someone was bound to see the SUV emerging from underground like an exotic beetle, but she couldn't worry about that now; she'd leave that for Sweetness.

Sure enough, a bunch of school kids were coming up the street when the Escalade entered the sunlight. The kids stared with surprise, but by then Max was on level ground and rolling in the opposite direction.

She didn't get far. At the next corner the traffic was jammed up because there were soldiers searching the cars ahead. Max threw it in reverse, turned around, and headed back the way she'd come.

She looked over at Adam, who was checking his mirror to see if they were being followed. Nothing so far.

"Our advantage is that I worked this side of town for ten years," she told him. "I know a thousand and one ways to the expressway."

"Then lead on, my sister."

She grinned and did just that.

Taking side streets, alleys, and a dizzying amount of turns through residential neighborhoods, they merged onto the expressway fifteen minutes later. From there she picked up I-75 going south.

"How do you think they found us?"

Max shrugged. "Maybe the car that hit the barrier had a friend and they saw us pull off the highway. I don't know."

Adam thought that as feasible a guess as any. What mattered, though, was that Max was keeping them one step ahead.

She glanced up at the mirror. "How's Ossie doing?"

Adam turned around so he could see. The big dog's rib cage was rising and falling in an even rhythm. "Sleeping like a baby, look's like."

"Good." She called out, "How you doing, Rube?"

Ruby barked, and a satisfied Max drove on.

The heart of the morning's rush hour was over, so the traffic was light. The area between Detroit and the nearby Ohio border was dominated by oil refineries and other smoke-belching factories. She wanted to make as much time as she could now, in anticipation of being slowed down by all the tankers and semis she'd soon be sharing the highway with once they neared the state line.

Max was still fiddling with the Escalade's controls. She'd mastered the wipers, the lights, and the air-conditioning. That was good, but she needed to know what the truck was packing, if anything. "Look around and see if you spot a CD. Myk should have left some kind of instructions for this baby."

"Instructions? As in an owner's manual?"

Max steered around an old woman doing sixty in the fast lane, then swung over again. "Sort of. See if it's in the glove box."

Adam looked, and sure enough found a gold CD with a black ace of spades on the label amidst the maps and registration papers.

"Put it in, would you, please?"

Seconds later they both listened to Myk's voice as he explained the Escalade's virtues. It had GPS capabilities, was armor clad, and equipped with what he described as a rolling communications system. "It's built into the dash and works like a walkie-talkie. Each time the phone is engaged, it draws on a randomly selected cell tower somewhere in North America so that a call made in Michigan will register as having been made in say, Georgia, or Oklahoma, or Toronto. According to the techies, the signal is impossible to trace because an eavesdropper won't have a clue as to the call's point of origination."

Then he added, "Portia's not the only one with elves."

Max and Adam shared a grin.

He went on to explain the truck's dual fuel tanks and the self-patching abilities of the tires. "You can roll over barbed wire, nails, glass, even a few bullets. Large armaments will do them in, though."

Adam asked, "Large armaments?"

"Missiles," she said casually while she passed a truck.

Adam stared.

Myk continued. "Speaking of large armaments, you have two, but only two. Let's hope it won't come down to that, but if it does, use them wisely."

Once again Adam stared. "We're carrying missiles?"

"Baby ones, yeah."

While Myk went on to talk about hidden compartments, trucker radio bands, and the like, Adam was so outdone he didn't know what to feel, ask, or say in response. *Missiles!* This was proving to be a novel experience if nothing else, and it was getting way too deep for him. Way too deep.

"Also," Myk added, "none of the good stuff like the missiles or the phone can be engaged without a code—which is the month and date of your mama's birthday, so if the truck falls into the wrong hands, you won't have to worry."

"Good to know," Max said, looking over at Adam.

"Well, that's it," Myk said. "Be safe and good luck."

Adam knew that luck had been on their side so far. He just hoped it held up.

Jan had his men bang on the back door of the old warehouse. According to Oskar's computer, the signal coded to Gary's cell phone had ended someplace in this area. During their sweep of the surrounding neighborhood, two crackheads swore they'd seen a man and a woman with some dogs enter the building last night. Jan didn't know whether to believe them but had given them a couple of counterfeit five-dollar bills for their trouble.

"May I help you?"

Startled, Jan swung around and stared into a pair of golden eyes that looked like they'd been forged in hell.

The gaze seemed to burn through to his soul, and Jan felt cold fear tingle in his blood. The light-skinned Black man was tall, bald, and dressed in a tailored black suit worn with the elegance of royalty. Flanking him were six armed Black men dressed in black.

Jan grabbed hold of himself and remembered that he was Afrikaner and not born to be intimidated by a man of color. "I'm General Walt Pearl. And you are?"

"What do you want?"

The icy stare made Jan want to shoot the mulatto for his arrogance, but he and his men were outnumbered. "We're looking for a man and a woman. There are two dogs traveling with them, too, we believe."

"Haven't seen them."

"According to—"

"Haven't seen them," the man repeated distinctly. "And unless you have a warrant, I'm going upstairs and to bed. I work midnights and I'm just getting home."

Jan snapped, "I am a general in the United States Army, I don't need a warrant."

The man tossed back, "Look around, Mr. General. This is not the United States, this is the west side of Detroit. There are seven of us and four of you. Do you want to open up and see who'll be standing when the smoke clears?"

Jan stilled.

The gold eyes flashed cold amusement. "We're done here. Good luck with the search."

That said, he and his entourage entered the building, leaving Jan and his wide-eyed companions standing outside in the morning sunshine.

Furious and humiliated, Jan called Washington and told his contact to put out an APB for Dr. Adam Gary.

To his surprise, the man said this would be his last favor and instructed him to never under any circumstances contact him or his office again.

As the call ended, Jan stood stunned. Had the man
suddenly gotten cold feet? Was he being watched? Had
the U.S. government gotten wind of what he and his
associates were attempting to achieve? Jan had no answers, but there was a chill in his bones.

Sixteen

Just as Max feared, the factory-lined corridor of I–75 leading to the Michigan-Ohio state line was fat with traffic. Semis hauling everything from enormous steel coils to new cars to pigs shared the lanes with double-barrel fuel tankers and single tankers sporting red stickers warning of hazardous waste. The scene could have doubled as a trucker's convention, and people driving personal vehicles did their best to flow through.

Because of the trucks, the going was slow. Max felt like they were crawling. She checked the speedometer. Twenty. They were crawling. That she and her crew were not out for a Sunday drive but trying to stay ahead of the bad guys was never far from her mind, and she made a point to keep checking her mirrors. Being forced to drive in what could only be described as a moving parking lot was not to their advantage. Safe harbor was still a good four or five hours away.

Max turned on the radio and switched it to the band that would pull in the truckers. She hoped their chatter would let her know what was going on up ahead. A few moments later she heard that a steel hauler had lost his load. Rods as big as sewer pipes were scattered all over the place, and the police were directing traffic off the highway so the mess could be cleared up. She looked over at Adam and sighed with frustration. "I hate detours."

"I can help you drive, you know."

Max had never considered giving up the wheel. "Really?"

"Sure. I may not know weapons, but I do drive. You've been going full steam since yesterday morning. Take a break."

She had to admit that her arms were tired from a day and a half of gripping the wheel, and her shoulders were bruised and sore from being tossed around during last night's close encounter with the Lexus and the concrete wall divider, but Max didn't like showing weakness, and getting him from point A to point B was her job.

Adam thought he knew her well enough now to imagine what she might be thinking. "Even Jinga had to rest sometime."

Max met his serious eyes. Emotions she had no names for swirled inside, touching her in places barred and shuttered for years. In that moment, she knew that of all the men in her past, Adam Gary had the potential to be the most dangerous. "Okay," she replied, concentrating again on driving. "You're on. Let me find a place to pull over."

She swung out from behind the semi they'd been trailing and stopped the car near the curb. "Let's stash the prototype and my toys first, though."

He nodded.

Keeping an eye on the traffic, she watched him place

the prototype, which was wrapped in one of Sweetness's fancy pillow cases, into the hidden compartment built into the body of the tailgate. Once she added her towel-wrapped weapons, he slammed the gate shut and they quickly got back in. He made the necessary adjustments to the seat and mirrors then merged back into the slow-moving train of vehicles following the detour.

Max had to admit that being the passenger was relaxing. She could look at what passed for scenery in the struggling neighborhood they were driving through, and could check on Ossie as often as she wanted and not have to worry about keeping her eyes on the road. Another advantage was that she could check out Adam, and enjoy that shadowy profile with its strong jaw and chin. Memories of their lovemaking drifted up hot and true, and she forced herself to think of other things.

Adam said, "Tell me about Sweetness. Where'd you meet him?"

"While I was working Detroit Homicide on a case involving his nine-year-old daughter. She was killed by a drunk driver on her way to school one morning."

"That's rough," Adam said solemnly. "Did they catch the person?"

"Somebody did. Caught him and killed him. Put him in his car then pushed it into the river."

Adam couldn't hide his surprise. "Was Sweet involved?"

She shrugged. "The driver also had a serious gambling problem and owed some pretty ugly people quite a bit of cash."

"So anybody could have popped him."

"Yep. Last I heard, no one was ever charged."

"So what does Sweet do?"

"This and that, and the less you know the better."

"Then that will be my last question," he tossed back with a smile.

She chuckled and turned back to the scenery.

They were finally merging back onto the highway. Adam took the Escalade up to the speed limit, then engaged the cruise. After settling in, he asked, "Ever thought about settling down, Max?"

She replied easily, "Oh, I don't know. Sometimes when I've been away from home for a long spell, or take on a job that really kicks my butt, I have a pity party for myself and think of throwing in the towel."

"What about kids?"

She shrugged. "This body is getting a little old to be reproducing, but I might want to adopt. Maybe. Jury's still out."

"Would you get married again?"

"Please. Only if my mama's life was in danger."

He chuckled. "You sound pretty adamant."

"Twice was enough. The first time was to a musician with an ego the size of Jupiter, and then Benny the Dog. Can I pick them or what?" She looked his way. "What about you. Do you want to get married?"

"Eventually. Like to have a couple of kids, too, before I get too old to enjoy them."

Max nodded understandingly. "Well, I'll probably wind up being one of those crackpot little old ladies holed up in her house with her guns and her dogs."

"Hey, you never know. Somewhere down the line you might meet a brother who'll rock your world."

"Yeah right, and pigs will be flying out of LAX."

"You have to have faith, Max."

"Why would I waste faith on something I don't want?"

"You don't want to have love in your life?"

She went silent. After mulling the question over for a few moments, she replied quietly, "Not if there's going to be heartbreak on the other side. Been there. Done that."

He met her eyes. "Not all men are that way."

Once again, muddled feelings filled Max's insides. "So I'm learning."

He used a bent finger to slowly caress her cheek. When her eyes slid shut from the power in his touch, he leaned over and gave her a short sweet kiss before turning his attention back to the drive.

Max was left zinging. Why this man? she wanted to know. Why in her thirty-fifth year would the fates put someone like him in her life? Parts of herself wanted the answer, but other parts wanted nothing to do with it.

Adam, meanwhile, wondered if Max had any softness in her life. He wasn't referring to the female kind of softness, because he knew Max was all woman, but the softness everyone needed. The kind of softness a man feels when he wakes up beside that one special woman. The kind of softness you feel coming home to the person you loved after a bad day. Who was her haven when she needed emotional shelter? What did she fear and who held her when things became too much to bear? He knew how tough she was, but even Superman feared losing Lois, and Kryptonite.

Adam set aside thoughts of Max for the moment and turned to a question that had been bugging him for a while. "If the President is so worried about the prototype falling into the wrong hands, why didn't he send a helicopter or something to take me to D.C.?"

"If the rumors of rogues are true, he probably wasn't sure who he could trust. Wouldn't want a chopper whisking you off to Afghanistan."

Adam saw her point.

Traffic flowed well for the next few miles, then, around Bowling Green, everything slowed and then stopped. Max groused, "Now what?"

Adam switched off the CD and turned the radio on so they could eavesdrop on the truckers again.

Police checkpoint. Less than five miles ahead. A worried Max quickly checked the cars around them in hopes of pulling off the highway, but the Escalade was in the middle lane and boxed in on both sides. She looked at the steep grades flanking the road and knew that even if they managed to escape the traffic, there was no way they could handle the incline. The Escalade was a lot of things, but not a mountain goat. They were stuck.

Adam asked, "Do you think they're looking for us?"

"I don't know but my gut's turning big-time."

She searched her mind for a way out. If this were a simple routine safety check, getting out of line would call unnecessary attention to themselves, but if this was a sweep intended to net them, they were caught unless she could come up with a way to go around it. "Any ideas?" she asked him.

"Nope."

Max sensed his worry matched her own. "Let's cut the AC and open the windows. We may need that gas."

Adam did as she requested and hit the button that controlled the sun roof. It slid open noiselessly, letting in fresh air and the rhythmic beat of a helicopter. Max craned her neck up to look past the windshield and saw a helicopter painted in military greens and brown hovering over the traffic. "Uh-oh."

Adam looked up at it, too, then over at Max. She slipped her Glock out of her purse and into her hand. To make matters worse, two armed soldiers appeared. They were walking through the stalled traffic scrutinizing the faces of drivers, then moving on.

She let out a soft curse. It had barely left her lips when a knock on the window beside her startled her. Turning, she saw the business end of an M-16 pointed her way and the hard eyes of the soldier behind it. "Put your hands up!" he barked.

Max sighed with frustration and anger.

"Drop the weapon!"

Max made a show of placing the Glock on top of the dashboard.

"Unlock the door!"

Adam complied, and the locks went up with a loud click.

"I want the woman to get in the backseat and I'll ride shotgun. You stay where you are, Dr. Gary."

That settled the mystery. The soldiers were after them.

Max stepped out with her hands up. She could see the concern and curiosity on the faces of the other drivers. As he gave her a light patdown, she wondered what kind of story the drivers would tell their friends and family about this when they reached their respective destinations.

"Where's your phone?" the soldier asked.

"On the seat."

"Get in."

Max did as she was told but wondered where he'd received his training. Anybody with sense would never have an unrestrained perp seated behind him. This small faux pas didn't tell her a lot about who she might be dealing with but it did tell her something: Either his training was lacking or he was underestimating her because of her sex. Since both could be used to her advantage, she sat back and waited.

While two other armed soldiers made the trucks and cars boxing in the Escalade open a hole in the traffic for them to squeeze through, the soldier seated beside Adam told Max, "If I have any problems with those dogs back there, I'll shoot them."

The threat didn't help Max's mood. She looked back at the strapped-in Ruby, whose furrowed face was directed at the soldier, and then at the sleeping Ossie. "One's drugged and the other will be fine."

Max then sat silent as Adam steered the Escalade to the shoulder. He was then instructed to drive down to the checkpoint that could be seen about a quarter of a mile away.

The soldier asked him, "Do you have the prototype?"

Adam looked over and replied, "How about we let your boss ask the questions."

The man's jaw tightened but he didn't respond.

Max beamed. *Good answer, Doc!*

When they reached the checkpoint, men dressed in Ohio State Trooper uniforms were taking down the sawhorses that had been blocking the highway. Once they were done, traffic began to crawl by, but not before the drivers took one last curious look at the commandeered Escalade.

Max and Adam waited as another soldier—a general, if all the stars and bars riding his shoulders were authentic—walked to the car accompanied by a pastyfaced man in a rumpled black suit. The soldier seated beside Adam said, "Roll down the window."

Adam complied, and the general stuck his head in. "I'm General Walt Pearl," he said importantly, "Army Intelligence."

Adam nodded. The man had coal black hair, cold blue eyes, and the voice of the "friend" on the phone. He was as tall as Adam and appeared to be in his late thirties or early forties. If he was who he claimed to be, Adam assumed Pearl was one of the Pentagon's rogues.

Pearl turned his attention on Max. "You must be Max Blake, the supposed housekeeper."

She didn't reply but silently wondered how he'd learned her identity. *Kent, maybe.*

"We ran your name through the national databases and it came back blank. Technically, you don't exist, Ms. Blake. Why is that?"

Max shrugged.

"Who are you, really?"

"The housekeeper."

Her blasé attitude didn't seem to sit well. Giving her an icy smile, he said, "Fine, stick with your story. You'll tell me the truth eventually."

His companion looked sweaty and nervous. In fact, he didn't even look like an American dressed in that bad suit. She wondered what his role might be.

Pearl ignored Max for the moment and asked Adam, "Do you have the prototype?"

"It destabilized last night when a car rammed us. I had to destroy it."

Max had been wondering if Adam could lie. Now she knew—not only could he lie, but he could do it with style.

The man in the rumpled suit snapped, "I don't believe you!"

The general looked at Adam as if trying to decide whether the scientist was telling the truth about the prototype. He then yelled over the traffic sounds at the soldier sitting next to Adam, "We'll go back to base and straighten this out. Make sure they stay close behind us."

The soldier cradling his weapon gave Max and Adam a sinister smile. "Don't worry."

Max was hoping the volume of oncoming cars would keep the Escalade and the Hummer holding Pearl and his party from merging back onto the highway together. That way, if the cars became separated, she might be able to take out the escort in the front seat and get the Escalade back on the road. But to her disappointment, a large break in the traffic facilitated a smooth entrance for both vehicles and they were soon on the way.

With Adam driving, the Escalade followed the Hummer for an hour, then trailed it up the ramp leading to a small town outside of Findlay, Ohio. They stopped to get gas. The soldier told Max, "Get gas, but don't get cute."

"I need my purse. It's on the floor by your feet."

He picked it up then began searching through the contents.

Max asked in a genuine-sounding voice, "Do you see my tampon in there anywhere?"

Her request turned him beet red. He quickly thrust the bag at her and a secret smile played over Max's face as she fished her credit card out of her wallet and stepped out of the truck.

Even though there weren't many other customers at the pumps, Max could have easily called for help and let the chips fall where they may, but she was sure the soldier would shoot her dogs if she did, and she knew Hannibal wanted as much info on Pearl and his people as she could glean, so she kept her mouth shut and pumped her gas.

Being outside the car also gave her an opportunity to discreetly check out how many people were in the Hummer. She saw two soldiers—one driving, the other pumping the gas—in addition to Pearl and his rumpled companion. Four plus the man riding with her and Adam. Five. The odds weren't too bad if she counted in Adam and the dogs, providing she could access a weapon. She thought about the helicopter they'd seen hovering over traffic at the checkpoint. The chopper could be problematic if it was under Pearl's control, but she'd deal with that if and when the time came. As she replaced the hose, she and Adam shared a silent look. Keeping her movements smooth and natural, she grabbed her receipt and got back into her seat.

The "base" Pearl had referred to turned out to be a shabby little motel that rented rooms by the hour. Max noted that the tacky place was located only a short drive from the highway. Apparently, the room arrangements had already been made because Pearl came over to Adam's side of the car and said to him, "Dr. Gary, you, Ms. Blake, and the dogs are going to be in the same room. Please park over there."

Adam parked and cut the engine. They got out.

Max asked their guard, "Is it okay if I let the dogs out now?"

He gave her a nod. "Don't do anything stupid, though."

Max opened the truck's tailgate where the prototype and her weapons lay hidden in the hollowed-out space between its steel panels. She beckoned to Ruby, who jumped down onto the pavement of the parking lot. Ossie was still knocked out.

Adam came around. "I'll carry him."

Grateful for his care and concern, Max stepped back so he could reach in. He carefully scooped the big dog up as easily as a child.

The motel had two levels, and all its rooms opened to the outside. As they walked toward it she noted that there were no other cars in the lot. The place looked abandoned.

Max and Adam were shown into a street level room that smelled of mildew and smoke. The interior consisted of a bed, a chair, and a tiny bathroom. The TV worked only if you fed it coins.

Adam placed Ossie on the small bathroom rug so he'd be undisturbed.

Pearl said, "We'll be here until our plane arrives, so make yourselves comfortable. My aide will bring you some food later."

Adam had to admit he was starving. His breakfast at Sweetness's had been cut short by their hasty departure. Add in the drama of the last few hours, and he was hungry enough to eat Guam.

Max said, "The dogs' food and water bowls are in the car. Can you send somebody to get them, too?"

Pearl scanned Ruby, who was watching him silently. "Nice animal," he noted. "Looks to be well-trained for a dog owned by a simple housekeeper. Why's the male asleep?"

"He gets carsick."

"Ah. I suggest you keep them under control if you want to keep them alive."

"You're the second person whose threatened them."

He met Max's eyes, but she didn't flinch.

He said, "You think you're a pretty tough bitch, don't you?"

"Doesn't matter what I think. Action is what counts, General Pearl."

He didn't reply to her bold statement. Instead, he turned to Adam and said, "We'll talk about the prototype shortly."

"Fine," Adam replied, "but I told you, I destroyed it."

"So you say." He turned to go to the door, but stopped and looked back at them. "There will be a guard in front of the door at all times, in case you're thinking of trying to escape."

A moment later they were alone.

Max looked at Adam and said, "I worked with General Walt Pearl when I first got into operations."

"Then why is he acting like he doesn't know you?"

"Because he doesn't."

Adam didn't understand.

Max explained coolly, "The real General Pearl was killed a few years ago in the Philippines."

Stunned, Adam searched her face. "So who is this man?"

"I have no idea, but I'd sure like to find out."

"So no big escape plan brewing in that brain of yours?"

"Not yet. I need to see what's going on here first. Even though there are five of them and only four of us, I figure the odds are in our favor because the guy in the black suit looks like he'll run at the first sign of trouble."

"Four on four, then."

"Basically."

Adam liked the odds as well, provided the general wasn't planning on doing to them what someone had done to Dr. Sylvester "Sly" Kent.

Seventeen

The soldier who'd ridden in the Escalade with Adam and Max entered a few minutes later with a bag of burgers and fries. He left, then returned a few minutes later with the bag of dog food and the bowls.

Once he was gone for good, Max poured food for Ruby and for the now stirring Ossie, then Max dragged the tall, half-filled bag of food into the bathroom, out of view.

"What are you doing?" Adam asked.

"I always stash spare toys in the food. Keep an eye out, would you?"

Adam grinned. He knew she wasn't referring to doggie toys.

Max stuck her arm deep into the bag and fished around until she found the Ziploc she was after. It held a Glock, ammo, a phone, and a few other surprises.

Adam, eating his fries, stood at the window and kept watch through the dusty lopsided blinds. He could see their guard standing outside the door. He was chowing down on a large burger. "So you do have a plan?"

"Nope, but in case one shows up, we have help."

He nodded approvingly, then said, "Uh-oh. They're searching the car."

Max joined him at the window. She watched one of the soldiers going through the gear in the back and fiddling around in the front seat. Even though he'd taken the keys from Adam earlier, without the code they couldn't access anything of importance. The dog blankets and clothes in the backseat wouldn't help them, either.

Pearl's face was set tight with irritation as he got out and slammed the door.

"He doesn't look happy," Adam noted while enjoying his chocolate shake.

"No he doesn't."

They shared a smile.

Max told him, "I meant to tell you how much I liked your lie about the prototype. In fact, remind me to take you along on my next job, you're a great sidekick."

He shook his head and said, "Oh, no. Once this is over, I'm going back to my nice quiet lab. This is way too much drama for me. You might want to think about slowing down yourself."

"Naw. I'm fine. I wouldn't know what to do if I wasn't doing this."

"Ever tried anything else?"

Max studied him. "No."

"You can't be Jinga forever, Max. You could get killed."

"True, but I could be killed crossing the street."

"I'm trying to be serious here."

"I caught that."

Their eyes met.

He said, "I just worry about you, that's all."

"And I appreciate it, but you don't have to. I'm well trained."

When he turned back to the window, she could see the hard set of his jaw. She didn't want this to be an issue between them, so she stepped over, wrapped her arms around his solid waist and placed her cheek against his warm back. "Adam, I'm never going to be one of those women waiting for her family to come home so that her life will have meaning."

"I know that, but—"

She cut him off by asking gently, "If the shoe were on the other foot and you were the one living my life, would you want to hear me asking you to make a change?"

For a moment he didn't respond, then he said, "Probably not."

"Is it because I'm female?"

He turned to look at her. "Yeah."

She gave him a bittersweet smile. "I like your honesty." Then she said softly, "Yes, what I do does scare me sometimes, and yes, I may die because of it. But it's what I choose to do. I choose."

"And the people who care about you? What about them?"

"If they really and truly care for me, they'd want me to be happy—no matter what."

Adam looked down into those sincere green eyes, and her indomitable spirit filled his heart. "You make it hard for a brother."

Her voice stayed soft. "That's what I'm here for."

The kiss that followed was one they both needed, a slow but searing renewal of emotions still waiting to be fully explored. They met tenderly, gently, holding each other closely while they reacquainted themselves with what they'd had to set aside since being on the run.

The door opened abruptly and they jumped.

Pearl walked in. "How touching. Sorry to interrupt, but Dr. Gary, it's time."

Adam was suddenly tired of all this; tired of running and ducking and being shot at. If Max didn't have a plan, he'd come up with one, because he'd had enough. All he wanted was to lose himself in his lab and spend the rest of the time enjoying Max's company for as long as she wanted to stay. But right now, duty called, he thought sarcastically. Giving Max a parting kiss on her forehead, he walked past Pearl and out of the door without a word.

Pearl told the soldier who'd been guarding her door, "Watch her."

They slammed the door and closed her in.

As silence resettled over the dingy little room, Max had Adam foremost in her mind as she asked the dogs, "Okay, who's got a plan?"

Adam was taken into a room two doors down. The decor was as bland as the decor he'd just left.

"Have a seat, Dr. Gary," the man with the accent invited.

"I'll stand."

Looking flustered, the man turned to Pearl, but Pearl said, "It doesn't matter."

Adam guessed Rumpled Suit wanted him to sit because of the great difference in their heights. It couldn't be a terrifying interrogation with the taller Adam glaring down from on high.

Pearl took over. "Where's the prototype?"

"Tossed it in a Dumpster."

"Where?"

"West side of Detroit, and I don't know the street, because I don't know the city."

"Explain again what happened to it."

"All the jostling from the car chase last night destabilized the formula. It started to corrode the casing so I got rid of it. The gas it releases is toxic."

The man in the rumpled suit said accusingly, "I thought it was perfected."

"I did, too. Guess that's why they call it a prototype." Adam turned away.

Pearl asked, "Do you think you can make one that is perfect?"

"Probably. Might take a year or two, though."

Adam could tell by Pearl's annoyed face that he hadn't cared for that answer.

"I think you're lying," Pearl said.

Adam shrugged. "Fine."

The short man said, "There are ways to make you tell us the truth, Dr. Gary."

Adam waited.

Pearl smiled. "He's right. How about we beat up on that lady of yours for an hour or two? Once Crane and Gibbons over there get through with her, those sweet lips you were kissing will be big as bananas, and those green eyes'll be black and blue."

Both soldiers smiled, and the one named Gibbons said, "Just tell us when."

Adam's anger was plain.

Pearl nodded with satisfaction. "Thought that would get your attention. Now, again, where's the prototype?"

"What part of 'I had to destroy it' don't you understand?"

The man with the accent snarled doubtfully, "You wouldn't destroy something so valuable."

"I can make another one. Remember?" Adam had said all he planned to, except for this, "Touch her, and I will kill you."

Pearl chuckled. "Spoken like a true lover." Then he added sarcastically, "You're a lab scientist. You don't know a thing about killing a person."

Adam's eyes glowed coldly. "I graduated med school at Johns Hopkins. If I hit you in the right spot, I can make your heart stop. I know ways to snap your neck and not even get my hands dirty. So, yeah, I can kill you, but the question will be, will I make it quick or make it slow?"

He looked over at Gibbons and saw fear flood the soldier's eyes before the man caught himself. Adam was satisfied.

Pearl said, "I want to talk to the woman. I'll be back."

Adam stiffened. Pearl gave him a cold smile then exited.

Two doors down, Max was seated on the bed when the door swung open. Pearl stood on the threshold. He told the guard, "Go to the other room. I want to talk to her alone."

Holding his gun on her, Pearl motioned her to go with him. Max stilled. "Where are we going?"

"To see your boyfriend."

Wondering how Adam was holding up and if they'd harmed him, Max saw the dogs stand up. She told them, "Stay. I'll be right back."

She followed Pearl outside, where sounds of the nearby highway could be heard in the distance.

"Down there," he said, and motioned with his gun. As Max walked, she realized she hadn't seen a soul upon their arrival and once again wondered if the place was even open. If it wasn't, she realized that if Pearl decided to dispose of them, their corpses might not be found for months. Not that she was planning on dying, but the thought was enough to keep her on her toes.

He made her stop in front of a room on the far end of the building, then motioned her inside. She twisted the knob with her left hand and stepped inside. He came in behind her and closed the door. The room was a twin of her own but there was no one in it.

She turned around to ask where Adam was but something in his eyes set off alarms.

Jan knew he was sexually attracted to this tall dynamic woman. Being who he was, he was accustomed to slaking his needs on women of color, and he was itching to get his hands between those long legs. "So," he said. "Do you want to tell me who you really are?"

Max was watching his vivid blue eyes. "I'm the housekeeper. Who are you?"

"General Walt Pearl."

She gave him a wintry smile. "Try again. I used to play poker with Walt Pearl before he died, so you can't possibly be him."

His eyes widened for a split second then his jaw tightened. "Undress."

Max went still. "Excuse me?"

"Take off your pants. I want us to get to know one another better."

"Oh, really?"

"We can make this easy or we can make it hard—makes no difference to me."

"So, we're talking rape."

He shrugged behind the raised rifle. "Call it whatever you care. As I said, hard or easy, it's up to you."

Max could see the smug triumph. She gave him another wintry smile. "Then by all means—let's make this easy!"

Max sailed the razor-sharp star hidden in her right hand with such speed and accuracy, it was embedded in the side of his neck before he could say, *rape*. The rifle hit the ground. His eyes bulging, he clawed at the disc.

By the time the furious Max picked up his gun and left the room, he was gurgling, clawing, and screaming on the floor. Striding to the Escalade, she pulled the extra set of keys from her bra and opened the tailgate. She didn't do well with threats of rape, and she was about to take it out on Pearl's friends.

She tossed Pearl's rifle into the hidden compartment, took out her own and slammed the gate shut. Her big gun now in tow, she went around and opened a side door, then crossed the parking lot back to her room. She threw open the door, grabbed her purse, and after putting the straps in Ruby's mouth, sent the dogs running to the car.

Max had no idea which room they'd taken Adam to, but she bet on it being close by because Pearl didn't have a posse large enough to guard a spread-out operation. She passed the room next door to hers. Nothing. The room next to it was the money ball. She could see them through the ragged venetian blinds and they could see her. The shock on the soldiers' faces put a grim smile on her face as she screamed out, "Adam, get away from the door!"

Opening up the weapon, she blasted the rusted hinges, then the lock. The old door was no match for so much firepower and crashed into the room. Then she was standing in the opening with her gun raised while the smoke and dust drifted around her like fog.

Not a man moved, including Adam.

Max swung her attention to the wide-eyed soldiers who'd been caught by surprise, their weapons hanging uselessly in their hands. "Drop 'em."

They checked out the size of her gun, saw the emerald death flashing in her green eyes, and didn't have to be asked twice. The guns clattered to the floor. Their hands went up and they stood absolutely still.

"Adam, get their guns, please, and the brunette has my phone."

Adam grabbed up the guns, then took her phone from the man's pocket.

Once Adam was out of the line of fire, she said to them, "Now, I'm going to ask you two some questions, and before you think you can lie, let me explain something. This gun has a high-tech lie detector built into it and will automatically send you to hell if you tell one."

Their eyes widened.

Behind her, Max heard the short man in the rumpled suit, scoff, "That's preposterous—"

Max swung the gun, blasted out a chunk of the wall behind him then swung it back. The man screamed like a little girl. Max growled, "You'll get your chance to talk next!"

The ashen-faced Oskar slid down what remained of the wall to the plaster-strewn floor.

For the next few minutes Max asked questions and Gibbons and Crane answered. She learned that they, like Pearl, were imposters. They weren't soldiers, but house painters. They first met Pearl six weeks ago in a Miami bar in response to an ad he'd placed in a third-rate soldier-of-fortune magazine soliciting men wanting action and adventure. He told them that they were going on a secret mission on behalf of the Pentagon and that Dr. Gary was to be taken into custody for offering the prototype to terrorists secretly hiding in the States. During Max's interrogation their eyes never wavered too far from the muzzle of her big gun. They seemed terrified by the idea of saying the wrong thing and being blown away, and as a result they gave her answers that were clear and succinct.

Max turned her wintry glare to the short man still sitting on the floor. "Name and country of origin," she snapped.

He hesitated, and Max shot up the wall beside him. He screamed and got on his knees.

"Answer me!"

Cringing and crying, he called out in a frightened voice, "Vlad! Vlad Oskar! Germany! Please don't shoot me!"

Max's smile was sinister. "Why are you in this country?" Then she added, "Remember what I said about this gun. Lie, and you die."

He whimpered in response to that then confessed, "I represent Afrikaners who want to set up their own country."

"Where?"

"On land taken from the present government."

"Taken, as in by force?"

He nodded. "They don't like the evolution of the South Africa their ancestors founded."

"So they want their own enclave."

Again he nodded.

Max shook her head. "Do they believe the South African army is going to just let them do this?"

"The group has weapons and pledges of support from military officials in the West. If there is a fight, they believe the present government will eventually capitulate and agree to their demands in order to restore peace."

"Tell me about this western support."

"Many of your own generals are not happy with the way your country has evolved, either."

"Our President, you mean?" Max knew that some Americans refused to accept the reality of the great-grandson of slaves being their duly elected commander in chief, but members of the Pentagon, too?

"Yes."

"So unhappy they'd risk treason?"

"Yes."

"How many?"

"Three, as far as I know, but we are gaining new supporters every day."

Max didn't like the sound of any of this. Even three rogues was an unacceptable number. "So why go after the prototype?"

"One of our scientists is convinced that in addition to its energy benefits, it can be converted to a powerful weapon. The sales of both would form the basis of the new country's economy."

Max had to admit it was a grandiose plan, but it wasn't

going to work, not if she had any say, and from where she stood, her say was all that mattered. She studied him, the fear in his eyes plain.

"What's Pearl's real name?" she asked, hoping he was bleeding to death.

Rumpled Suit seemed surprised by the question and again hesitated. Max's gun blew out a portion of the wall a few inches to the right of his head, then took out the wall to the left. "You don't want to play chicken with me!" she barked. "His name!"

His eyes were wide as plates. "Jan Kruger!" He was covered with plaster dust, and the wet stain covering the front of his pants revealed just how terrified he'd been by the weapon fire.

"Country of origin?"

"South Africa. He works for the ambassador to the U.S."

"I want the names of those generals."

He hesitated only long enough for Max to tighten her grip before firing. Seeing that, and knowing she wouldn't hesitate to reduce him to plaster, he cringed. "Brunner. Calhoun. Brice."

"Thank you."

She glanced around at the rest of them. Each man seemed to be holding his breath. "Adam, are you ready?"

He answered grimly, "Yeah." He'd never seen anything like the display she'd just put on, and again he was glad she was on his side.

Max hoped Adam now understood why fearing for her safety was unnecessary. She could take care of herself. Carrying the guns that had belonged to Crane and Gibbons, he joined her at the door.

She told the men, "If I were you, I'd stay here until we're gone. I'd also find another line of work."

That said, she and Adam departed. As they hastened to the Escalade, Max took a moment to blow out the Hummer's tires.

Finished and satisfied, she looked to make sure they weren't being followed when fire exploded in her back and shoulder. The force buckled her. Surprise and confusion filled her face, then she saw the staggering Pearl, gun in hand, poised to fire again. Fury overriding her pain, Max gritted her teeth against the agony and opened fire, hoping to blow him to hell. Blood spewed from his chest and he went down. Apparently they'd had guns stashed away in both rooms because now the others were firing too. Turning on them, she sent lead their way. They ducked back inside the doorway, out of sight, as Adam was yelling, "Max!"

Then he was at her side, helping her to the car and in.

While she rested against the door, each breath seemingly made of fire, Adam was behind the wheel. He roared them away while the shooting furious men did their best to make them stop.

Adam's adrenaline was pumping overtime. Shocked and shaken, he tried to keep one eye on her and one on the road. He looked for signs that might lead him to a hospital. The dogs were whimpering and crying, and he was so blown away he couldn't think. *He told her this could happen! Told her! Dammit!*

Max was having trouble breathing, "Stupid," she whispered. "I should've checked the rooms. Stupid and cocky."

"I'm taking you to an E.R."

"No!" she protested. "Portia. Portia."

"Hospital!"

"Portia's or so help me I'll get out and walk."

Adam sighed with frustration. There was no doubt in his mind that she'd do just that.

"Call her from my phone."

By now the dogs had jumped into the row of seats behind Adam and Max and were doing their best to see Max for themselves. Max wanted to reassure them, but reaching up sent heat hot as napalm up and down her arm and back. She gritted her teeth. "Don't worry," she told them. "Adam will get us to Portia and everything will be fine."

They whimpered. Ruby threw back her head and her mournful keening filled the interior.

Adam met Max's sleepy-looking eyes, and she gave him a soft crooked smile, then whispered, "This is what I get for showing off for the smart cute boy next door."

He lowered his head, trying to hide his smile, but couldn't do it. "You're a mess, do you know that?"

"No other woman like me in the world."

"You got that right."

She then asked, "Portia's?"

"Let me look at the wound first."

"I've been shot before, Adam," she said sluggishly. "This is bad, but not fatal. I'd know, I think."

Adam steered the car to the shoulder, got out and ran around to her side. He pulled open the door and she slowly leaned up so he could see. The gray upholstered seat was red with her blood. The thin blouse had been no match for the bullets. The fabric over her shoulder was as torn up as her flesh. It was an ugly wound. He probed it gently, using his medical training in an attempt to determine if she were in mortal danger. "Let's clean it up, if we can."

He went around, looked into the cooler built into the well between the backseats and grabbed a bottle of water.

"Lean forward again for me, sweetheart." He gently poured a slow stream of water over the black-edged wounds, and she sucked in a long breath that let him know how painful the bathing was. "Sorry. I have to clean it."

"I know."

He could see how much effort she was using to move and speak, and he wanted to get her to a hospital so bad he could taste it. Using some clean toweling from a roll resting on the backseat, he did his best to mop up her wet back, but stopping the bleeding was a priority. Because he had nothing else on hand, he immediately stripped off his shirt, bunched it up and gently placed the mass against the wound. "Lean back now."

She did and said, "Hurts like hell, but it feels better."

"You need to go to the E.R. How far are we from Portia's?"

"Two hours, tops."

"You could bleed out by then."

"Only if we stay here arguing."

He sighed. Her point taken, he fastened her seat belt, then closed her door. Getting into the driver's seat, he told the dogs. "Guess we're going to Portia's."

He put the car in gear, merged it back into the evening traffic, and headed south for the drive to Dayton.

Jan Kruger was dying and he knew it. Every inch of his body was in pain. His life's blood seemed to be pouring from everywhere. *Damn that bitch!* He could see Oskar and the others standing over him. They were wavering as if they were made from smoke. It wasn't supposed to end this way. He was supposed to be triumphant and feted for restoring the glory of a new world, not lying on the grounds of a ramshackle motel. He wanted to scream his rage! He wanted to curse that bitch through time! Instead he closed his eyes, thought about his wife and sons, and then the world went black.

Eighteen

Adam got Portia on Max's phone. He put her on the speaker so he could concentrate on driving. She sounded surprised to hear his voice. "Has something happened to Max?"

"She's been shot and we're headed your way."

"Oh dear. How bad is she?"

"Bleeding pretty bad, and she won't let me take her to the E.R."

"That's because she shouldn't. Technically, Max doesn't exist. Unless she's near death you're right to bring her here. I'll have a surgeon ready."

Adam shook his head. "What do you mean she doesn't exist?"

"All of her records have been purged. Because of her job, she isn't registered anywhere anymore. No Social Security number, legal billing address, none of that."

Adam remembered Pearl mentioning the same thing. At the time, he hadn't seen that as something he needed to be worried about. Now? "How do I get to you?"

Portia gave him the directions, and he punched the coordinates into the GPS system. Once that was set, he relaxed a bit, safe in the knowledge that he could get where he needed to be so Max could get help.

"Tell me what happened," Portia said.

Adam told her the story. He began with their capture at the checkpoint and ended with their escape. She asked a few questions to clarify some of the tale, then took down the names of the rogue generals: Brunner. Calhoun. Price.

"I'll put this on the wire right away," Portia said. "It shouldn't take long to get this mess cleaned up now that we have some names. Thank you."

"I'll celebrate when I know she's okay."

"She alert?"

"Not really. She's been nodding off and on."

In truth, Max could hear the entire conversation quite well, but she felt as if she were floating miles and miles away. Getting too close to full awareness unleashed the dragon fire in her upper back and shoulder, so drifting was better.

"How're the dogs?" Portia asked.

"As worried as I am."

"Hang in there. You'll be here shortly. Call back if you need to."

"Thanks, Portia. I'm looking forward to meeting you."

"Same here."

And she was gone.

Adam glanced over at Max. Her eyes were closed but her breathing appeared to be as even as it could be, considering the circumstances. He looked up into the mirror at the dogs and saw that their attention was trained on her. He shook his head. *What a crew.*

For the next two hours he drove as fast as the early

evening traffic would allow. He kept an eye out for
Ohio Highway Patrol cars because the last thing he
needed was a ticket and to explain Max's condition. He
hadn't checked the bleeding since giving up his shirt.
He didn't want to take the time to stop.

He finally saw the signs for Dayton and followed the
GPS prompts to the suburbs west of the city. After pass-
ing them, he found himself driving through farmland
down a pitted and rut-filled dirt road that caused Max to
moan every time the Escalade rocked. Concerned, he
reached over and placed his palm on her forehead. It was
dewed with sweat and her skin was hot with fever. He
didn't dare drive faster for fear of causing her more discomfort, so he grimly plowed on. Five miles later he
made one last turn and came to a stop before a two-story
farmhouse sitting beside a large weathered gray barn.
He punched up Portia. "We're here."

"Great," she said, her voice filled with relief.

"Drive into the barn. The back wall will open. Follow the tunnel."

Adam was confused. During the ride, he'd taken on
the habit of talking to the dogs the way Max often did,
and he asked them now, "Did she say follow the tunnel? What tunnel?"

Ruby barked excitedly. Ossie, miserable from the
ride, looked up once then laid back down.

"Okay," Adam said, shrugging, and slowly steered
over to the barn. The door looked to be made of a cor-
rugated metal. While he waited for whatever might
happen next, the barn door began to rise as if it were a
window shade. He drove in.

The lighting inside revealed hand tools hanging
neatly on the wall. In the corners were heavier

equipment like tillers, lawn mowers, and snow blowers.

As he sat there trying to figure out where this tunnel Portia mentioned might be located, the wall in front of them slowly split in half and opened like the doors of an elevator. Before him now stood a metal-clad passage that shone under the bright lights mounted on the walls. "This must be it," he said aloud, but inside he asked himself, *Where the hell am I?*

Adam slowly steered down the incline and past the shiny walls. It reminded him of one of the top secret installations in Hollywood movies, but this was real, and so were Max's injuries.

He gave her another concerned glance, and seeing her lying against the door so silent and still, his heart twisted. He drove another few feet and saw the tunnel end. A middle-aged woman with Hispanic features and long black hair threaded with silver was waiting there. Beside her stood two men and a woman, all of them wearing what appeared to be white medical coats. Propped against the wall was a stretcher.

Filled with relief but still worried about Max, he opened his door and stepped out. The medical people rushed to the passenger side, and while Adam and the dogs looked on, they helped Max out and gently assisted her into lying down on the stretcher. She opened her eyes, smiled at Adam and whispered, "Thanks for getting us here in one piece. I told you you were a great sidekick."

He took her hand and gave it a tender squeeze. He placed a kiss on her fevered brow and knew in his bones that he wasn't going to be okay until she was better. She squeezed his hand back with all the strength of a baby bird, then gave him another smile before they whisked her away. Adam knew he'd take that parting smile to the grave.

"Dr. Gary?"

He'd all but forgotten the presence of the woman he knew by the sound of her voice to be Portia. He shook her outstretched hand. She was very beautiful, but the long scar running from just below one eye to her chin was startling. He forced himself not to stare. "Thanks for your help," he said genuinely.

"No problem, and don't worry about my face. The cut draws attention wherever I go, so I'm used to the stares."

"My apologies."

She waved him off. "Not necessary."

She then said to the dogs that had trotted to her side, "Hello, my babies. Dr. Adam got your mama here in one piece. It's good to see you." He could see the happiness in their eyes as they jostled to be the one she petted the most. She scratched their necks affectionately. "Jesse and James aren't here," she said, "so you'll have the place all to yourselves."

They barked. Portia grinned and said, "Dr. Gary, come, let's get you settled so you can relax."

He was more than happy to comply. Still looking around in wonder, he followed her and the dogs up a short flight of stairs. To his surprise, they exited inside of a large well-stocked pantry and then stepped out into an even larger kitchen.

"Are you hungry?" she asked.

Adam checked out the old-fashioned wooden table in the center of the room and the sleek modern appliances. "I am, but I need to come down for a minute first. Where'd they take Max?"

"We have a small operating theater here."

Adam found that amazing. "I'm medically trained. I can help."

"If they need your assistance they will let you know."

Adam supposed that was true but it didn't diminish his worry. "What is this place?"

Portia said simply, "My home." She then said, "Come with me and we'll find you a room you can use while you are here."

From the impressive gadgets and software Portia had developed, Adam knew that the house was more than just her home, but he didn't press for a deeper explanation. He was her guest, after all, and he respected that.

Portia let the dogs out to play in the large field surrounding the farmhouse, then took him up the stairs to a bedroom on the second floor. It was decorated in dark blues and grays. There was an attached balcony that looked out onto the open fields and a small stand of trees. In the corner of the balcony there was a small table and a chair, in case the room's occupant wanted to sit outside.

Portia asked, "Will this be okay?"

"This is fine. Thanks. How long do you think they'll be working on Max?"

"When they're done, they'll let us know." Portia smiled. "Dr. Gary, relax. She is in good hands."

Adam's lips thinned. "Sorry."

"It's okay. You're worried about her. I am, too, but we can help more by staying out of the way and letting the doctors do their job."

Adam wasn't accustomed to feeling so powerless, and he was having a hard time with it.

"You got her here, safe," Portia reminded him. "Give yourself credit for that."

"It's not enough."

Portia didn't respond for a moment, and then, after studying him silently, asked, "You care for her, don't you?"

He didn't lie. "Yes."

Portia nodded. "Then it will work out, you'll see."

"She's a very unique lady."

Portia chuckled. "Oh yes. One of the most unique women I know." She then asked him, "Do you need anything? Clothing, toiletries?"

"I have stuff in my bag in the truck. Is it okay for me to go back down?"

"Of course."

"I'll bring the prototype, too."

Portia grinned happily. "Good. I've been wanting to see it."

"Then let me go and get it."

"And in exchange, I will show you my lab."

It was Adam's turn to grin. "I'll be right back."

"I'll meet you down in the kitchen."

The two scientists spent the next two hours discussing their work. Adam was impressed with Portia's lab and the room she used as her communications hub. She was impressed with his prototype. When the dark-haired Dr. Maria Lorenz walked in a few minutes later, both Adam and Portia waited tensely for the prognosis.

"She came through the surgery just fine," the lady doctor said reassuringly. "We were able to remove the bullets and repair her shoulder. She's going to be real sore for a while, and there will be a pretty ugly scar, but she should make a complete recovery, providing she takes it easy so she can heal."

Those were the best words Adam had heard all day, until Dr. Lorenz said, "She's asking for you, Dr. Gary. You get five minutes. No more. She needs to rest."

Inside, he shouted for joy. He looked over at the dogs lying on the floor by the stove and asked, "Can the dogs come along?"

The doctor seemed amused by the request. "Sure, why not? But they have to share your five minutes."

Adam didn't care. He knew how Max felt about her babies and he was sure that Ruby and Ossie wanted to see her as badly as he did. "Come on, guys, let's go see your mama."

They got up immediately, their eyes bright. Realizing how far he'd come in dealing with the two rottweilers since they first entered his life, he was happy to have them trotting alongside while they followed Portia and the doctor to where Max was waiting.

She was lying in bed in a small bedroom filled with monitors. IVs were hooked into her veins and a young Black man in a white coat was taking her pulse. As Adam neared the bed, he could see that her eyes were closed, and he thought she might be asleep. Unsure if he should disturb her, he looked to the doctor for direction.

She responded kindly, saying, "Call her softly. It's okay."

"Max?" Adam waited tensely for a response, and a few moments later she opened her eyes.

She gave him a groggy smile. "Hey," she whispered. "If it isn't the cute boy next door."

Happy and relieved inside and out, he replied softly, "Hey. How are you feeling?"

"Like a woman who's been shot," she tossed back with dry amusement, "but the doc says I'll be fine and I'm holding her to that."

Adam doubted she knew how relieved and moved he was to see her and to hear her voice. "Portia and the dogs are here, too."

Ruby and Ossie took that as their cue to come to the bed. Both animals stuck their large heads on top of the bedding, and she stroked their muzzles weakly. "Hi guys," she said to them. "You two okay?"

They barked in response, and that made her smile. "Good," she whispered. Her eyes drifted closed for a few long seconds. When they opened again, she said to Adam, "Portia spoils Ossie and Ruby. Make sure she doesn't let them run too wild while we're here."

Adam looked over at Portia and saw the secretive smile on her face. Amused, he turned back. "Okay."

Unable to resist the urge, he slowly traced a bent knuckle down the smooth warm planes of her brown cheek then kissed it gently. Adam was immediately struck by the myriad emotions the contact evoked. He and Max might have come together in lust at first, but what he was feeling now was different, stronger, wondrous. "We should let you rest."

She nodded almost imperceptibly.

Adam placed another tender kiss, this one on her forehead, as a farewell. "Get some sleep."

"I will. Can't wait until you can kiss more."

Chuckling at her indomitable and, yes, scandalous spirit, he shook his head. "We'll see you in the morning."

"Okay."

Lord knew he didn't want to leave her, and it must

have shown on his face because when he turned to Dr. Lorenz, she was smiling, but told him quietly yet firmly, "No."

Busted, he hung his head, and Portia didn't bother hiding her amusement. Adam gave the now sleeping Max one last parting look, then he and the others slipped out, so that the medical team could continue her care.

Later, as Adam lay in bed in the dark, he glanced over at the luminous face of the digital clock on the night table. Midnight. Although he'd had a hellacious day and was very tired, he was still too wound up to sleep. Unable to conquer the problem, he got up. Hoping it might help him to relax, he walked out onto the balcony attached to the bedroom. Above him was a velvet black sky studded with stars. Back home in Michigan the night had always been accompanied by the sound of the waves, but here he heard a symphony of insect songs and the wind blowing through the chimes hanging on the balcony's edge. Thinking about the house in Michigan made him realize what an amazing two and a half days it had been. The day before yesterday he'd awakened in his own bed to the sounds of surf and the cries of gulls, and now he was in the remarkable home of a remarkable woman named Portia in the farmlands of central Ohio. It was one more entry on an increasingly long list of amazing events.

Casting his mind back on the chaotic last twenty-four hours, all he could see was Max and that big gun. He had to admit that when she walked into the room, the gun still smoking and her eyes full of death, she'd scared the hell out of him, too. He'd never seen anyone, much less a woman, handle a weapon with such ferocity and confidence. If the men with Pearl or Kruger or whatever his damn name had been had any sense, they'd be at the airport right now trying to fly home, because if they ran into Max again, injured or not, he knew they would see hell. She had not been playing.

That same ferocious confidence had gotten answers, too. Portia had already wired her contacts about Pearl and the renegade generals. The South African ambassador had also been alerted and vowed to start an investigation into the people wanting to replunge her country into death and anarchy. Adam hoped everyone involved would be caught, tried, and jailed for a long time. As far as Adam knew, Sly Kent's murder was still unsolved, but he was sure that would be figured out eventually, too. He made a mental note to call Kaitlin, then remembered he no longer had a phone. He'd deal with that later.

For now, though, thoughts of Max filled his mind. Truthfully, he couldn't imagine a day that didn't include her swaggering bossiness. He knew that they lived totally opposite lives and that when this adventure ended he'd go back to his life and she to hers, but he wanted to put that off until he learned everything there was to know about her remarkable self. What was her favorite color? Who were her sheroes? Did she like spinach? Adam didn't know the answers to any of those inconsequential questions, but relationships were built on the inconsequential, too, and a relationship is what he wanted to have with her. It was the first time he'd allowed himself to admit that fact. There was more to her than mayhem and guns, and it was those parts buried beneath the Iron Maiden exterior that he wanted to explore, connect with, play with and make smile.

Would she have him, and could she be convinced to give up her dangerous lifestyle? Those were two more questions he didn't have the answers to, so for now he chose to be content and glad that she was alive and well.

Adam sat outside awhile longer. He thought about his mother and how she was doing, and that he should go and see her as soon as he could. He wondered if he was still going to get to meet the President, and how cool that would be if he did. He thought about the prototype and how he owed Myk Chandler the most expensive bottle of aged cognac he could find for all of his help. And again, Adam thought of Max. Beautiful, sexy, dangerous Max. *Lord have mercy!* As she'd said, no other woman like her in the world.

The next morning he awoke at six to the sound of the alarm on his watch. He'd set it so he could get up and take his morning run, but he was so whipped, he'd already decided to skip it and go back to sleep when he saw the dogs. Ruby and Ossie were standing by the bed looking at him. They'd become accustomed to going with him, and he supposed to them every day meant *every* day. "Okay, okay," he grumbled, throwing back the sheet. "Let me hit the bathroom first, then we'll go."

Ten minutes later, after leaving a note for Portia on the kitchen table, he and the dogs were outside. Because Adam had no idea where to go, he said to the dogs, "Lead the way."

They took off across an open field and Adam set himself a steady pace and tried to keep them in sight. When they got back to the house, Portia was seated at the table enjoying a cup of coffee. "Morning," she said. "Coffee."

"Let me shower first."

"The President called just a while ago wanting to speak to you."

Adam went still.

"He's going to give you and Storm a medal at a state dinner in the fall."

"Who's Storm?"

"Max. He calls her Storm after the X-Man super heroine. You know. Halle Berry played her in the movie."

Adam was amazed. "That woman has more names than the Book of Genesis."

Portia smiled around her raised cup. "That she does."

"Why's he want to give me a medal? Max, I can understand, but I didn't do anything."

"Your lie helped keep the prototype out of enemy hands. No telling what we'd be facing if they'd gotten hold of it, and you brought Max home safe. She's one of Hannibal's favorite people, you know. He just wants to say thanks."

"But—"

"Go get your shower. I'll feed the dogs."

She stood, called to Ruby and Ossie, and they left the amazed Adam standing alone in the kitchen.

Max was dreaming, or at least she hoped so because she and Adam were getting married. They were standing at an altar. She had on a hot red dress, Adam had on a tux and the preacher in the robe was Myk Chandler. Ruby was walking on her hind legs. She was six feet tall, had a bouquet of flowers in her front paws, and was wearing a dress that matched hers. Chandler told Adam to kiss the bride, but she was looking at the choir. Pearl was there with a gun. He began shooting. Her bouquet morphed into a gun and she fired back. People starting running and then she and Adam were in a red canoe out on the lake drifting in the sunshine. The water was calm and shining. She felt at peace.

After finishing his breakfast, Adam was allowed in to see Max. She was asleep, so, with Dr. Lorenz's permission, he pulled up a chair and sat. A few moments later, as if Max sensed his presence, her eyes opened.

"Hey," she said.

"Hey," he responded softly. "How you doing?"

"I dreamed about you."

"Oh yeah?"

"Yeah." She paused for a moment as if trying to remember. "We were in a canoe. Ruby was at some kind of wedding. She had on a red dress and was walking on her hind legs. She was as tall as you."

Adam laughed quietly. "Maybe Dr. Lorenz needs to cut back on your drugs."

"Maybe. Myk was in the dream, too. I don't remember the rest."

"Sounds like that might be a good thing."

Her eyes drifted closed for a few moments, then opened again. "How are the dogs?"

"Fine. Having a good time playing outside."

She smiled. "Good. They like you."

"I'm liking them better, too."

"Knew you would. Once you got to know them."

He nodded.

"I think I'm going back to sleep. Will you stay a little while?"

"Rottweilers couldn't tear me away."

She chuckled faintly. "He's got dog jokes now, folks." She reached for his hand and he gently closed his around hers. "See you in a bit," she whispered, and she slept.

That evening, a light-skinned brother wearing sunglasses and a long army-looking trench coat sailed into Portia's kitchen while she and Adam were going over the schematics of some of Portia's electronic prototypes.

"Saint!" Portia exclaimed in a happy and surprised voice.

"Evening."

Portia made the introductions. "Saint, this is Dr. Adam Gary."

"Hello," Saint said.

Adam nodded a greeting.

Saint asked, "How's our girl?"

"Okay considering she got back-shot."

"Damn. Can I see her?"

Portia tossed back, "Probably not in that coat."

"What is it with everybody and my coat?"

"If you washed it even occasionally maybe it wouldn't need a toxic warning sticker on it."

Saint looked to Adam and said, "Women."

Adam grinned.

Portia said, "Go on back, but I'm telling you now, Dr. Lorenz isn't going to let you in wearing that thing."

Sighing, Saint shook off the coat and tossed it over one of the empty kitchen chairs. "Better?"

Portia grinned and waved him on.

Saint said to Adam, "Don't let her touch my coat while I'm gone."

Adam said, "I got your back."

"Thanks, man." Then he walked off in the direction of the sickroom.

Saint returned a few minutes later. "I need to get going." He put his coat back on.

Adam had to admit the coat was not the cleanest article of clothing he'd seen lately.

Saint said, "Doc, I'm here for the prototype."

"Sure, let me get it."

Once the shades-wearing Saint had the device in his hand, he studied the swirling black liquid encased inside. "Looks like a liquid black mood ring."

Adam nodded. He'd never thought about it that way, but the man was right.

"It's not going to blow up on me or anything?"

"Nope," Adam assured him. "Even if you hit with a hammer it won't break."

"Cool." And he dropped the cylinder into one of the inside pockets of his coat. "Doc. Nice meeting. Portia, see you later."

"'Bye, Saint."

He strode out, the hem of his coat moving with his steps.

Adam looked at Portia, and she, smiling, shook her head. "He's one of a kind."

And Adam thought, *Just like Max.*

Nineteen

By the fourth day of her confinement Max had recovered enough for the doctor's restrictions to start giving her the blues. She knew she wasn't able to leap tall buildings with a single bound yet, but she could at least sit in a chair outside in the sunshine. When she asked Dr. Lorenz, the doctor said, "No, Max. Maybe in a couple days."

So later that day, when Adam walked into the room with her lunch on a tray, she was sulking even though she was thrilled to see him. "Is there a file hidden in that soup somewhere so I can break out of here?" she asked.

He laughed. "Sorry. Just noodles and chicken."

She sighed. "If I have to stay in this bed much longer I'm going to go insane."

"Lighten up. The bed rest is for your own good."

"So you say."

He placed the tray on the small bed table she used when eating. After positioning it over her sheet-covered middle, he took a seat in the chair beside the bed. "Eat and stop bitching," he said affectionately.

"Only for you."

His amusement was plain. "What's Dr. Lorenz say about commuting your sentence?"

"A couple more days."

"That's because everybody knows you aren't going to take it easy if she lets you out, so she's going to sit on you for as long as she can."

"I suppose," Max said, trying to spoon out soup with her left hand. She was normally right-handed but her wounds were on that side so she was forced to be left-handed until times got better. The liquid sloshed down the front of her T-shirt.

"You want some help?"

"No."

He watched the next spoonful of soup miss the mark, then he sat back and shook his head. "Nothing wrong with needing a little assistance, Miss You."

"I'm fine."

Her shirt continued to be the main beneficiary of Portia's homemade chicken soup, but Adam knew the more he hassled her, the more hard-headed she'd act, so he didn't say anything else. "Have Ruby and Ossie been in to see you today?" More soup dribbled down her shirt, and an amused Adam stayed silent.

"They dropped by earlier." Then her green eyes lifted to his. "You're laughing at me, aren't you?"

"Who me? Nope."

She grinned. "Liar." Then she said, "That's one of the things I like about you, though."

"What?"

"That you let me be me, even when I'm being stubborn."

"No sense in arguing with a woman who knows her own mind."

"And you have never tried to compete with me. That's usually the first thing most men I'm around want to do—show me how manly they are."

"Nothing to compete with you about. I'm bigger, stronger, faster."

"Hey, wait a minute."

"I am. You're badder, of course—without a doubt—but in my world, being a badass won't get you a Nobel, so I've no interest in outtoughing you."

Max asked, "You really think you're faster than me?"

He nodded. "And stronger. I'm a man, Max. It's in the physiology."

"When I get well, we'll see."

He chuckled, "Okay. Now, when I beat you, what do I get?"

"When I beat you, what do I get?"

"Oh, it's like that, is it?"

She nodded. "Yeah, Mr. Jesse Owens Gary."

"I ran track in college. My time for the 220 is third best in school history."

Max tossed back, "That was what, fifty years ago?"

"You're wrong girl. Wrong."

They were both laughing and enjoying each other's company, then Max said seriously, "I miss hanging out with you."

"Miss you, too. Thanks for not dying on me."

"You're welcome. Would you do me a favor?"

"Whatever you want."

"Would you feed me this damn soup. I'm so hungry I could eat the bowl."

He threw back his head and his laughter filled the room. He then picked up the spoon and helped her out.

*   *   *

By day six Max was allowed to leave the room, but only in a wheelchair and only for twenty minutes at a time. The doctor was pleased with the healing. She worried about a setback if Max tried to do too much, though, so Adam became the designated keeper.

The first time he wheeled her out into the hallway she was immediately mobbed by the dogs. They were jumping and barking and prancing around as if it was the happiest day of their canine lives. Max's returning kisses, scratches, and hugs added to the chaos. Her jubilance equaled theirs.

Adam said, "We only have twenty minutes, you all. How about we take this celebration outside."

Ruby, who'd managed to work herself onto Max's lap, barked happily. The tickled Adam pushed the now heavier chair forward.

Max couldn't believe how wonderful it felt to be outside with the sun and the breeze on her face. Because of the uneven ground, the wheelchair couldn't go any farther than the edge of the patio, but she didn't care. She could hear the birds, see the clouds, and smell the nose-twitching scent of the fresh manure Portia used as fertilizer on the hundreds of acres of farmland. Being out of the sickroom easily outweighed the stink, so Max didn't let that spoil her mood either. "Thank you," she said, looking up at the handsome Dr. Gary. To her, he was just as gorgeous as the June day.

"You're welcome."

Ruby and Ossie were chasing each other around the trees. The squirrels and birds, apparently accustomed to the presence and antics of their canine siblings, Jesse and James, didn't pay them any attention. Max, however, enjoyed watching them acting like the dogs they

were. Sometimes the job didn't allow them much freedom or fun, but being here and at home in Texas always
seemed to reenergize them.

Adam could see the happiness in her face and it
made him happy as well. "So, how's this?" In his mind
the fates had provided the perfect day for her breakout
from the Big House.

"You're going to need a whip and a chair to get me
back inside." Her eyes were bright with humor as they
met his.

"I was afraid of that."

The look they shared became so prolonged, the humor faded and neither seemed able to break the contact. They fed themselves on the sight of each other. It
had been a while since they'd been intimate, but what
they were feeling at that moment wasn't lust. As Adam
noted, the connection pulling at them was different,
stronger, wondrous.

He had to lean low to touch his lips to hers, but he
didn't complain; neither did she. The sweet richness of
the kiss obliterated all.

Max cupped his cheek with her left hand. Caressing
the soft hair there, she leaned up so they could better
enjoy the coaxing, teasing, and nibbling. She felt as if
an eternity had passed since they'd been alone and
could be with each other this way. Her breathing increased and so did his. The embers of their previous
encounter had never been fully extinguished, and as
passion began to warm their blood, the sparks glowed,
then caught, making the lovers deepen the kiss.

Adam squatted to decrease the distance between
them and bring their bodies closer. Moving his kisses
to the hollow of her throat, he ran his hand over her

mouth, her jaw, and the trembling skin above the lacy border of the thin green nightgown she had on beneath the matching terry robe. He knew she was in no condition to be loved the way he wanted to make love to her; fully, totally, and scandalously, but it didn't stop him from enjoying the scents of her skin or the soft moan she let out when he cupped her breast.

"Ahem!"

They both jumped.

Dr. Lorenz walked into view. "Your twenty minutes are up, madam."

Max stuck out her lip like a sulking child and Adam did the same.

Laughing, the doctor said, "You two are too much. Take her back inside, Dr. Gary."

"Yes, ma'am."

So Adam pushed Max back to her room, then helped her into the bed, all under the watchful eye of Dr. Lorenz.

In bed now, Max said to her, "You ruined a perfectly good kiss."

She chuckled. "For now, that is my job."

"Well, you're too good at it," Max mockingly groused.

She exited the room but not before calling out, "Five minutes, Dr. Gary."

All he could do was shake his head.

When they were alone again, he said, "She's tough."

"As a Marine drill sergeant."

Adam sat down on the edge of the bed. He leaned over and kissed her gently. "I owe you for that kisses interruptus," he whispered.

She said sassily, "I love it when you talk dirty."

Adam had never met a woman like her before in his life. "You are so outrageous."

"But you enjoy it."

His voice softened. "Yes. Yes, I do." He stroked a lingering finger down her cheek. "Rest up. I'll come back and break you out again later."

In the bed and supported by the pillows, Max could feel herself drifting away and thought maybe she wasn't as ready to rock and roll as she'd led herself to believe. "Promise?"

He slowly crossed his heart. "Cross my heart."

"Good," she whispered, pleased. "I'm going to sleep now."

He kissed her forehead. "Sweet dreams."

And they were sweet because she dreamed of a tender caring man named Adam.

That evening, Portia told Adam that the Bureau had captured Pearl's rumpled companion Vlad Oskar at a small airport near Miami. He'd been busted trying to jack a private plane and was held by the local police until the agents arrived. At the preliminary court hearing, the federal prosecutor had little trouble convincing the presiding judge that the man was a flight risk, so his passport was confiscated and he was remanded without bond to the Dade County jail.

"Good," Max said when Adam relayed the news to her later on. They were outside enjoying the peacefulness of the night. Max was in her wheelchair and he was seated in a lawn chair beside her.

"Now that you're technically done guarding me, what's next?"

Her shrug made the stitches in her shoulder pull and she winced silently. "Don't know. Home to Texas for sure, but afterward? Probably sniff out another job."

He went quiet.

Max asked him, "That bothers you, doesn't it?"

He looked her way. "I can't lie."

"This is what I do."

"And it almost got you killed. What if there's nobody around next time to drive you? What if you get shot in the gut? Suppose it's your heart?"

Max reached over and placed her hand on top of his. They were destined to have this conversation, she supposed, but at what cost? When he linked his fingers with hers, the emotions that flooded her were so strong they tightened her throat.

He said to her, "Max, I'm not a super hero or an international spy—none of that. I'm just a regular everyday brother who has a thing for a remarkable woman he'd like to see grow. Watching you get shot almost killed me. Then, because you have this secret life, I couldn't even take you to the E.R."

Max closed her eyes and tried to delude herself into believing that the pain emanated from her shoulder wound and not her heart.

He told her, "If you and I aren't on the same page, fine. I'll slink off into the sunset and we can stop this conversation right here, but I have to tell you how I feel."

"And I appreciate it," she said. "And just so you know, I do care for you, Adam. A lot. I'd like this thing between us to grow, too. But."

"You're not going to change what you do."

She shook her head in the dark. "No."

He shrugged. "Then I'll have to respect that, even if I don't like it."

When he gently withdrew his fingers from hers, she knew their time together was coming to an end, and all the tender brightness he'd brought into her life began withering inside her like a dying rose.

Over the next few days, Dr. Lorenz gave Max five-pound hand weights to lift so that the muscles in her shoulder and upper back would regain their strength, flexibility, and tone. Adam was no less caring or concerned, and he and Max were able to enjoy each other's company, but things had changed between them and they both knew it.

One evening at dinner, Adam announced that he was going back to Michigan and his work. Now that the prototype was safe, he had no reason to hang around. "I talked to the NASA people this afternoon and they want me to come down and supervise some tests on the prototype. They're thinking it might help power some of their interplanetary probes."

Portia said, "Sounds promising. I can take care of your flight arrangements home if you'd like."

"That'd be great." Adam planned to attend the President's dinner in the fall, but frankly, all he wanted to do now was go home and lick his wounds.

Portia said, "I've enjoyed your company, Adam."

"And I've had a good time. Thanks for the hospitality."

He looked over at Max, who met his eyes and said, "Have a safe trip home."

"I will."

Max was able to walk under her own power now, and she stood and left Portia and Adam at the table.

Portia didn't say anything for a moment, but seeing Adam's tight jaw and the distance in his eyes, she finally offered, "You can't turn a lioness into a house cat."

"I know. That's why I need to go back to my life."

"I'm sorry, Adam," Portia replied, her voice sad.

"So am I."

Then he left the table to gather up his meager belongings in preparation for the morning flight back to Michigan.

Max looked up at the moon and wondered what was wrong with her. After her second divorce, she'd never allowed a man to give her the blues. Over the years, she'd had trysts with matadors, race car drivers, and even a few European captains of industry, and once the flames burned out with each of them, they'd said *Ciao* and parted with no regrets. All were men of action drawn to her strength and drive the same way she'd been drawn to theirs. But what she felt in response to Adam's leaving was new, and scary as hell. *Why him*? she asked herself for what seemed like the umpteenth time. What was it about Adam that was tearing her up this way? Why did the prospect of maybe never seeing him again leave her so depressed? She ran her hands through her short hair, confused, frustrated, and angry that a mild-mannered but very sexy *lab scientist,* of all people, would have the audacity to ask that she take a look at changing her life.

She was realistic enough to know that she couldn't run around playing Storm until she was old and gray. She'd readily admit to not being as physically sharp as she'd been a decade ago. Skills eroded, reflexes slowed, and eventually people like her had to find other employment in order to keep themselves, their colleagues, and their missions out of harm's way. So her question became, was she mad at him for wanting her to change her life, or was she just mad, period, because she knew he was right? Truthfully, she was scared to look at the answer, and because she wouldn't know what to do with the answer even if she had one, Max chose not to deal with it at all, at least for now. Instead, she looked up at the moon and hoped the misery would eventually subside.

It didn't. When she woke up the following morning, she was just as blue as she'd been going to bed.

Breakfast was a forced affair.

When she came into the kitchen, he and Portia were already there. Good mornings were exchanged. Max looked at him. Adam looked back. Max sat.

Portia said, "Adam and I have been talking about collaborating on some future projects."

Max forced a smile. "That sounds exciting." She glanced over at him and found him watching her. Whatever he was feeling was hidden deep beneath that unreadable mask. "Looks like a good day to fly," she said, needing to break the lengthening silence. Unlike her mood, it was sunny and bright outside.

"Yeah, it does," he replied.

Neither had anything to say after that.

When it was time for him to go, she pasted on her false smile and walked with him out to the cab waiting to take him to the airport. The dogs trotting alongside were subdued and silent. They seemed to have picked up on the fact that he was leaving and had followed him around all morning.

Adam opened the cab door and tossed his duffel inside. He then looked down at the woman he wanted to share life with but couldn't. "Thanks for everything."

"No problem."

Both felt the words that could be said, but Adam thought it best if they made this parting short. "Call me sometime and let me know how you're doing."

"I'll do that. You do the same."

They both knew they wouldn't unless one or the other relented.

Adam wanted to kiss her, hold her, feel her heart beating against his own, but he didn't. If he touched her, he'd shatter, so he said, "Take it easy, Max."

"You, too."

He gave the dogs an emotion-filled scratch across their backs. Ruby whined and Ossie began to bark. Adam took a deep breath, got into the cab and closed the door.

As the cab drove off and took Adam Gary out of Max Blake's life, she stood in the driveway watching, but he didn't look back.

Adam took a cab home from the airport and was surprised by the yellow police tape over the opening in the gate. The fence was still torn up from where Max had punched the Honda through, but he didn't understand the reason for the tape until he walked into the house.

The interior had been trashed. Sledgehammers had been taken to the walls, the kitchen cabinets and what had been inside them strewn everywhere, and the refrigerator lying on its side, its contents puddling on the floor. The big glass door leading out to the patio had apparently been shot out, with bullet holes in the trim and shattered glass covering the furniture and floor.

Adam ran down to the lab, noticing more destruction to the walls on the way. He assumed the destruction had been carried out by the men on the jet skis and their friends looking for the prototype. His lab was in shambles. Busted equipment, monitors, and books littered the place. A herd of cattle couldn't have done more damage. Grim-faced, he picked his way through the broken glass and forest of papers just to make sure the carnage was total, and it was. Nothing was intact, not his computers, copiers, or anything else that had been kept in the lab and the outer office. The only saving grace was that because he'd taken Max's advice, he had everything on portable disks. That knowledge didn't lessen his anger at the damages or at the fact that ten years' worth of work was now about as valuable as napkins from Mickey D's blowing down the street.

He also took solace from knowing they hadn't been able to find the prototype. Max's face floated across his mind, but he pushed it aside. The less he thought about her, the better he'd be able to handle her not being around.

The second floor had taken a hit, too. Bedding was slashed, his bookcases had been turned over, and the drawers of his dresser tossed across the room. Kaitlin's pink and white room had not been spared, either. While surveying her damaged things, he made a note to call her later.

But at the moment he had other calls to make. The first was to the police. They expressed regret that they hadn't been able to catch the perps who'd annihilated the house, and they assured him the investigation would be ongoing. He thanked them and made a second call, to his mother. She didn't pick up, so he left her a message, saying he'd be there sometime tomorrow and would call later with the specifics. His last call, aided by directory assistance, was to the local Cadillac dealer. Adam didn't own a car, but because of all the patents he'd sold over the years, he had plenty of money, so by seven o' clock that evening a salesman knocked on his partially attached front door and handed over the keys to a black, fresh-out-the-box Escalade that was parked in the drive, gassed up and ready to go. Adam took the keys, signed the paperwork, and named the powerful new truck Ossie.

The day after Adam's departure, Max made her own preparations to leave. She and the dogs would be flying home to Texas, and after that she wasn't sure. She didn't want to jump into another job right away, mainly because she hadn't completely healed, and because she wasn't real interested even though she knew keeping busy would help banish her ennui. Adam stayed on her mind in spite of her determination not to think about him. His leaving seemed to have left a hole in her life she didn't know he had filled. *No use crying over spilled milk, the man's gone.* Life as she knew it would continue.

But was it a life she wanted? she asked herself on the plane ride home to Texas. Until meeting him, the world had been her oyster, and whether she wanted it raw or fried, the choice had been up to her. After two bad marriages, the idea of a long-term hookup with any man was about as desirable as root canal without an anesthetic, but who knew she'd meet a man with a brain the size of Texas and a heart to match? He'd even bitten the bullet and taken a liking to her dogs, and with his history, that was a major undertaking. Yes, he'd acted like a complete jerk the first day they met, and she'd been convinced he was carved from stone, but beneath the lab coat was a man she'd enjoyed cooking for, laughing with, and walking on the beach alongside. She could relax around him, and having to prove she was the baddest bitch on the block wasn't necessary because he didn't care. He came from a world that valued brain power, not firepower, and if she wanted to walk in his world she'd have to lay down her guns—not because he believed a girl shouldn't have them, but because he preferred her alive. Max had no problem with that. She liked being alive, too. However, the life she led had meaning, purpose, and she was proud to be one of the shadowy shape shifters fighting the world's crime. For a small-town girl with a GED, she'd come a long way, and she wasn't ready to get off the ride, at least not yet.

Her mama, Michele, was waiting for her in Baggage Claim. They shared a long embrace, a mutual affectionate grin, then went to retrieve her bags. It took almost thirty minutes for the dogs to be transported to the terminal, but Max knew her mother would've waited until Christmas for her granddogs to arrive, as she affectionately called Ruby and Ossie.

The dogs were happy to see her as well, and stood patiently while she attached their leashes. After taking a short walk from the terminal to the parking garage, the reunited Blakes got into Michele's new green Navigator and she drove away from the airport.

Max could feel herself physically and mentally relax

as they rolled by the familiar landscape. Although the Blake land was outside of the city, Max was home.

Her mother said, "First your sister, and now you."

Max turned. "What do you mean?"

"She's here, too. Got in last night."

"JT's here?"

"Yep."

Max liked hearing that. Because of their jobs, they rarely got to hang out except during the winter holidays. Max loved her big sister. "How's she doing?"

"Okay, I guess. Usual drama with those basketball boys, but some man is giving her the flux. She's here trying to figure it out."

Max leaned her head back on the seat. "Aren't we all?"

"You, too?"

"Oh, Mama, you just don't know."

Her mother said with amusement, "Lord. Do I need to put a sign saying 'Heartbreak Hotel' out front?"

Max grinned. Her mother was a crazy woman. "Hold off, but I'll let you know." Max looked over at the woman who'd given her birth, taught her to read, and turned her sixteen-year-old self over to the juvenile authorities because it was all she had left. Max loved her like she loved breathing. "I'm glad to be home."

Her mother smiled back. "I'm glad you're here, too, babygirl."

Twenty

Adam had grown up in suburban Chicago, and when he drove up to the house he'd lived in most of his life, his mother was out front watering her flowers with the hose. Dressed in her sneaks, jeans, and a faded T-shirt, she didn't look like the nation's premier African-American woman of letters, but she did look like his mama.

She turned toward the street to see who was parking in front of her house, and when Adam stepped out and came around the truck, a smile spread across her still youthful face. Hurrying to turn off the water, she wiped her hands on her jeans and held out her arms.

The grinning Adam hugged her close and twirled her around until the laughing began. "Put me down, boy!"

But he knew she loved it. He'd been greeting her this way since high school. He kissed her on the cheek then did as she'd asked.

"I got the call from the government folks saying you were on lockdown. Are you done with the prototype? Should I start looking for something to wear to the Nobel ceremonies?"

The grin spread across his face. "Nothing on the Nobel, but you might want to start looking for something to wear to the White House."

She asked skeptically, "The White House?"

He nodded. Thoughts of the fall ceremony made him think about Max.

His mother must have seen the clouds roll across his mood, because she asked, "What's up with you, Adam?"

"Long story."

Lauren McDonald Gary looked up. "Oh really? Does it explain why you're driving somebody's Escalade?"

Adam's humor returned. "It's mine."

"Yours?"

"Yeah. Why do you look so surprised?"

"When was the last time you owned a car?"

He stopped and made a show of thinking. "Well, let's see?"

She waved her hand. "No no. Who are you and what have you done with my used to be really boring son?"

Adam began to laugh. "I'm the same me."

"Not if you're driving that. The story behind this must be a whopper, so come on in and tell all. By the way," she added as she hooked an arm affectionately around his waist and walked them up the stairs, "it's wonderful to see you, babyboy."

He pulled her close. "Good seeing you, too, Mom."

When they entered, Adam went straight to the kitchen. "Is there anything to eat?"

Her dark eyes sparkled with mirth. "Now that's the son I know."

She fried him up a quick hamburger, which he devoured with all the gusto of a twelve-year-old.

"Why's the table set in the dining room?" he asked, coming back in the house after getting his bags out of Ossie. "If you're having company over, I can stay at a hotel if I'm in the way."

"Please. It's just your dad. I promised him dinner while he's in town."

Adam said, "Well, now."

"Don't start. I do it every now and then. When he's been on the road like he has for the last month or so, a home-cooked meal gives him a chance to catch his breath."

Adam sat in the chair across the table from her. "He still loves you, Mom. Are you going to make him stand out in the rain forever?"

"He loved me when he was married to me, but that didn't keep him from cheating. Besides, a little rain never killed anybody."

"But it's been a long time."

"Yes, it has. Hope he's been buying good umbrellas. Now, enough about me. What's been going on with you?"

They'd been each other's confidante for as long as Adam had been alive. Pregnant and married at sixteen, she'd lost his father, Craig, to the war in Vietnam in 1967. She'd married Ray Gary when Adam was five and divorced him ten years later. No matter the trial or the triumph, she'd always been there for Adam, and he'd walk through fire for her. "Do you want the short version or the long one?"

"Door number two. The long version."

So he started at the beginning with Max's arrival.

Partway through, she interrupted and asked, "Dogs?"

"Rottweilers."

"Oh, lord."

"It's okay. I'm fine with them."

"Really?"

He nodded.

"Okay," she said, sounding doubtful, "go ahead."

From there he gave her the highlights: the jet skiers, the car chases, and Max's confrontation with Pearl and his men. Then he told her about Max being shot.

"Is she okay?" Lauren asked anxiously. "Girlfriend sounds like Linda Hamilton in *The Terminator*."

"She was healing up when I left."

"I'm glad she was with you, and that you're in one piece."

"So am I."

Lauren studied him. "So what happened between you and Max that made you go out and buy an Escalade?"

"Nothing,"

She sat back, folded her arms and waited.

He sighed. *Mamas*. He didn't stand a chance of getting out of the kitchen alive unless he told her something. "I could honestly see me spending the rest of my life with her, but she doesn't want to give up being Linda Hamilton."

"Why should she?"

Adam placed his forehead on the table for a few long seconds, then looked up. "When you and Pops were first together and totally in love, how would you have felt if one of his crazy lady fans some kind of way got on stage and shot him right before your eyes?"

She stiffened.

"The force knocks him down, blood's everywhere—"

She held up her hand. "Enough."

"I couldn't even take her to an E.R. because of who she is and what she does."

"You really care for her, don't you?"

He nodded. "I do, but it's not going to happen, so life goes on."

"I'm sorry, Adam."

"Nothing to be sorry about. I'm a big boy. I'll get over it."

But he wondered if it would be in this lifetime or the next.

When Raymond "Sweet Ray" Gary showed up at the house, the sight of Adam made him break out in a surprised grin. "Adam!"

The two men shared an emotional embrace. Ray was the only father Adam had ever known, and he loved him as much as he did his mother. When they stepped back, Ray said, "Lauren didn't say you were coming in when I called her yesterday morning."

"I didn't know," she said easily.

Adam checked out his pops looking dap in his sky blue stage clothes. "I'm liking those blue gators."

Ray looked down at the alligator skin shoes. "Picked these up the last time I was in Detroit. Gator capital of the world, you know."

"I do." Adam thought about his own adventure in Detroit and another man, with the nickname Sweet.

Ray said, "Your mother and I tried to call you for days after we saw the news about the prototype but couldn't catch you."

Lauren ushered the men into the dining room. "That's because Mr. Wizard here was costarring in his own James Bond movie."

"What?" Ray stopped, looked at his stepson and asked, "What's she talking about."

So while they had dinner, Adam told the story again.

Ray cut into his pork chop. "Am I right to assume the Lady Max is fine?"

Leave it to Pops to ferret out the truth. "I didn't say that."

"You didn't have to, I could hear it in your voice. Chocolate, caramel, or vanilla?"

Lauren was looking at him sideways.

"Caramel," Adam replied.

"Eyes?"

"Green."

Ray looked up from his plate. "Whoa."

Adam never ceased to be amazed by his pops. "But nothing's happening."

"Why not?"

"Because Wonder Woman fights better when mild-mannered Clark Kent isn't hanging on to the edge of her cape."

Ray met his eyes, studied his son for a moment, then asked, "You want to clip her wings?"

"Nope, just her gun hand."

His mother said, "But that gun hand kept you alive, right?"

"Yeah, but—"

"It must have been terrible seeing her hurt like that, but would you give up chemistry if she asked you to?"

"It's not the same, Mom."

"Why not? Suppose you accidentally mix the wrong chemicals. You wind up in the burn ward looking like the mummy, and she says, 'Oh please, Mr. Wizard, no more chemicals.' What would you say?"

Adam sat silent.

Ray forked up some of the green beans on his plate and said to Adam, "I don't even know why you started this. You know Ms. Debate Queen over there was going to beat you down, especially on something that could be called a woman's issue, quote unquote."

Lauren shot her ex a look but there was a smile behind it. "Why should men be the only folks allowed to blow stuff up?"

Adam met his mother's eyes. "So you think I'm being overprotective," he declared.

"No, darling, I think you're in love."

High-powered sports agent Jessi Theresa Blake, aka JT, looked over at her baby sister Max lying on the pool's edge and asked, "This is *the* Dr. Adam Gary, the inventing brother who was on the cover of *Time* magazine last year?"

Max nodded.

"Since when did you start hanging around with men with IQs?"

"Shut up," Max said, chuckling from behind her shades. The sun felt good. "It was a job at first. Now?" Max shrugged.

"Now you're wishing you'd read more than just *Fanny Hill* in school, I'll bet."

Max snorted. "I will shoot you, you know."

JT yelled to Michele, who was inside the house watching a DVD of *For Love of Ivy* with her grand-dogs. "Mama! Maxie said she's going to shoot me!"

Michele yelled back, "Maxie! Only plastic bullets. Okay?"

"Okay, Mama!"

The sisters laughed, then Max tossed back, "From what I'm hearing, I'm not the only one with manly issues."

JT sighed.

Max turned over on the warm tile and propped herself on her side. "Spill it."

Brown eyes met green ones, then JT said, as if confused, "I think I'm in love."

The wonder and surprise on her sister's chocolate face made Max start to laugh. "Really?"

"Yeah, I think so."

"I thought I was in love, too, twice, remember? Sure it's not the flu?"

JT grabbed one of the pillows off the chaise and threw it at Max. Max yelled out, "Mama!"

Michele hollered back, "Interrupt me with 'Mama!' one more time and you're both going to your rooms!"

They fell out.

Once they regained some sense, Max asked seriously, "Why do you think it's love?"

"Can't eat, can't sleep. Think about him all the time. Dream about him."

"Then why are you here instead of where he is?"

"I don't know," she said glumly. "Scared, I guess."

"Of him?

"No, of me. I've been by myself for so long. What am I going to do with a man?"

"He treat you good?"

"Always. A little arrogant, though, but hey, so am I."

"Then what's the problem?"

She shrugged. "I suppose I just need to figure out what I really want."

Silence settled between them.

JT finally asked, "What about you?"

Max rolled over onto her back and sighed with the same frustration JT had a moment before. "I don't know, either. He's so smart. He's kind, nice, and fabulous in bed, by the way."

"Then I'll throw your question back: Why are you here instead of where he is?"

"He wants me to give up the Life."

JT's response was blunt. "I ain't mad at him. Mama and I worry about you all the time. Where you are. Are you alive?"

"I know," Max replied softly. Because her sister and mother loved her, they rarely expressed their fears about what she did for a living, but Max could see it in her mother's eyes every time a new assignment called—the fear that maybe that good-bye would be the last.

JT pointed out, "Even Pam Grier got too old to play Coffy, Max."

Max smiled under her glasses.

"So what are you going to do?"

Max gave a minute shrug. "Who knows, but if I turn in my stuff, it'll have to be because *I* want to, not because somebody else does. I do that and I'll be letting folks chip away at my soul for the rest of my life."

"Deep."

Max tossed back with a smile. "Thought you'd like it."

* * *

That evening, Max called Kaitlin. They'd exchanged numbers a few days before Kent's death. Max had begun to like Kaitlin toward the end. Finding out how the young woman was doing in the wake of her father's death was long overdue.

"I'm doing, okay," Kaitlin replied in answer to Max's question. "After the autopsy, I had him cremated. The service was last week."

"I'm sorry for your loss."

"Thanks. The Bureau agent in Grand Rapids said his murder had something to do with South Africa?"

Max just said, "Hmm."

"They didn't tell me a lot because they're still doing the investigation. Now tell me what happened to the house."

"What do you mean? Which house?"

"Adam's house on the lake. Sheriff Ramos called me and said the place was wrecked."

Max sat up straight. "Really?"

"You weren't there?"

"No. It must have happened after Adam and I left to deliver the prototype."

"Supposedly there are big holes in the walls, and I guess Adam's lab is completely ruined. They jacked up all the computers, busted up his counters. Do you think it was somebody looking for the prototype?"

"Probably." She assumed the jet ski riders were the culprits, and Max's heart went out to him. Luckily, he'd downloaded his work, but still, it must have been hard to walk in on something like that.

Kaitlin said, "Is he there with you?"

"No. We parted ways after we took care of the prototype."

"Oh," was all Kaitlin said, then added, "he left me a message and gave me his new number. I tried calling him back, but I got his voice mail."

"Give me the new number, maybe I'll try and run him down, too."

Kaitlin gave Max the number and she wrote it down.

"Thanks for letting me know about the house," Max added sincerely.

"No problem."

"Again, my condolences on your loss."

"Thanks."

Max clicked off. Kaitlin's description of the house's damage was disturbing. If it was as bad as she'd made it sound Adam probably had to find someplace else to stay. She wondered if she should call him. After all they'd been through together, she was naturally concerned, and a part of her wanted to hear his voice badly, but other parts were jumping up and down shouting *No!*

Max bit the bullet and called him. While it rang, she took in a few deep breaths. On the fourth ring she was kicked over to his voice mail. She thought about what she could say, but her thoughts and emotions were so jumbled, she couldn't get it together. In the end she cut the connection and silently wished him well.

Adam and Lauren spent the evening at the concert Ray had come into town for. They had a good time watching the show from backstage. It had been years since Adam had seen his pops perform. The pipes weren't as tight and his range wasn't as wide, but he could still bring down the house with the signature ballads the women loved.

"Nice show," Adam said to her as they drove home in the Escalade.

"The man can still sing, I give him that."

"He could be singing just to you, if you'd let him."

She remained quiet for a moment, and he could tell she was thinking back. "Your mama's too old for heartache. The first time around almost killed me, remember?"

He did. The divorce became final a few months after Adam's fifteenth birthday. It was a painful time for everyone involved. "He still sending you flowers for your birthday?"

"My birthday, your birthday, his birthday. Lord, that man."

Adam heard the wonder laced through her chuckle. "You still love him?"

"Never stopped."

They were at the curb in front of the house. "Well?"

She turned his way. She knew what he was asking. "I don't know, babyboy. We'll see."

He nodded. It was all he could ask.

Upstairs in the guest room that had once been his bedroom, he checked his calls. When he saw her number, he went still. *Max.* All sorts of emotions flooded him. It had been nearly a month since they had seen each other last, and in that time the memories hadn't dimmed. He wondered what made her call. He checked his watch. Eleven-thirty. He knew she was a night owl, and so, taking the chance that she was still up, he hit redial.

When she picked up, he said, "Max?"

"Hey," she said softly. "How are you?"

Hearing her voice made his need for her swell inside

with such intensity he had to close his eyes and wait for the sharp sensations to subside. "Doing okay. How're you? How's your shoulder?"

"Good and good."

He smiled.

Silence.

Adam kept his tone light. "I see you called."

"Yeah, I did. Just checking up on you. Kaitlin gave me your new number and told me about the house."

"They hit it pretty good. I'm looking for a new place."

"Where are you now?"

"At my mother's. Outside Chicago. You?"

"Texas."

Adam wanted to talk with her until sunrise. "So things are okay?"

"Yeah, they are. How's the work going?"

"Pretty good. Still dealing with the NASA thing. A couple of other projects in the pipeline, but finding a new place to live is at the top of the list."

"Makes sense."

Silence.

He asked, "How are the dogs?"

She said, "Fine. My mother's spoiling them worse than Portia, though. Always does. She calls them her granddogs."

"Tell them I said hello."

"I will."

Silence rose again.

She broke it by saying. "I didn't want anything when I called. Just wanted to see how you were doing."

"Glad you called."

"Me, too. Well, I should let you go. Take care, Adam."

"You, too, Max."

And it was over.

Down in Texas, Max held the now silent phone against her heart and looked up at the moon. Hearing his voice brought back all the memories she'd been trying to run away from. Lord, she missed him.

JT stepped outside to join her. "You okay?"

Max said solemnly, "Yeah."

"Was that him?"

Max nodded.

JT said softly, "We're a mess, you know that?"

Max smiled.

"I'm going back to L.A. in the morning. You want to come? We could do some major shopping and call it retail therapy."

Max grinned. "Nah. Think I'll hang here for a little while longer."

Jessi said, "Okay."

"I'll take you to the airport in the morning, though."

"That'll be cool."

After a few moments of silence, JT said, "I'm going to bed. Don't be out here all night."

"I won't. Good night, Jes."

"Night, Max. See you in the morning."

Three days after JT flew out, Max made a few calls. There was a job in Singapore with her name on it, if she wanted it. She agreed to the terms of the contract then made the necessary arrangements to fly out the next morning.

Her mother drove her to the airport. Michele held onto the leashed Ossie and Ruby while Max took the bags out of the back of the Navigator.

Once she had everything on the curb, Max held her mother tight. "I'll see you, Mama."

Michele squeezed her tight, then whispered emotionally, "Come back to me. Okay?"

"I will. Don't worry." But Max knew her mother would worry despite her reassurances and it tightened her heart.

Michele said a final good-bye to her granddogs, then wiping at the tears filling her eyes, gave Max a parting smile, a wave, and drove away.

Max watched until the Navigator left her sight, then she and the dogs headed for the airport check-in and the plane ride back to her life.

Twenty-one

In Singapore, Max and her dogs joined a team of shadows hunting down a gang of smugglers trafficking in ancient Cambodian artifacts. Most of the stolen goods were being plundered from temple sites in Thailand and from the fabled temples of Angkor Wat in nearby Cambodia. Among the hundreds of items missing were stone statues of the Buddha, handrails from nine-hundred-year-old Buddhist structures, and busts of mythical angels, known as *apsaras,* being sold on the down low in the West for sixty thousand dollars apiece. Most amazing to Max were the reports of entire stone walls, beautifully carved and decorated with symbols of the Buddhist faith, stolen from the temples, even though some of the slabs weighed as much as ten tons. The antiques were sent from Cambodia, then via Singapore on to Thailand. From there they were shipped to buyers in the United States and Europe.

It was a grueling investigation. The Cambodian countryside where most of the smuggling originated was thick with heat and insects. Max didn't know who was more miserable, the people on the team or her dogs.

Ruby and Ossie were especially susceptible to the blood-
sucking beasties that swarmed over them, looking for
lunch, but as always, they were troopers. The team spent
many days hacking their way through heavy vegetation
to check out temple sites inaccessible by car, with long
climbs through the sometimes mountainous terrain, but
were finally successful in making a bust.

They'd received a tip that took them to the home of a
prominent Danish businessman in the city of Ayut-
thaya, the former capital of old Siam, located a few
hours drive from Bangkok. Apparently, the Dane's
wife, angry over her husband's affair with one of the
couple's female servants, had gone to the authorities
and dropped a dime. Max and her people raided the
house the next day and hit the jackpot. The home and a
storage structure behind it were filled with antiques.

That night, Max stood in her hot, cheap hotel room
in Bangkok and looked at herself in the mirror. Her
face and arms were covered with bites. Her legs bore
the scars of leeches and her tied-up hair was through.
She was so tired and so ready to go home she could
have walked. Ossie had scratched himself raw in some
places because of all the bites, and Ruby hadn't fared
much better. It was the end of August. They'd been on
this mission for eight weeks, and she was glad it was
finally over.

She'd also come to a decision. After eight weeks of
fighting through jungle, eating government-issue prefab
food, and sleeping on the ground, it was time to find
some other way to pay the bills. She no longer had the
head for what she was doing. The decision hadn't come
to her as an epiphany but over the course of the job. The
long days were no longer filled with excitement, as

they'd once been. It had been stone hard work, and on those steamy hot nights when it had been too uncomfortable to sleep, she'd had time to evaluate her life. She thought about the look of worry in her mother's eyes. She thought about JT's sisterly fears, and she thought about Adam. She hadn't spoken with him since leaving the States, and the void of not having him around was still open and raw. In the past, working had always been good at banishing whatever ailed her, but not this time. The more she worked, the more she thought about him, what he might be doing, and if he'd found someone else to spend time with. Basically, she had the same symptoms JT had described, and like JT, she had come to the conclusion that in spite of her previous denials, she was very much in love.

Max turned from the mirror and plopped down onto the thin mattress on the wobbly bed. Tomorrow she and the dogs would be flying out of Southeast Asia for the long trip home. Once there, she planned to make a few phone calls to cement her decision to back away from the Life, then call Adam.

Adam looked at the beautiful golden-skinned woman seated across the table from him and wished he were elsewhere. He'd met her a few weeks ago at the gym where he worked out, and she'd seemed nice enough, not to mention that her height and build reminded him of Max. They'd had a few conversations, a couple of coffees at the Starbucks next door to the gym, and when he asked her to dinner, she'd shyly agreed. Apparently, the shyness had been an act. She'd been talking nonstop since he picked her up at her apartment. He knew all about her hospital administrative job and why she couldn't stand working there—apparently, they were hassling her about being fifteen minutes late to work every day. He heard about her family, and that she was suing her sister for credit card theft. Last but not least, he was given a too-vivid description of why the men her girlfriends were dating were all dogs.

"You know, I Googled you," she said then. Her name was Shanté.

"Really?" he said, trying to be polite. Luckily, he could see the light at the end of the tunnel. They were having dessert and he wanted her to hurry up and finish her cheesecake so he could take her home.

"You're really famous, Adam. When you said you were a chemist, I thought you might be like this other brother I dated a few months ago. He claimed to be one, but turned out to be a janitor at a water treatment plant."

Adam had no idea what to say to that, so instead he took a bite of his apple pie à la mode and waited to hear what she'd say next.

"That thing you invented must have made you a lot of money. Probably set you up for life."

Adam studied her. *Here we go.* "I'm okay," was his only response.

"Good-looking brother like you needs a steady woman." Then she asked in a sultry voice, "You wouldn't happen to be holding auditions tonight, would you?"

Adam told the truth. "No. I'm flying to D.C. in the morning. Need to turn in early."

"I don't have to stay all night, you know," she offered with a sly smile. "Do a little bit of auditioning tonight and a little bit after you get back from D.C."

"Thanks for the offer and I'm real flattered, but I'll have to pass."

She took offense. "What? You gay?"

Adam looked around, and when he caught the eye of his waiter, raised his hand and said, "Check, please."

After dropping her off, Adam drove home to his new condo in a downtown Chicago high-rise overlooking Lake Michigan. There was valet parking, a 24/7 grocery, an on-call maintenance crew, and maid service, to name a few of the amenities. For all the money he paid, he thought it should have come with season tickets to every sports franchise in town, too, but he liked the place. It was large without being cavernous, spacious but welcoming. He'd purchased furniture, art for the walls, new electronics—including a flat screen for his media room, and one for his bedroom—then settled in to enjoy it.

That had been in late June, and now in late September he had to admit that he felt like a changed man. After having spent the last ten years holed up in his lab hunched over his work, he'd forgotten how much energy there was to be found in big cities like Chicago, and how revitalizing that energy could be. The people, the myriad offerings of food, entertainment, and sports, all worked together to spur his decision to take a hard look at his life and make some adjustments.

He'd decided to take a year off. No labs, no work, no nothing but what he wanted to do. Because of the prototype and his other patents, if he never worked another day in his life he could still live to the fullest and pay his bills. With that in mind he was going to kick back and try and figure out how he wanted his future to play out. Did he want to start a new project? Teach? See the

Great Wall of China, maybe? He could cruise around the world if he wanted, or join a dig in Egypt's Valley of the Kings. He had given himself the permission and the freedom to do whatever he wanted in the next twelve months, and he planned to take full advantage.

He walked to the windows and looked out over the dark lake. *Where's Max?* In the last two months the question had gone from a roar to a whisper, but it was still there, haunting him, coming to him in the middle of the night. *Where's Max?* Adam didn't know. Back in July, he'd tried calling her, but her number was no longer active. He'd called Portia a few days later to talk to her about putting their proposed collaboration on hold. At the end of their conversation, when he asked about Max, all Portia would say was that she and the dogs were out of the country.

Tomorrow he would be flying to D.C. to attend the state dinner promised by the President, then receive the medal Adam still didn't think he should be getting. Max was supposed to be getting one, too, but he had no idea if she was still abroad or back in the States. He'd find out soon enough. One part of him hoped she would be there, if only to see her and reassure himself that she was okay. Another part, still fixated on a relationship that would never be, hoped she'd sent her regrets instead.

Max flew into D.C. for the dinner a day early so she could handle some business and so her mother, who'd never been to the nation's capital, could see the sights. Leaving JT and Michele to explore the Smithsonian after lunch, Max hopped into a cab and directed the cabbie to take her to the White House.

Her credentials got her through the security checkpoints and she was soon standing outside the Oval Office, waiting for her appointment with the President. When her time came, a female aide ushered her in then left her alone. When she came in, he stood and said affectionately, "Ah, Lady Storm."

"Afternoon, Mr. President. How are you?"

"I was fine until I heard you were resigning."

Max gave him JT's line. "Even Pam Grier got too old to play Coffy, sir."

"And a pity that was, too. Though she did look good in *Jackie Brown*."

Max chuckled. "Your wife know you have a thing for Ms. Grier?"

He nodded. "Just like I know she has a thing for Denzel." He then motioned her to a chair. "Have a seat. The Thai ambassador sends his regards for the excellent work."

"I'm glad we were able to get it done."

Once they were settled in their seats and comfortable, she asked, "How'd the South African thing play out?"

"Last I heard, the government was still rounding up the conspirators. They have recovered quite a few weapons, too. Planes, stingers, and a huge cache of counterfeit U.S. Treasury bills. They're keeping us posted."

"Good. What about the renegades?"

"We're rounding them up, too. Some will be given a chance to resign, others we plan to try for treason."

Max was glad to hear that.

"I've signed your resignation request, but you know I didn't want to. We'll miss you a great deal."

"I appreciate that, and truthfully, I won't mind being called every now and then if you get in a pinch."

"I'll keep that in mind. So, what are your plans?"

"Depends."

"On what?"

"On what happens when I meet up with a certain scientist again tomorrow evening."

He looked surprised. "Really?"

Max nodded.

"That's interesting. Anything I can do to help?"

Max smiled. "I think I have it covered."

"Well, if anything comes to you, give us a call. His stepfather has agreed to perform for us, you know."

"No, I didn't. My mother's going to have a fit. She loves him. My sisters and I grew up listening to his songs."

"He and his ex-wife have confirmed."

A young female aide stuck her head in the door and said quietly, "Sorry to disturb you, sir, but the senators are here for their two o' clock."

"Thanks, Linda."

Linda withdrew and the door was closed again.

Max stood. "Let me get out of here so you can do some work. Thanks for everything, sir."

He stood. "You're welcome. Your country appreciates your service, Max."

The former lady Marine gave the general a crisp salute.

He returned it sharply, then Max headed out.

Adam gazed around the ballroom and felt like Where's Waldo in a celebrity magazine. Everywhere he turned he saw the famous in science, film, literature, and music.

Now that he no longer lived underground, he could connect faces to who they were and what they were known for: like the brother across the room whose directing won him an Oscar this year, and the blond sister in the tasteful green gown whose hip-hop CD was riding the top of the charts. It was a heady, eclectic gathering, and Adam, nursing a small cognac, was impressed and honored to be there. A jazz group was playing background to the all voices and the visiting of the guests, and the music fit the atmosphere seamlessly.

His mother walked back to his side after having spent a few moments talking to the First Lady. Lauren, like all the other elegantly gowned women in the room, looked gorgeous in her black dress and jewels. Adam and the men were wearing tuxedos.

"Isn't this fabulous?" she asked, her eyes sparkling with excitement.

"Yes, it is. Have you seen Pops yet?"

"Nope. Not yet."

Two Marines wearing dress blues were announcing the guests as they entered, and when Adam heard one of them call out, "Introducing Ms. Michele and Ms. JT Blake of Texas and New York," his head whirled to the entrance. Two tall, elegantly dressed women who bore a striking resemblance to Max entered the room.

Then the Marine announced, "Ms. Max Blake, accompanied by Ossie and Ruby Blake."

Adam's heart started pounding. There she stood, gorgeous in a flowing off-the-shoulder red dress and a silk wrap. Ossie had on a formal bow tie and Ruby a red bow. As she strolled into the room with that walk of hers, holding the fancy after-five leashes of the very elegant and poised rottweilers, she looked like Josephine

Baker striding in with leased leopards, and people openly stared in amazement.

His mother was one of them. "Is that her, Adam?"

"Yes, it is." He couldn't take his eyes off of her. She had a walk as fluid as a river and as seductive as a moonlit sea. Watching her presence electrify the room made every moment he'd spent with her flood back; from the first day she'd crashed like a meteor into his life, wearing shades and green cowboy boots, to the times they'd spent tossing Frisbees to the dogs, to the cab that rode him away from Portia's farmhouse and out of her life. And yes, he remembered their lovemaking. He could still taste her; recall the softness of her skin and the sweet wild pressure of her legs clapped around his waist. From all of the attention she was drawing from the men in the room, he sensed they were wishing for memories, too.

He watched her make her way through the crowd, stopping to smile and chat here and there then moving on to greet others in the room whom she seemed to know.

His mother said, "She's gorgeous, Adam."

Adam could only agree. The diamond-edged rubies strung around her neck and hanging in columns from her ears were as fiery as her dress. He fantasized on what might be under all that silk, but took another sip of his cognac and decided to leave that alone.

As if she could feel his thoughts, she looked across the large stateroom and met his eyes. Time seemed to stand still. Adam saluted her with his glass.

Max acknowledged the greeting with a short nod of her head, and she swore her suddenly tight nipples did too. She willed her heart to slow down but it didn't seem to be paying much attention. She ran her eyes over him almost hungrily. He looked real good in his formal black and white attire. In her opinion he was the finest thing in the room. And was that a small gold hoop in his ear? When had he pierced his ear? Apparently something was up with the staid conservative Mr. Wizard, and excusing herself from her family, she and the dogs walked in his direction so she could check him out. The dogs were going to spend the evening outside, behind the scene, until it was time for their medals, but she wouldn't deny them a visit with Dr. Adam.

Seeing her walking his way, Adam wondered how he was going to get through this evening without snatching her into a closet and showing her how much he'd missed her and, yes, loved her, because he did love her. His mother was right. On the plane ride this morning he'd come to the conclusion that he didn't care what she did to make a living. His desire to have her no matter what far outweighed his concerns about her safety. If she wanted to stock the house with enough guns to storm Normandy, he didn't care, as long as he could wake up with her beside him every sunrise.

The dogs saw Adam and began straining at the bit to get to him, and Max totally understood.

Adam greeted her with a strong hug, and Max's eyes slid closed from the sharp sensations. *Lord he felt good.* Ever mindful of their surroundings, they kept it short, but that first contact had been electric.

"Max, this is my mother, Lauren. Mama, Max Blake." Adam felt drunk, not from the cognac but from Max's scents and warmth.

"Pleased to meet you," Lauren said, looking up at Max in wonder.

"Nice meeting you as well," Max replied, and wondered if anyone could tell that she could still feel the heat of Adam's body through her thin red silk dress.

Adam dropped down to acknowledge the dogs, and the sight of him greeting the large rottweilers with such affection, and the affectionate way they responded, left Lauren speechless.

Max saw the look and said to her, "He's their buddy. They've missed him." Then she added, while holding Adam's eyes, "I've missed him, too."

"And I've missed you," Adam said.

The current arcing between them was so intense it was almost visible. "Come," she said to him. "Let's take the dogs outside, then, I want you all to meet my mom and sister."

So Adam and Lauren followed Max and the dogs outside, and then they crossed the room. Adam and Max tried not to show how hungry they were for each other, but with each glance embers came to life like stoked coals.

The introductions were made, and while Lauren, Michele, and JT chatted, Adam and Max stood next to each other. He leaned over and whispered in her ear, "Think we'll get in trouble if we cut out?"

Max whispered back, "Our mamas will kill us."

True dat.

So the two held hands instead and tried to tell themselves it was enough for now, but they were lying.

Michele Blake looked over at her daughter holding hands with the handsome Dr. Adam and asked with humor-laced suspicion, "What are you two plotting?"

Max chuckled. "Nothing, Mama."

Lauren checked them out, too, then said in patented

mama tones, "I do have my belt in my purse, just so you'll know."

They all laughed at that, but it was easy to see that both mothers were pleased to see their children so obviously happy.

Dinner began a short time later, and Max knew she had the President to thank for seating Adam directly across from her.

They spent the elaborate coursed meal sharing small talk with each other, and with the guests seated to their right and left, but the silent sensual conversation between Max and Adam continued. At one point Max extended her leg beneath the cloth-covered table and brushed her ankle lightly up against Adam's calf. He choked on his wine. Shooting her an amused warning glance, he grabbed up his linen napkin and made his apologies. Once the conversation around them began to flow again, he looked into her twinkling eyes and mouthed, *Behave.*

She just smiled.

As they left the table after dinner, Adam walked with her back to the ballroom and said for her ears only, "You're awful playful tonight."

"You ain't seen nothing yet."

He stopped short, but she floated away and went to find her mother and sister. Eyes glowing, Adam knew that from that point forward the game was on.

They played their cat and mouse game for the rest of the night through the presentation of the medals and the President's remarks on how proud he was to have Dr. Adam Gary be the first recipient of the newly established Lewis Latimer award for science; through the round of congratulations that followed for Max,

Adam, and the dogs; and through Ray Gary's fabulous performance.

Ray's cover of the old Bobby Womack tune, "Just Trying to Hold onto My Woman," was sung straight into Lauren's eyes. The lyrics, so poignant yet powerful, were of a man letting the world know how much he cared, and when Ray walked over to his ex, got down on one knee and sang the last refrain with such emotion, there wasn't a dry eye in the house.

By the time the dancing commenced, there was so much love in the air the partygoers could taste it. Max looked up at Adam as they danced to the slow sweet music of the band. She couldn't ever remember being happier. "Do you think your parents are going to get back together now?"

Adam could see Lauren and Ray in the crowd, slow-dancing like 1970s high schoolers. She had her head on his chest and he was holding her tight. "I think so. Pops put on a helluva show."

"Well, if your mama doesn't want him, I know my mama does."

Adam looked down into the green eyes of his dreams and asked, "And what do you want?"

She didn't stutter. "You."

Knowing he was the happiest man on the planet, Adam eased her in close and whispered, "I want you, too."

The President strolled over and tapped Adam on the shoulder. Adam turned with Max in his arms and said, "Yes sir."

"My wife has asked that the two of you go out into the garden."

Max asked, "Why?"

He smiled and said softly, "You're generating a lot of heat, shall we say, and some of the older ladies are—"

"Jealous?" Max asked coolly.

"No. Envious. It's obvious you two are in love, and they and my wife think you might like some privacy."

Adam and Max both laughed, and an uncharacteristically embarrassed Max dropped her head on Adam's chest for a moment.

Adam, still holding her, said with all seriousness, "Sir, if I've been disrespectful—"

The President raised his hand. "No no. It's nothing like that. You two haven't been carrying on like teenagers by any means, but it's in your eyes," he said knowingly. "Makes me want to take the First Lady out on a stroll in the moonlight myself."

Max shook her head.

Adam looked down at Max and asked in an English-sounding accent, "Would my lady like to see the gardens?"

"I believe she would."

So, when the musicians finished their tune, Max and Adam and a few other couples took a walk. As Max and Adam passed the First Lady talking with Michele, JT, Ray, and Lauren, the President's wife came over to Max and whispered for her ears alone, "The Lincoln bedroom is available."

A shocked Max stared, and then laughed until tears stood in her eyes.

Twenty-two

After the warm ballroom with all its people and conversations, the night air felt good. As they walked through the darkness, Adam, holding Max's hand, asked, "What did the First Lady say to you?"

Max told him.

"Oh really?" He laughed, then said with amusement, "She might be almost as outrageous as you."

Max cuddled close as they moved farther out into the dark gardens. "That could be true."

By now they were alone and hidden from the crowd inside, and the first thing Adam did was ease her in front of him and give her the kiss he'd been wanting to bestow since leaving her in Ohio.

Max moaned like a woman in need, slipped her arms around his waist and let herself enjoy what she'd been craving since that day, too. The feel of him, the warmth, the familiarity of his embrace, made her want more.

Adam reacquainted himself with the smell of her hair, the shape of her ears, the softness of her mouth. Her tongue played with his, and his manhood soared with desire. "Lord, I've missed you," he husked out.

"I've missed you, too. . . ."

Adam couldn't help himself, his hands were roaming over the curves and valleys sheathed in red silk, and Max's hands were wandering all over him. They were like eager hormone-heightened teenagers in a high school back hall. She moved her palm shamelessly over the placard on the front of his pants because he'd freed one of her nipples from the top of her dress and was feasting scandalously.

"Ahem!"

They stopped and glared. There stood one of the ceremonial Marines with his back turned to them.

"Can I help you?" Adam asked in a voice ragged with impatience and desire.

The obviously embarrassed Marine replied, "The First Lady sent this key."

Adam could feel and hear Max's uneven breathing behind him as she hastily fixed her dress. When he sensed that she was ready, he walked over and took the key. The Marine stepped quickly back the way he'd come.

Max and Adam looked at each other, laughed, then ran like kids to the Lincoln bedroom.

Once inside the bedroom historians believed Lincoln never actually slept in, Max slowly peeled off her dress in the soft glow of the lone lamp they'd turned on and stood for a moment and let him look.

And look he did. Adam was entranced, spellbound, hot, as he ran his eyes over the Woman with Many Names wearing nothing but a black thong, killer Brazilian heels, and, around her waist, tiny rubies strung together on a delicate gold chain. Smiling like the seductress that she was, Max turned herself slowly so he could get a good look at the open-work laces on the back of the thong, and he growled, "Come here, you. . . ."

So she did.

While she stood before him, he slid a possessive hand over the thin triangle between her thighs and played until she caught fire. Only then did he turn her around and give his attention to the man-hardening lacing over her fine behind. He undid the tie slowly, greeting each newly exposed portion of skin with kisses, caresses, and such scandalous licks that Max groaned and shimmered. Her legs were shaking so much she was having trouble standing, but that issue was erotically resolved when he invited her to lie down on the bed, lazily pulled off the thong and slid to his knees.

Max was so hot that at the first touch of his wanton greeting she came gloriously, twisting, arching, and gasping.

Adam chuckled but didn't stop until a second coming buckled her. As she lay there riding out the echoes of her completion, eyes closed and her long legs positioned lusciously just for him, he stood and began to undress. His prior celibacy had given him the stamina he'd needed to keep his own desire under control, but it wouldn't last forever, and neither could he.

The first coupling was fast, hard. Their need to consummate their months-long separation had no time for technique or artistry. The powerful orgasm that resulted made her cry out and left him thrusting and pumping like a man just freed from prison. Afterward they fell back, breathing hard, fingers entwined, and enjoyed the pleasure of finally having each other near.

When their hearts and lungs regained some semblance of normalcy, Adam moved the short distance to her side and propped himself up on an elbow. He looked down into her face and all he felt inside filled his heart. Sliding a tender finger over the curve of her lips, he asked, "Is this the part where I'm supposed to tell you I love you?"

"I think so."

"Good, because I do. And, you need to know that I don't care what you do for a living, Max. I seriously don't. I just want you in my life. If you want to play Jinga forever, I'm down with it and I'll try not to hassle you as long as at the end of the day you come home to me."

Filled with emotion, Max reached up and caressed his cheek. She asked softly, "Is this the part where I'm supposed to say I love you, too?"

He grinned. "Think so."

"I do love you, Adam, very very much, and you'll be glad to know that the President signed my resignation yesterday."

His eyes widened. "What?"

She smiled. "Yep, and it was *my* decision, the way it was supposed to be."

Adam fell back, then raised himself. "You wouldn't kid a brother, would you?"

"Not on something like this. I'm all yours now, my brother, so whatcha gonna do with me?"

He dragged her on top of him. Max fit him inside and then melted with the sensations.

"How about this?" he asked slyly.

As he began to move and she began to slowly ride,

she said, "I always did like the way that Einstein brain of yours works."

"Good, because I'll be thinking of stuff like this for the rest of our lives."

"Promise?"

"Forever."

Epilogue

Max threw the Frisbee down the beach, and Ruby and Ossie went tearing after it. Ossie, being stronger and faster, got there first, so Adam threw another and called out, "Here you go, girl!"

Ruby raced after it and brought it down.

Max and Adam had been playing with the dogs for over an hour. "Time for a Kool-Aid break," she said, picking up the pitcher and the two glasses perched on the sand.

Adam shook his head. "That stuff is going to freeze out here."

She poured two glasses of the lime Kool-Aid and asked, "Well, when are you going to invent something that makes it warm this time of year. Mr. Wizard?"

He hung his head.

It was early November. It had taken every day since their wedding a week after the White House medal ceremony for the workmen they'd hired to put the lakeside house back together. They'd moved in three days ago. The place was still filled with packing boxes, but they'd be emptied eventually.

Max said to him, "I'm glad we decided to come back here."

Adam looked up at the house standing like a sentinel on the bluff and agreed, "Me, too."

The government had handed over the title as a wedding gift, engineered by the President and his First Lady. Max and Adam had to pay for all the repairs, but between them the new Mr. and Mrs. Adam Blake had quite a bit of green, so they spared no cost having the place lovingly restored to their specifications.

The November wind was brisk coming off the lake, and soon snow would come. Max pulled up the collar of her heavy jacket, then drained the last of her lime drink. "It's cold out here. Time to go in."

Adam smiled. He called the dogs, and the canines headed up the dune to the patio. Max hooked her arm in his and said to him as they walked down the beach to the stairs, "My doctor called a little while ago."

"Are you okay?" he asked with concern.

"Yep, I'm pregnant, though."

Adam's eyes widened and he stared.

Max nodded. "Probably all that history making we did in the Lincoln bedroom."

Adam grinned.

Max was pleased with the news, too. She was a bit concerned about her age, but the doctor was convinced that with the proper care she and the baby would be fine.

Adam said, "I think I want a girl."

"Okay," Max chuckled. "Whatever the gender, the baby will probably be born with a pocket protector in one hand and an AK-47 in the other."

Adam laughed, "I can't wait."

"Neither can I."

The following June, Max gave birth to a nine-pound-eight-ounce baby girl that she and Adam named Lauren Michele. Young Miss Blake didn't come into the world packing a pocket protector or an AK-47, but she was healthy, loud, and had Granny Loreli's green eyes, just like her mother. Both parents were proud.

Author's Note

Max and Adam were two characters I loved getting to know, and I hope you readers did as well. Wild ride, wasn't it? Max Blake has to be one of the fiercest females I've ever encountered, and I hope she and Adam and little Lauren live happily ever after.

Max was born in my kitchen when a girlfriend asked why all the NIA agents had to be male. "Why can't we have a female agent?" friend Alicia asked, and immediately Max was born. So thanks, Alicia.

The great Angolan queen Jinga, known also as Nzingha and by other accounts as Ginga, fought Portuguese slavers for thirty years. When she died on December 17, 1663, her death reportedly fueled other rulers on the continent to take up the resistance against the slave trade and European dominance—rulers such as: Madame Timbu of Nigeria; Nandi, mother of the fearless Zulu warrior, Chaka; and Dahomian King, Behanzin Bowelle and his female army. Further information on this fascinating African queen and others is just a Google click away, so enjoy reading the history.

Speaking of Zulu warrior Chaka, while I was

working on Adam and Max's story, the 2006 Westminster Dog Show was held in New York City. To my surprise, pride, and delight, for the very first time in Westminster's 130-year history a rottweiler took first place in the Working Group class. This was not just any rottie, folks, but one with the glorious name of Champion Carter's Noble Shaka Zulu. So a hearty BJ shout-out goes to breeder, owner, and handler Mr. Keith Carter, a brother who during his college years played linebacker for Florida State University. I was proud watching history being made, and I know Ruby and Ossie were, too. ☺

In closing, do you all realize that I have been spinning published stories for twelve years now? My, how time flies when you're having fun, but no way could I have done this alone, so a big thank-you to my editor, Erika, for her patience and brilliance; my agent, Nancy, for her wisdom and great phone calls; Adrienne, Pam, Tom Egner in Art, and all the other folks at Avon and Harper for their faith in me and in my work. Last, but certainly not least, beaucoup thanks to my readers. Your love, devotion, and prayers keep me writing. Stay blessed.

See you next time,
B.